# HER SOLDIER

## OF THE

# QUEEN

She always did as she should do
and never became the woman
she was meant to be until she met ...

# HER SOLDIER

## OF THE

# QUEEN

### DOROTHY DOWNS

**IRIE
BOOKS**

ISBN 978-1-5154-1727-9
Copyright 2019 by Dorothy Downs

Cover and interior design
by Nancy R Koucky, NRK Designs

*Her Soldier of the Queen* is published by
Irie Books, Santa Fe, New Mexico
For information, contact www.iriebooks.com

IRIE
BOOKS

To Every Soldier
Who Served Their Country

"A soldier's life is terrible hard."
From the poem *Buckingham Palace*
by A. A. Milne

# Contents

I

# Part I
# No Coincidences in Life

It is said there are no coincidences in life. We are given the experiences we need, whether we are looking for them or not. The best are totally unexpected. She sat at her desk and ran her fingers over the glass jar filled with seashells. It was pear-shaped, tactile, full of never-forgotten memories from the 1980s. It contained shells varied in shapes, sizes, and colors, and a small piece of driftwood, patterned by the ebb and flow of the sea, as her life had been. They reminded her of the soldier of the Queen who came and went into her life, always an ocean away. He said, "I go where I'm sent."

# I

# The Train / London / Edinburgh

A long row of taxis, like enormous black ants, moved in and out of London King's Cross railway station. The driver inched along until he found an opening and pulled next to the curb.

"This is it, ma'am," he said, opening her door and dropping *Liberator* on the sidewalk. Ginny had nicknamed her big, black, wheeled suitcase *Liberator* because it set her free. Made it easier to manage luggage on a trip.

"Is this enough?" She asked, nervously counting the unfamiliar coins, giving him what seemed like a more than an adequate tip. The driver touched his cap, climbed back into his taxi and drove away.

Tightening the strap in her hand, she gave *Liberator* a testy little tug. The wheels squeaked. The suitcase barely moved.

*Blasted books*, she thought. *Liberator's* sides bulged at the seams, stuffed with the many books she'd bought during her stay. After visiting museum collections, there always was time left over to spend in the museum stores, temptingly stocked with British publications she would never be able to find in her hometown of Miami. Now they'd be a weight problem all the way to Scotland and back.

She gave the strap another tug and the wheels reluctantly began to roll. The station was not too crowded, but being unaccustomed to train travel, she found the bustling station completely overwhelming. She was used to airports. Train stations were new to her. No one around to check her in and point her in the right direction, and the immediacy of the trains being right there and ready to leave was intimidating.

With renewed determination, she pushed back her shoulders and began pulling the wobbly suitcase through the terminal, while trying to look as composed as possible.

A row of trains stood waiting for morning travelers, some of them milling about with baggage, others scurrying and climbing aboard. There was a loud shout of "BOARD!" as a train lurched and pulled from the station. She looked around in confusion.

*Please, God, don't let that have been mine*, she thought in a flurry of panic. A large uniformed man standing by an iron gate leading to the trains studied a watch on a chain. He was the perfect image of a conductor.

She handed her BritRail pass to him and asked, "Which way to catch the *Flying Scotsman* to Edinburgh?"

He studied the ticket, handed it back to her, and without a word, pointed to track eleven.

"Car D. Ah, here we are," she said to *Liberator*, heaving the suitcase onto the train and shoving it into the aisle. Plenty of people were already in the drab Second-Class coach. Heads turned to see her, but no one took interest in her struggle. Suitcases were piled in a luggage compartment at the front of the coach. She pushed *Liberator* in with the others, glad to be free of it at last.

Then, checking the numbers on the seats, she located her window seat, with an empty seat beside it. Finally she took off her London Fog coat, stowed it in the rack overhead, and sank into the worn blue velvet cushions. Second Class was far from elegant, but she was grateful to be here and would get to Edinburgh just as fast as those in First Class.

Two women were seated across from her. Judging from their faces, a mother and daughter. They had the same stout build, and the younger woman wore a dull tweed suit with a faded print blouse. Her salt-and-pepper hair was tightly curled.

Both women wore matching eyeglass frames. But the mother's blue eyes had a spark of humor that unfortunately had not been passed on to her daughter. They read the Sunday *London Times* and chatted softly as they read and shared.

Ginny glanced at their newspaper, seeing the headlines and photos of violence in Northern Ireland over Bobby Sands and other prisoners on hunger strikes. The dateline was March 15, 1981.

*Funny*, she thought, remembering she had an article about Florida Indians being published in *The Miami Herald* on that very day. She wasn't there to see it.

Across the aisle from the mother sat two German-speaking girls reading travel guidebooks in awkward English. The seats across from them were empty.

Just as the train was about to pull out of the station, a tall, attractive man entered the coach, looked around and slid into the aisle seat across from Ginny. The train jerked and the wheels started clicking on the tracks.

The conductor made his way through the coach, checking tickets. Ginny fumbled in her bag and handed the BritRail pass to him. The conductor frowned, told her in a voice that all could hear, "Madam, you did not have your rail pass validated at the station. You must do that first thing when you get to Edinburgh."

All activity stopped and her seatmates stared. She felt her face flush.

"Sorry, I'm new at this," she said. "This's my first train trip in England and I still don't know all the rules." She could tell that he enjoyed seeing how nervous she was.

London to Edinburgh on the express train, the *Flying Scotsman*, usually took four and a half hours on weekdays. The ticket agent had warned her that because they made repairs on the tracks on Sundays, the trip could take up to six hours. She really didn't care because she had never seen the English and Scottish countryside.

Soon the train left the depressing outskirts of London and began to roll through an exquisite landscape. Ginny lost herself in the view of field after field of men and boys playing Sunday soccer. Little villages with old parish churches and ancient cemeteries gave her a sense of storybook England. She smiled to herself. How far away Miami seemed now.

She took her camera from its case and started taking snapshots. Each time the film advanced it made a noise which seemed oddly loud in the confines of the train. The man across the aisle was watching her. She saw him duck back into his book.

She wondered what he saw in her.

The old English countryside sped past. How great to be out of the Florida heat. The motion of the train was hypnotic. Ginny closed her eyes and felt the rhythm of the rails. Her unhappy home life was behind her now.

She was glad to be away from the chaos. *Now I will get my real work done,* she thought. Research, the thing she loved most about writing.

*This is what she had hoped for.* With that thought, she opened her eyes just as the train passed another church and graveyard. The sight gave her a shiver. Miles of close row houses and ugly factories followed; then the train zoomed through long black tunnels which eventually gave way to more rolling countryside and villages with neat houses set on kept yards.

Ginny looked up just as the man across the aisle returned from what she guessed was a trip to the "loo," as the Brits said. His six-foot plus frame moved with the grace of a professional runner. The man sat back down and immersed himself in his book, *The Bourne Identity.*

Now Ginny watched him as he had watched her. He was casually dressed in a blue wool crew-neck sweater, a striped Oxford shirt open at the throat, dark gray trousers. He had a nice profile. His thick chestnut hair was slightly curly.

*I'd love to run my fingers through that hair,* she thought. Then she realized this was an impulsive urge she'd never known before.

As she studied him she saw his bright eyes darken. There was a strange sadness about the man. A hardness, too.

*Am I imagining that?* she wondered.

Her speculations wandered.

*Maybe he's a doctor who has lost patients to terminal illnesses, she thought. He probably has a lovely wife and three adoring children meeting him at the station.*

The conductor made his way down the aisle: "Reservations for lunch."

The German girls and mother and daughter eagerly bought tickets for the first seating.

"Is the food good?" Ginny asked the women across from her. "We rarely travel on trains in America anymore, so I can't imagine what it might be like here."

"Oh, very good," the younger woman assured her.

The conversation ended abruptly and Ginny felt more alone than ever. After a while she got lost in the scenery and the German girls chatted among themselves as if she wasn't there.

After a little while she glanced over at the book reading man.

For a split second their eyes met.

Ginny sensed the curiosity was mutual.

She swiftly turned again to the scenery. *Had he seen her fidgety hands, her nervousness at being so alone on a train?*

Suddenly she had an urge to open her handbag. She zipped it open and stared vacantly at its contents. Across the aisle those eyes caught her every move. She could feel him staring at her and perhaps saying to himself, "Can't you sit still?"

The first seating for lunch was called. The German girls and the two other women grabbed their purses and hurried to the dining coach. Relieved to have the space alone, from her bag she pulled out her makeshift lunch of the morning croissant, a can of processed Cheddar cheese, and the can of tomato juice she brought from home.

The eyes across the aisle, she sensed, were once again, she imagined, disapproving.

Another quick glance on her part told her the man had unwrapped a neat little sandwich, white bread crusts evenly trimmed.

*Who could have made that for him?*

They lunched in silence. A long time passed before mother and daughter returned from the dining car. Their cheeks were flushed with the rosy glow that comes with wine and a full meal.

"What did you have for lunch?" Ginny asked. Neither replied.

*Didn't they hear me?*

Young men in their early twenties from a coach ahead now made trips down the aisle, lurching back and forth, she guessed going to the bar car. Most of them were punk types, some with their hair combed up in crazy styles, numerous earrings dangling from their ears. Some of them had arms that were virtual art galleries of elaborate tattoos. One young man's arm was graced with a colorful Kabuki dancer that would have made the Japanese artist Utamaro proud.

Suddenly a weird announcement rang over the loudspeaker: "To the lady with the ginger-colored hair, the prison matron will be waiting for you on the platform."

A loud chorus of laughter broke out in the coach as everyone looked around for the lady with the ginger-colored hair. Ginny turned and saw that the man across the aisle was smiling at her, his eyes now dark blue and fixed upon her. They shared the moment with a quick smile and then she felt uncomfortable and checked her handbag again.

The older woman gave her a little wink.

Abruptly, the reading man looked up from his book and smiled. " I heard you say that you're from America," he said softly. "Whereabouts?"

"Florida," Ginny said. "Miami. And you?"

"London."

There followed a moment where the train did the talking with the clicking of the rails.

"Have you ever been to America?" Ginny asked, hoping to be heard over the train. "We seem to see a lot of British travelers now in Florida."

"Haven't been to Florida," he told her. "Been to New York and Philadelphia to visit friends. I guess that's quite different from Florida, though, isn't it. But I hope to get there in the future." He paused, then said, "Are you on holiday?"

"No, business." She gave a moment's thought on how to explain her reason for traveling.

Then: "I'm an art historian. My background is in Native American art. I'm in England and Scotland to research the influence that eighteenth century British, and especially Scottish Highlander, traders, soldiers, and settlers, had on the culture, legends, and art of the American Indians. I go out on the reservations a lot and talk to the people. It's very interesting work, but pretty esoteric ..."

"British immigrants? Would never have imagined it." He chuckled and his accent was wonderful, his laugh soft and beguiling.

Ginny laughed too. She could tell that he hadn't taken her seriously.

Another group of boys bolted by for more beers and she gave him a puzzled look.

"Soldiers on leave," he told her.

She wondered how he knew that.

"Are you on business?" she asked.

"No, on holiday. In fact, I'm going up in the Highlands."

"Are you going golfing? I hear the courses in Scotland are the best in the world."

He laughed. "I'm hardly the type. I'm going to a ski resort up there."

Ginny had never even considered there were ski resorts in the Scottish Highlands, realizing how little she knew about Scotland.

Their conversation was brief and not flirtatious, and there was nothing left to say. The silence said it all. With more uninterrupted miles, Ginny sensed the curious eyes across the aisle observing her every move. Eventually, after he had dozed off, she took a long look at him. His book lay open-face on his lap. *What is so intriguing about him?*

She selected a small cosmetic mirror from her bag and studied her face for a moment. Ginny had always been a wholesome American girl type, the sweetheart of a high school boys' club and her looks reflected this. *Why am I not more confident here?*

With this thought, she ran a brush through her hair.

*Do the lines by my eyes seem deeper? Hopefully they add character.*

Her recent forty-third birthday was a milestone in more ways than one. She had accomplished the career goals she had set for herself. The passing years had heightened her ambitions. In a silent laugh, her eyes brightened and crinkled in the mirror's reflection. She smoothed her beige cashmere turtleneck then put the mirror back into her bag.

As the train approached Scotland, the mother suddenly perked up. She was obviously happy to be going home. She began pointing out the sights and talking about where she lived in Edinburgh, how beautiful it was, and how much she loved the city.

Soon they were pulling into the station and the travelers began to gather their belongings. Ginny was ready for the next part of the adventure, but worried because she didn't have a hotel reservation and really didn't know where to go. People at the Tourist Board in London said their colleagues in Edinburgh would help her and there should be no problem finding a reasonably priced room.

The mother and daughter kept their seats when everyone else was getting up. They had made this trip many times before and there would be no surprises for them in Edinburgh. It was back to the tedium that must have comprised their daily routines.

When the train came to a full halt, the man across the aisle stepped in front of her, holding his bag and jacket, adjusting his tweed cap.

*How rude*, she thought. *He could have at least let me out first instead of all but knocking me down.* She put on her coat, and as they moved to the luggage storage compartment, she reached for *Liberator.*

The man reached in front of her and asked, "May I help you with that? Here, take these." He handed her his bag and jacket and pulled the suitcase from the rack. Grateful, she knew there was no way she could make a graceful exit dragging it.

"It's very nice of you to help me, but it's really heavy," she warned.

He rolled his eyes and laughed at the weight.

As they walked to the Way Out sign, she asked, "Where do you go from here?"

"On a train to Perth, where I'll be met by friends. Then it's an hour ride to the resort from there. And you? Are you being met?"

"No. I don't even have a place to stay yet. I have to check with the Tourist Board for a hotel listing."

"I heard the conductor say that you didn't get your BritRail pass validated. You had better stop and do that, and we can also check on the next train to Perth."

She was right; he had been watching her from the beginning of the trip. She had her BritRail pass validated and he checked on his train schedule. He had an hour to kill.

As they walked toward the Tourist Board, she asked the question only an American would venture. "What do you do?"

"I'm a British army officer," he said, with some noticeable pride.

"Had I known that, you would never have shut me up on the train. I have so many questions about the British military, especially historically."

"That's what I was afraid of," he said with a laugh. "Come on, let's find you a room and a taxi."

They walked up the steep ramp, following signs to Tourist Information. He shifted the weight of the suitcase a couple times, chuckling at the uncommon weight.

"Are you sure you can manage that thing? It's really awful. It has wheels. You can put it down and pull it, you know."

"What've you got in here? The kitchen sink?" He then set *Liberator* on its wheels, and they moved more smoothly. His mood seemed to change as they walked.

"We didn't say much on the train," she said teasingly.

He smiled, said nothing.

"I was fidgety, wasn't I?"

"Not really. You're just a typical American, I think." He gave her a sideways glance, and added, "I like Americans. I fought beside a bunch of them in Vietnam."

"You were there? I didn't know the British were there. But then, I wasn't paying much attention. I thought the whole thing was awful and blocked it out of my mind. I've never been too concerned about things I can't control or change. It's too frustrating. Fortunately, I didn't know anyone who was in that war."

"The British weren't officially stationed there. I'd served in Borneo, and was only an advisor on jungle warfare in Vietnam."

As they reached the Tourist Board at the top of the ramp, a broad-shouldered man with a ruddy complexion stepped in front of them, interrupting their conversation with a deep Scottish burr.

"Do you have a place to stay? My friend has a guesthouse near here. It's clean, nice, and a good price just for you."

"No thanks," her companion said. "We're going to the Tourist Board to get some information."

"They're closed," the Scot informed them. "Closed at one today."

"Thanks," they said in unison. The Scot was right though, the door was closed and locked. With a mutual sigh, they made their way down the ramp.

Ginny was glad to have her impromptu escort. *On my own I would have gone off with that Scot and been sold into white slavery ... you couldn't find a more gullible traveler!*

"Look, I'm going to be at a really nice place in the Highlands, sort of a resort for army personnel. If you're interested in the Highlanders, why don't you come up for a day and I can show you around? Friends up there will have a car I can use. Or if you're too busy, I could come down to Edinburgh and take you out for dinner."

"I really don't have time for a side trip. My time's so limited now and my schedule's jammed with visiting libraries and museums. But thanks for the offer anyway."

*A trip to the Highlands! But I'm here for work, not play. Besides, I don't even know this guy.*

"Well, I'd like to talk to you if I may. Let's get some coffee and then find a taxi for you."

This seemed safe enough. Her mind went back and forth ... *trust a stranger, don't trust a stranger.*

They walked into the terminal coffee shop. He seated her at a table so she could watch their luggage while he stood in line for coffee. She studied him as he stood across the room, above the crowd. It seemed that no woman alive could help being struck by his good looks. He was statuesque, emblematic. Whether he was conscious of it or not was another matter. He was what he was, and he didn't seem to know it in the way that she did. And that was a good thing.

"Tell me about your work," she asked as he settled down and two cups of coffee steamed.

"Right now, I just finished a tour of duty in the Royal Palace Guard," he told her. "You know, trooping the colors and all of that. But I'm also a paratrooper and an officer. You Americans call what I do Special Forces or the Green Beret. We call it Special Air Services. SAS."

Green Beret clicked with her but SAS didn't.

"Do you wear a big black hat?" she asked. This was a favorite American fantasy, the guards at Buckingham Palace. It reminded her of a nursery rhyme from *Winnie-the-Pooh*. Christopher Robin's nanny, Alice, took him to Buckingham Palace to watch the changing of the Guard, and now the little rhyme ran through her head. Alice was marrying one of the Guard.

"How exciting! I've actually met one of the Guard," Ginny said, but realized she should have paid more attention to the last line " … a soldier's life is terrible hard." She then remembered the white rabbit. *Perhaps Alice is a cautionary name.*

"The hat is the skin of a female bear," he said breaking her thoughts. "And the white pants are very tight. Everything has to be shined perfectly. That's not what I was doing, however."

"I'd love to see you in uniform."

"No, you wouldn't. You wouldn't like it at all. And in London I have to wear a three-piece suit, with a bowler hat and umbrella. I always have to be properly dressed, no jeans. Too stuffy. I'm much happier like this."

"Good," she said.

"My job was a nightmare," he went on. "I had so much responsibility for the royal family and special events. We're very worried about the Irish Republican Army assassins and bombers. The scheduling was abominable. But I've just completed that eighteen-month tour and had a farewell party before leaving London. When I get back from the holiday, I'll leave for my next tour, in Belize. It's warm and not much is going on there, just training young soldiers in the jungle. It should be pretty pleasant, all things considered. It's just a short flight from Miami, and I'm told that's a nice place to relax."

"Miami? Great! I can show you around." She raised her coffee cup. "Tell me more. What's it like to be a paratrooper? I have a bad case of acrophobia, and no desire whatsoever to ever jump from a plane. I don't even like Ferris wheels, or looking down long escalators. My knees go weak." She took a sip of coffee, then set the cup back down.

"I had to be pushed out the first time. There was no way I'd just jump from that thing. They had to undo my fingers, one by one, and shove me out the door. And by the way, I'll never be a dead hero either. I've known too many of them. There's no future in that. But you get used to it all. The army's been my life. I hated school and didn't know what else to do, so I went into the military. Figured it was the best way I could make something of myself. I went in when I was seventeen and have been in for twenty years now."

Quick arithmetic told her that he must be thirty-seven. *Well, best to get it out in the open.*

"I'm forty-three," she said and felt herself wince.

"Doesn't matter. It's just a number. That's not important. Let me see your passport. Where all have you been?"

They exchanged passports and he eagerly searched her information, name, address, and stamp-markings of the countries she had visited, but only on package group tours.

It was then she realized they hadn't even introduced themselves yet.

Apparently, he realized it at the same time, and laughed. Such a nice laugh.

"Virginia Thomas," he said." I didn't even know your name! As you see, I'm Lieutenant James Byrd Evans." He pronounced it "Leftenant," the old, formal British way.

Ginny searched her wallet and brought out a business card from the museum. "We've been talking like we've known each other forever," she said. "Actually, I find this a bit amazing. It's nice to meet you, Lieutenant James Byrd Evans. Do you have a card?"

"Army officers don't have cards. We're never in one place long enough."

She again studied his passport and generic photograph, the unsmiling face wearing glasses with dark frames looked little like the handsome man seated next to her. Flipping through his passport, she noticed that it was almost full, while hers had a very few entries.

"I have other passports that are full," he told her. "I've really seen the world. Not always under the best circumstance, sorry to say. Why are you alone in Scotland?"

"It's actually best to be alone for a trip like this," she said. "No one else would be interested and I can get more work done. Fewer distractions. Besides, I think I like traveling alone. I've done some brief research on Cherokee Indians in the mountains of North Carolina and really enjoyed it. I haven't had much freedom, really. This is my first solo venture across the ocean, and I'm starting to love it."

"Are you married?"

"I am. And you?"

"No. Never."

That cleared some of the air. *How can I begin to explain my current chaos to a stranger without dwelling on it and sounding pathetic. Or worse -- maudlin and helpless.* "Let's just say things, frankly, aren't going too well right now. Guess I'm needing more breathing room. Well, to say the least. It's hard to explain. I just want to be more free."

"I love my freedom too. My only close relative, my father, died last year, and I have no one to answer to. If this is your first trip abroad alone, what will be your next?"

"Let me get through this one first."

"Tell me about the Highlanders. Are you serious, or is that just an excuse to get you out of the house?"

"No, I'm serious. Honest. I'm seriously involved in this research and have found some other people pretty interested in it over here too. They've seen articles I've written. Look, hand my bag to me and I'll show you what I mean."

She pulled out some photographs of old portraits of Indian and Highlander men. One Indian chief had the last name of McIntosh, and his father was a trader from the Highlands. His mother was from a prominent Indian clan. The chief wore a fur bonnet trimmed with a white egret plume, and he held an heirloom broadsword. Men in both groups wore kilts or skirt-like attire, finding trousers unmanly. The similarities in their dress were always astounding and, yes, convincing.

"You win, but please think about coming up to the Highlands to spend a day with me. You really should. Let me give you a number where you can contact me if you change your mind. Just ask for Lieutenant Evans."

He wrote his name and a phone number from the town of Glenshee on a piece of paper and handed it to her. She said, "I really can't come, but my address and phone number are on the business card that I gave you. On second thought, since things are so shaky now, you'd better have my post office box number. That's more private. It's my business mail address and the phone number is my private line with an answering machine on it. You can write or give me a call when you come to Miami. Leave a message on my machine if I'm not there. It would be fun to show you around my hometown."

"An answering machine? I hate answering machines! Never know what to say to them. Let's get your taxi now. I have to catch my train to Perth."

James grabbed up *Liberator* and hailed a taxi in front of the terminal. He told the driver to take her to the Charlotte Square area, somewhere not too expensive but nice, and loaded her suitcase into the front seat.

"Please think about coming up," he said again.

They shook hands and then said goodbye. As the taxi crept its way through the traffic and up the ramp, she watched James move toward the train to Perth. He put down his bag, and then waved for as long as the taxi was in sight.

*How sweet.* She waved back. But her return was sort of discreet.

*My marriage is in shambles and the last thing I need now is to get involved with a man, but that just may be the best offer I'll ever have. Why did I have to say no?*

She eased into her seat and stared out the window.

# 2
# Edinburgh / Scottish Highlands

The taxi driver took her to the Hotel Rothesay, a small bed and breakfast hotel in the quiet Charlotte Square neighborhood. The price was reasonable, and the large clean room had a private bath; but she soon found that it was freezing cold. Ginny opened her suitcase, hung some clothes on hangers, washed up, then left and walked around the corner in search of an early dinner.

There were several inexpensive restaurants close to the busy intersection. She chose an Italian restaurant, *Rosie's*. The pasta was good but as she ate, savoring the food, Ginny began to feel alone in the world. As if she'd lost a friend. Had she?

Walking back to her hotel, she passed an old church, busy with Sunday evening. Though she hadn't attended church in many years, the milling crowd and the happy sound of singing somehow made her feel even more like an outsider. A blast of cold air increased the feeling of loneliness. For a dreary moment, she watched the fallen leaves swirling at her feet. Then, feeling heavy and out of balance, she went back to the Rothesay.

Things appeared different. The hotel now looked depressing.

*Is anyone staying here besides me?*

The manager was the only spark in the emptiness that surrounded her. Yet, though he was polite, there was something dark and brooding about him. He sat alone in his sitting room, the only light and sound coming from a small jittery television.

She got into the creaky metal lift cage that passed as an elevator, went directly to her room, and dressed for bed.

Her long johns, thermal underwear decorated with pink roses she had packed for chilly Scotland, were a wise choice under her flannel gown. The room was freezing.

"This definitely is not a sight I would want to share with anyone," she said to herself as she filled the bed with books and notes, climbed in and pulled the covers to her neck as she planned the next day's research.

*God, it's cold! Don't they have any heat in this place? I can see why it's cheap, empty, and irretrievably lonely.*

No thermostat in sight.

She began planning. If she could get a lot done on Monday, maybe, just maybe, she could squeeze in a trip to the Highlands on Tuesday.

At least I'll have someone to talk to.

James was right. *If I'm writing about Highlanders, I ought to visit the Highlands and see firsthand what the countryside is like. It would surely give me more insight into the people. There is no excuse not to go.*

So if James had a car, and naturally he would, he'd be a wonderful guide.

*I was crazy to refuse his offer. At this point, no regrets, right?*

*I said no but I meant why not? Am I always so contradictory? I thought I'd left the negativity behind in Miami but it seems to have followed me here.*

It was hard to screen out the husband, as she sometimes called him. He demanded ownership of her. But then took her for granted. He refused a marriage counselor, and each time she brought it up, he got angry. There was no changing him, only the chance to change herself.

Ginny fell asleep, thinking of James. His alert, lively expressions. His handsome attire, matching his handsome face. He was, as she fell asleep, a dream come true.

Next morning, she and the manager were the only people in the breakfast room. He also was the waiter, and probably the cook as well. Looking outside, she saw a big horse clopping down the street, pulling a wagon loaded with bottles of milk. How strange it all seemed, a charming time warp.

Returning to her room, Ginny picked up the phone to call the number James had given her. The manager also apparently operated the switchboard, and she read him the number.

After a couple of rings, someone answered. But she wasn't quite sure of the voice. "May I speak to Lieutenant James Evans?"

"Speaking."

"James, this is Virginia. Didn't expect to find you in. Thought I'd have to leave a message. What a nice surprise. I've decided to come up tomorrow, if the offer's still open. What should I do?"

"I was hoping to hear from you. I'll call this evening, about seven, and give you some train information."

Ginny gave him the name and number of her hotel. As she hung up, pleased with her decision, she knew this day would be a busy one.

"Never go away with strangers," her mother had always cautioned. Ginny, always chatty and friendly with everyone, caused her mother to believe that one day she'd run off with a serial killer. For some reason, NEVER GO AWAY WITH STRANGERS was the very slogan used by Laker Airways for ads that were plastered on the sides of all of the big red double-decker buses that rumbled through Edinburgh. She saw them and heard her mother's voice in her inner ear.

Her first stop was the National Portrait Gallery, where she would search for obscure portraits of Highlanders who might have been in North America during the Seven Years War or the American Revolution.

Ginny's arrival was expected, as she had been corresponding with the Curator, or Keeper, of the collection, and had called her from London. She was a friendly woman, eager to please. She also shared Ginny's interest in the cross-cultural synchrony. And there were full-length portraits of Highlander officers, wearing kilts and bonnets and carrying broadswords. These, she found out, were unpublished, and real finds. Ginny photographed them and made notes of their clan names.

Afterwards, Ginny thanked the Keeper and asked her to phone ahead to set up her appointment with Mr Ross, Keeper of the Scottish United Services Museum at Edinburgh Castle. She had written to him months ago. In his return letter, he sounded cranky and uninterested in her "fool theory." She knew that appointment would not be easy to make. It would help to pave the way if this Keeper would make the introductory call.

She was right. When on the phone, Mr Ross, angrily said to her, "Didn't you get our letter? I doubt if we can help you and coming here would be a waste of your time and ours."

She sensed that he had no desire to have another American snooping around, likely looking for some long-lost Scottish ancestor. Ginny persevered, saying, "Please just let me come and explain this to you. I have some interesting Indian portraits from America that you probably haven't seen which document my theories. I think it's important that we meet."

This piqued Mr Ross's curiosity just enough for him to agree to a meeting. "How soon will you be able to get here?"

She looked at her watch. "Is an hour too soon?"

"Fine. See you then."

Ginny made the mistake of walking. It was farther than she realized, but the scenery was special. Princes Street, the main thoroughfare, was lined with the kinds of stores you find in many cities the world over. There was a Woolworth's, department and electronic stores, mixed with tourist shops selling tourist trinkets, native tartans, kilts, and cashmeres. The highlight was the rugged hill, formed by the core of an extinct volcano that was topped by Edinburgh Castle. It was impossible not to be impressed by the haunting beauty of the old fortress.

By the time she climbed the high hill to the castle, Ginny was out of breath. And there at the entryway was a formally dressed sentry on duty at the gate.

"Excuse me, but I have an appointment with Mr Ross. Could you give me directions to his office? My name is Virginia Thomas."

"Been expecting you," the guard said. "I've been asked to personally escort you to Mr Ross's office. Might show you around a bit on the way."

Walking through the grounds, he seemed to feel it his duty to comment on the history of the castle, pointing out the Batteries, Governor's House, hospital, and Scottish War Memorial. They stopped briefly for her to look at the small pet cemetery reserved for the mascots of the regiments, then crossed the cobblestone courtyard of Crown Square and stood before the impressive castle, its tall tower housing her destination: The United Services Museum.

"This is it. Be sure to peek inside at the Crown Room. The crown, scepter, and sword of state are magnificent! Then go up the stairs and you will find Mr Ross waiting for you." They shook hands and Ginny thanked him for the guided tour.

The Scottish Royal regalia was as spectacular as expected. She climbed the dark, narrow, winding wooden staircase and two men greeted her. They introduced themselves as Mr Ross and his equally ancient assistant, Mr Graham.

After immediate pleasantries, they gave a long discourse on the fact that the Highlanders in North America were few in number and probably did not wear their kilts.

Ginny could not believe her ears and wondered if they were just testing her. *Are they trying to throw me off track to get rid of me, or did they know surprisingly little about Highlander activities in the colonies? There's no question that they are experts on military dress.*

The discussion was long, but very informative. At the end of it, Mr Ross asked Ginny to return on Thursday. They promised that they would have many rare documents and original drawings to show to her. Both sides had won because of the valuable exchange of ideas.

"We always enjoy a good fight," Mr Ross said, laughing, as she made her way to the exit.

Outside, Ginny stopped at the Argyle Battery, part of the main northern defense of the castle. She was exhilarated by the stimulating conversation and brisk Scottish air. The view of Princes Street and Edinburgh was splendid, but the ocean stretching beyond reminded Ginny how far from home she was.

The day was upbeat and productive and Ginny was feeling comfortable in her skin for the first time.

*I guess I deserve a "Highland fling,"* she thought, even though she couldn't believe she actually had the courage to go and meet with James. *It's only for a day. This is an opportunity I just can't pass up. And why should I?*

She decided that she would do her best to talk James into a side trip to the Black Watch Museum in Perth, which she guessed should be fairly painless for a military man. The history books were full of information about Black Watch regiment activities in North America, especially Canada. Stopping in a small pub for a beer and early dinner, she then returned to her hotel to wait for James's call.

Which came right on time. James was enthusiastic, telling her, "Catch the train to Perth at Waverley Station at nine forty-five tomorrow morning. I have a car and will be waiting for you at the station at Perth. By the way," he added, "the weather's been awful, so pack a small bag in case we get weathered in."

*Likely story,* Ginny thought. *Are you going to fall for that one? Well, if you are, you know what could happen.* She carefully considered the 'what ifs,' deciding, *may not be all bad,* and laughed. She may have lost her mind, but at least she hadn't completely lost her sense of humor.

Planning to meet a handsome and interesting man who was little more than a stranger, and being ready for whatever might happen, brought about excitement she had never experienced. She was even looking forward to it. Having been married since she was eighteen, never once had she ever thought of doing anything like this before. If only things had been different at home. Yes, if only...

She deserved a chance to do some interesting things, and maybe this was a push of sorts, a chance to start really re-thinking her life.

Ginny packed her tote bag, looked over her notes, and turned in early, though had a tough time falling asleep, the nervous excitement of tomorrow's possibilities buzzing and fluttering through her. The next morning, the courteous but cheerless manager served up another filling breakfast. He certainly wasn't chatty.

"I'm going on an overnight trip and will return sometime tomorrow," Ginny told him as she finished her meal and gathered her belongings. "I'll be keeping my room and leaving my suitcase here if that's all right." The manager nodded.

"Will you please call for a taxi to Waverley station?"

At nine forty-five, the train pulled out of the station. Ginny looked out the window at the Scottish countryside. She saw sheep and new spring lambs in the fields, but her thoughts were on James.

*How will this go? Will we have as much to talk about? Am I really doing this? Am I going to meet someone I hardly know? Guess I can't turn back now. It's only for a day. Maybe. He was so nice, an officer and a gentleman for sure.*

He hadn't been pushy with her on the train. It seemed the natural thing to do, as if part of a plan gently unfolded.

A coincidence? Despite her hasty exit from Miami, the trip had seemed like following an unknown but carefully set plan, no complications. She had followed her intuition all along, and so far, everything had gone well.

Somehow this, too, seemed like the thing to do. Enthusiasm percolated inside her about the prospect of seeing the Highlands and spending some time with James.

The train slowed and pulled into the station at Perth and Ginny scanned the platform. When she stepped off the train, James emerged from the small crowd of greeters.

As soon as she saw him, Ginny knew that she had made the right decision. *He's even nicer looking than I remembered---and that smile!*

"How was your trip?" He placed an arm around her shoulder and guided her to the car. Ginny already felt a sudden jolt of warmth.

"Beautiful! Wonderful scenery. The lambs are so adorable," she said.

"I've been waiting here since about nine-thirty. That's even before you left Edinburgh. I thought, What if she doesn't come? I'll just get on a train and go down to Edinburgh and find her. "

The car his friend loaned him was a new, small European Ford Escort, a sporty bright orange and black, with a black and white tweed upholstery interior. Nothing like her conservative silver Honda back in Miami.

"James," she said as they climbed in the car, "I have one request. Just a little work to do. There's a museum, the Black Watch Museum, that I must see in Perth if for no other reason than to justify my conscience. Can we find it and have a quick look around?"

"Sure, no problem."

James pulled the car away from the train station and turned left onto Leonard Street. When he saw a tourist information sign, he pulled in and parked. He ran in just long enough to grab a map of Perth and a handful of tourist pamphlets. Handing them to Ginny, he then headed on their way again.

"Tell me about yourself," James said.

"What do you want to know?"

"Everything, I guess. I want to know everything about you. Start at the beginning."

*Where to begin? How can I make it brief?* No one had ever cared enough to ask her about her life before. She'd never seriously considered the subject in this way.

"Are you sure?"

"I'm sure," he said.

"Well, the beginning," she drew in a breath, then let it out. "I was born and raised in Miami, great weather, eternal sunshine, lush tropical landscape. A young, exciting, modern city. Who couldn't love Miami as a hometown? Miami and Miami Beach are great tourist destinations, connected by a causeway over Biscayne Bay. Dolphins rolling in the bay. Miami Beach is very glitzy, famous for huge luxurious hotels on the ocean. I rarely go there. Miami is more of a hometown."

James nodded, keeping his eyes on the road as he made another left to

St. Andreas Street, with gothic, medieval, and revival style buildings.

"Recently, I was guarding the Royal family and exposed to lots of luxury. Huge castles but not much sunshine," he said, as they came to a roundabout. "What did you like to do?"

"I've been an artist as long as I can remember. Started as a little girl, when I first picked up a pencil to draw, or crayons to color, and then a brush to paint.

"My father died when I was almost thirteen. Horrible brain cancer, devastating. That had an awful effect on my life. My distraught mother, sister, and I moved in with my grandparents, who then lost their freedom. There were lots of arguments and much tension, so I was very unhappy. I could always escape in art and my imagination."

"Sorry, " James said. "That couldn't have been easy. What was school like?"

"I was in high school in the 50s. Try to understand that growing up in America in the 50s was what we called later, a real trip. I was popular enough, plenty of girlfriends and several boyfriends. Some wrote in my yearbook about liking my paintings. I was remembered for painting clowns, smiling, with a tear rolling down one cheek. Guess that says a lot.

"I dated Wayne Thomas in high school. I was so unhappy at home, I was glad to escape that sad house and we married when I was eighteen and he was twenty, just before we started at the university. He was a first-year law student and I was a freshman art major. We graduated together.

"After graduation, Wayne enlisted in the army and was an officer in JAG. I guess you know that means Judge Advocate General, the legal branch of the American armed services."

"JAG of British Forces," James said.

I had no role models for a great career, and no idea where art would take me. In my family, women married young and stayed at home to be the perfect wife and mother. I resigned myself to that fate."

"Sign of the times,"James said.

"Yet, I guess hidden in the back of my mind was a totally sublimated wild side, a curiosity gene somewhere. In college, being around other artists, I often wished I could just run off to New York or Paris, where the art action was, to live the artist's life. I became interested in Asian art, Zen Buddhism and Alan Watts, who wrote about it. I wanted to see Japan. However, I always did what was considered *right*, and gave up those dreams of travel early. I was a real product of my generation."

"Well, our stories couldn't be more opposite. I've always had my freedom. I was born in 1945, in war-torn London, and not the best part of London, East End. My father was Cockney, my mother was Irish. The area was bombed heavily during the war. My family had to deal with the destruction, severe hardships, and rationing. Certainly never posh.

"When I was sixteen, the headmaster of my school and I came to an agreement. He didn't want me in school and I didn't want to be there, so I took my snooker cue and ran away. I ended up in Singapore, supporting myself by shooting pool. I had excellent hand-eye coordination, great depth perception, and was good at it. Then I decided to put that skill to good use with a rifle and make something of myself, so I joined the army It's been my career since I was seventeen."

"Wow! What a way to enter the military," Ginny said. "Wayne was stationed in Missouri, so we moved to Fort Leonard Wood, a training camp, known as Fort-Lost-in-the-Woods. At night, while doing dinner dishes, I could hear the endless rounds of gunfire in the distance and knew young soldiers in training were crawling under live bullets. Very scary and I worried about them. It was an honor for Wayne to serve. He had his job, friends, respect.

"Not in my plans. I was isolated Nowhere. Literally, it was in the middle of nowhere; not Florida, New York, Paris, or Kyoto. I had only lived in large cities and the wilderness army post was like prison to me. I didn't meet any wives I had anything in common with, and few opportunities to make friends. I did get to teach some painting classes at the Officer's Wives' Club. I'll admit, I hated every minute of it. Sorry, that's how I felt.

"When we first talked over coffee, I just didn't think to mention the one good thing I got from Fort Wood. We have a son, Eric. A bundle of joy that kept me busy. He was born in the army hospital, as we planned, and he's quite proud of that. Eric's twenty, doing well in college, away a lot on his own now, and a fun good guy. I love him, always very glad when I can see him, and I'm proud of him."

"Congratulations on your son. I understand about Missouri, because I've been stuck in awful places for long tours, too. My army perk is that I've traveled a lot in the service," James continued.

"Africa. I love Africa and would happily go back there. Berlin. The Congo. Vietnam; I was at Da Nang. Because of my experience in Borneo, I was training Americans in jungle warfare, but the British were not in Nam officially. Northern Ireland; I had two tours there and was in the bloodiest fighting in Northern Ireland, 'Bloody Sunday' in Londonderry, Derry, 1972. I've also learned to speak a number of languages: German, French, Greek, and some Irish dialects. Guess I've seen a lot of combat, but I'm not the blood-thirsty type. Some are, you know. I just go where I'm assigned and do the job."

James was quiet and Ginny continued telling her story. "I have nothing so exciting to report. After the army, we moved back to Miami and Wayne joined an old, established law firm. He changed. There were many good years, but unhappy times as well. I guess I put my life on hold to raise Eric and keep house as expected, but I was full of resentment. I had to live through others."

"I had to follow military orders, but other than that I was quite inde-pendent," James explained and then Ginny spoke again.

"I realized that there was more I was capable of doing — I had this strong stirring, a deeper spiritual need, to find out what life was really about. Painting became too easy. I was selling well, but it wasn't a challenge anymore, needed more depth in content. I was seriously interested in people of other cultures, Native Americans, Africans, others, their art, religions, ways of life, and their stories. When Eric was old enough and I felt he was on the right track, I decided that it was my time to do some of the things I wanted to do."

"Getting near your museum, but please continue," James said.

"Well, I went to graduate school, studying anthropology and art histo-ry- tribal arts. I wanted to know about the people and art of other cultures, not just through books, but to go out to the reservations to observe and in-terview, listen and talk. I work with many Native Americans and they're my friends. I'm not good with languages, but of course the people I work with speak fluent English and their native languages.

"I like museum work. Now I have a part-time job at a museum with good future prospects, but I've been absolutely badgered. My husband can neither understand nor approve of the great things happening to me, ca-reer-wise, as well as the changes in my life and attitude. He prefers to think I've simply gone crazy, mostly because I'm just not marching to his drumbeat anymore. He's jealous of my time and my passion for research and he argues with me all the time. He's away on business or at meetings much of the time, so I'm either very lonely or harassed, rarely anything else."

She gently bit her lip and sank a little deeper in her seat. "I've said more than I wanted but that's how it is and I'm pretty miserable. I smile on the outside, like the clowns I painted, but a lot has been bottled up for so many years. Our son knows what goes on, how unhappy I am, and understands. I've only told one friend the extent of my frustrations. No one ever asked or cared before. Sorry, that's pretty much the story and the other reason why I'm here, away from it all. Guess you're sorry you asked."

"No, not at all. I can understand your pride in your success. I know that feeling, but no one was holding me back. Thanks for sharing with me," he said.

"And you?" she asked. "Tell me more about you."

"Here's your museum. I'll finish later."

They pulled into the parking lot of the small and picturesque castle museum and went inside. James suggested that they stop to look at the military uniforms and silver trophies on display and explained the awards of the Black Watch regiments. Ginny took a few notes and photographs, bought a book on the Black Watch and a print of a Highland officer, and they left the museum.

The day was sparkling, with a cloudless bright blue sky. The air cool and crisp but not too cold, they traveled on roads that became narrow and winding.

"I'm taking the back roads so you can see more. Can't see much speeding along the highway."

She was grateful, looking out at spectacular woodlands.

"Never been married," he continued. "But I believe I've experienced all of the emotions; love, caring, hate. The military's been my life."

She wondered how he ever escaped marriage, thinking he must be pretty elusive.

"Once, I led a patrol in Nam to rescue two American nurses who had been captured. After we got them out, I started seeing one of them. She was beautiful. They sent her back to the States. When I got a chance, I went over to visit her. I found that she was happily living with someone. The part that really hurt was that it was another girl. Was that ever awful for my ego."

"I guess," Ginny said.

We went through narrow lanes, passing farms and fields, some with game birds behind white fences.

"Look at the pheasants. Beautiful birds! Too bad they aren't free. Know the feeling," she said.

The land opened up to rolling hills and glens. Ginny was awestruck by the region's natural beauty.

"The glens are named after the rivers that flow through them, with names like Glenisla and Glenshee," James explained.

"Glenshee? Is that where we are? I have no idea of where we are going. Glenshee means 'Glen of the fairies' in Gaelic. It's considered a magical place. I read about it in *The Fairy Faith in Celtic Countries*. Guess you probably haven't heard of or read it. Published in 1911, the author was Evans Wentz, as I remember, He interviewed people who told of encounters with fairies and Little People. There's an account that Glenshee was once considered full of fairies, until the screech of the steam engine drove them underground, as Wentz put it. Fascinating. Native Americans have similar stories of Little People, too.

"Those similarities are just the kind of thing I'm looking for. Of course, in contemporary times, the belief in fairies and Little People is considered superstition. I respect all ways of thinking except those that are prejudicial. I listen and tape record tales told by natives who want their stories preserved for fear of losing the oral tradition altogether. American Indians I've known and worked with respect the spoken and the written word. I think the human imagination is boundless and belief in myths is universal. The people change but the myths stay the same, rooted in the past. The trouble is, we're in too much of a hurry to preserve them."

"I suppose you're right, but I never really thought about it that way,"- James said.

"It's understandable that the Indians and the Highlanders were compatible. The two groups shared many common social and religious customs and attitudes. Both were tribal and organized into clans. They had close ties with nature, consulted oracles, and believed that supernatural spirits, including 'Little People,' inhabited the woods. They even had comparable rituals, including sacred fires, and harvest dances."

"Interesting. This is all new to me," James said, watching the curved road ahead.

"By 1750, Indian trade in the Southeastern Creek Indian nation was virtually monopolized by the Highland clans of the Chattan confederation. More trading licenses bore Scottish names such as McGillivray, McIntosh, and McQueen.

"Highlander men had Indian wives from prominent clans and together they raised families. They're matrilineal, and their sons became powerful in their communities as chiefs. I should imagine there was a lot of pillow talk and I wonder what they taught their children in Indian languages and Gaelic. Sorry for the long rambling lecture, but that's what I've put together. I want you to know I wasn't making this up, being here is so exciting, and I need to thank you for inviting me."

James smiled. "I knew you'd love it, from what you told me while we were having coffee," he said. "You're sure enthusiastic and I see how serious you are about this. I'm learning a lot I didn't know.

"You had to see the country. As for the Highlanders, there are lords who own the land and everything on it, for as far as the eye can see. That castle over there belongs to Lord Gibbs. He owns all of this. The sheep painted with blue on their rumps belong to him, but those with red belong to someone else. They plant turnips and the sheep eat the tops. The cattle are fed the vegetables."

Ginny was so glad she'd come with James ... what if she'd followed through on her no go idea?

*My life is so sheltered in Miami. Right now, I feel like a tropical bird freed from its cage. James' life is different. Who knows, maybe it's even heroic, in a certain way. One thing for sure, he knows the world like the back of his hand. But here we are together and he seems to appreciate my love of storytelling and the world of the imagination. I'm sure he's not faking it.*

"Hungry?" he asked.

"Very," she told him.

"Time for lunch then."

He pulled the car into the parking lot of an old inn; Glenshee Inn, the sign read. It was small and pleasant, and inside they were the only diners other than the owner, who chatted with a friend. They took a table next to a glowing peat fire. The menu was written on a chalkboard and listed "Baked Tatties," and a number of topping selections. James ordered for them, a French topping with mushrooms on their baked potatoes and two half pints of dark beer.

Seated across from each other on the wooden benches, they sipped the creamy foam from the Guinness and exchanged smiles. Their eyes locked. It was the first time they openly looked deeply at each other. He took her hand.

"I have this fantasy of being away with someone in a cabin, with a nice cozy fire on a long, snowy weekend," James said softly.

Ginny's eyes sparkled. "That's a fantasy I could easily share."

They finished their lunch saying little.

The tour continued. "We're getting near the ski area now," James said. "There's a party tonight and my friends want to meet you. Remember the two German women on the train? They stayed up here the other night but are gone now."

"Too bad," Ginny said. "It would've been fun to see the looks on their faces when we turned up together. They would never have guessed. We said so little on the train and it was very discreet. The lady across from me did notice the one time you and I smiled at each other. That was when the strange announcement came for the lady with the ginger-colored hair."

Ginny added, with a laugh, "I felt your eyes on me, as well, and sometimes they *were* disapproving."

James said, "Admiring. Not disapproving."

They drove on to the foot of the Glenshee chairlift on Cairnwell Mountain, in the Cairngorms range. Skiers made their way down the deep slopes. There were numerous army trucks, Land Rovers, and skiers sloshing in the little snow that remained. The weather was too nice to hold the snow, which was mushy. Terrible for skiing. The Peter Stuytevant Tobacco Company had spent a fortune promoting this annual event, Snow Fun Week, so the lack of snow and the low attendance had to be disappointing.

Soldiers in khaki fatigues spotted the car and waved or yelled a greeting. Ginny wondered if they had been the guys on the train. James stopped, excused himself, and walked over to talk to a soldier in a Land Rover.

Returning, James said, "I have a message to check on. I'll show you where I'm staying. I have a room in the building over there." He pointed.

They wound around the narrow road and approached a white farmhouse. James indicated a nearby woman chopping firewood. "They lead a very hard life here. Few luxuries." He stopped the car and went inside to check on his message.

Ginny was alone in the Highlands. She got out of the car to experience the quiet beauty of the mountains and glens, took a deep breath of fresh, cool mountain air. So peaceful. Only the chirping of birds cut into the silence. The whole view was like a painting. The white farmhouse was accented with a bright blue wooden door and window frames. A red phone booth stood in front of the house.

All was quaint and perhaps a little too perfect. *Have I stepped back through a time warp? The woman chopping firewood. Was that real?*

Actually, this reminded Ginny of the hills of North Carolina, where she spent many a summer with her family. North Carolina, the Land of the Cherokee, and where Highlanders and other Scottish or Irish immigrants had settled. How similar the Smoky Mountains must have seemed to their homelands, with mountains, the gentle rolling hills, sparkling rivers, and bubbling brooks. Dragonflies skimmed the streams, wings fluttering like in stories of fairies of Scotland. No wonder they felt at home there. Her research had taken her full circle. The Highlands. A place where she'd lived, and now a place she'd dreamed of ...

James emerged from the house. "Strange," he said. "I'm to call my office in London tomorrow at ten o'clock."

"What for?"

"I don't know. Wonder what's up. Come on. Let's go."

Winding down the road and away from the farmhouse, Ginny asked, "Where to now?"

"To a hotel. You're going to need a little rest if you're going to the party tonight."

"And you?"

"Same."

A warm feeling touched her cheeks. Then a puzzling sense of tension. *Well, we couldn't go on driving around forever.*

She decided to relax, settle back, go with the flow. She nestled in her seat and didn't say anything, savoring the moment.

"I didn't know how to come right out and tell you how much I wanted you to stay with me tonight," James told her. "That's why I suggested that you bring a bag, in case the weather was bad. A terrible white lie, and I apologize, but I hope you'll stay."

Ginny didn't know how to reply. "Hmm," she said, and snuggled deeper into the seat. *Well, at least he's honest about that.*

He turned the car into the parking lot of the Glenshee Inn again, and stopped. "I booked the room when I paid our lunch bill. I hope this is okay because everything else in the area is full."

As they unloaded the car, Ginny asked, "Should I bring my book?"

James smiled. "Don't think you'll need it."

She blushed, realizing her naiveté.

The proprietor took them up the stairs to a large room with a bath next door. "No private baths here," he said. "But this is the closest. I don't expect many other guests anyway. There's a coffee pot down the hall."

He showed James around and Ginny stared at the snow out of the window as they talked. The room was cold. Soon the door closed and Ginny felt James behind her.

His arms slid around her waist, and he pulled her close.

Then there was a knock at the door.

James opened it. The proprietor again.

"The bar opens at five."

"Thanks." He exited and James closed the door, laughing.

Ginny looked out the window again. At the same time, she felt his arms come around her. Slowly, he turned her, touched her face, raised her chin until her eyes met his.

*His deep blue eyes, so deep you could swim in them.*

"Ever since the first moment I saw you on the train, I knew I had to be with you. That's why I sat where I did. So I could see you."

The words were so unexpected and sincere that she felt her heart skip a beat. He drew her close and gave her a kiss. A lingering kiss.

Slowly, as she allowed herself to relax, the kiss kindled a growing ember inside her.

Ginny felt their bodies merge, closer and closer.

James's British reserve was gone now.

They sank onto the bed. "We're overdressed," he said.

The room was cold and without words they quietly undressed and, minutes later, found each other under the covers. He touched her and she moved closer to him.

They made love, alternately giving and surrendering, until they both lay still for a moment, breathing heavily. After a moment or two, they found each other again. This time their bodies knew what to do without a single thought. It was a dream pantomime of pure love.

The soldier came with a shudder that Ginny found vulnerable and beautiful. Hers was long and almost continuous. In her mind, it lasted forever.

When they could finally speak, James whispered, "I like the name Virginia."

"Ginny, please. But Virginia, if you like it that way. So, do your friends call you James?"

"Mostly. But Americans call me Jim. You can call me that, if you want."

"Jim. I like that."

"Tell me, what color are your eyes?"

"Hazel, green and brown. Yours are the deepest blue I've ever seen."

"You didn't look close enough. They're blue-green."

They both laughed.

After which they made love again and again. At last they were too tired to move.

"I'll be honest with you," he said. "This is heaven; you're heaven."

"What's happening to us?" Ginny asked.

"Quite simply … we're falling …"

"… in love?"

Sometime later, they dressed and went out.

Ginny asked herself, over and over, am I really in love?

In the car, in the fading dusk, she asked, "Where're we going?"

"Somewhere for a nice dinner. Alone," he said. "I just want to talk to you and be alone with you."

"But what about your party? You were looking forward to it."

"You can't talk at parties."

He drove the slow descent into Blairgowrie and parked in the center of town. There were several hotels with restaurants in the area. After checking them all out, they agreed on the Angus Hotel.

The restaurant was crowded. Jim left his name on the waiting list with the hostess, who sent them to the cozy bar. There they found a corner table and ordered gin and tonics.

There was so much to talk about. He filled her head with war stories, tales of exotic places and sights she could barely imagine, and, somehow, longed to see. Ginny let go of herself. She'd never been so charmed.

He told her, "Your Highlanders are still fearful warriors, you might be interested to know. Once, when I was in Northern Ireland, thousands of Irish were gathered and ready to storm the British. We would've been greatly out-numbered, but there was a large Highland regiment on duty at the time, and they lined up in full battle dress and fixed bayonets. They marched down the street, and the crowd quietly dispersed."

His name was called and they were soon seated in a booth. Again Ginny preferred that he order for both of them: prawns, steak, salad and a carefully selected German white wine.

"Do you have a confidant?" Jim asked.

"Yes, a best friend that I've known for many years. There are no secrets between us," she said. "Her name is Dr. Marjorie Henning, Margie, a university professor. She is my mentor."

"Are you going to tell her about me?"

*I wonder if Margie would believe the story.*

Ginny quickly changed the subject. "Do you have someone *you* talk to?"

"Yes," said Jim. "I don't see much of him, though. Remember when they had the bomb on the QE II? He's the specialist they dropped in by helicopter to defuse it. Exceptionally delicate work and a tremendous risk. Great friend, though."

"What a friend."

There was a silence while they sipped their wine.

"Ginny, do you know what you must do when you get home?"

"What's that?" she asked.

"You should assert yourself, and above all, straighten out your life, whatever that really means. If you're this unhappy, consider a clean break. Get a divorce and a real job. I'm saying to you, *jump!* Take that leap of faith -- but I won't catch you. You'll have to learn to land on your own two feet. I see you have greater strength than you realize; it shines bright in your eyes. Go ahead and put everybody out of misery. It's the best thing for everyone."

"I know you're right. Of course, easier said than done," Ginny said.

"I'll be over in Belize soon and will come to Miami as often as possible. You won't be able to lead a double life. You'll have to do something about it. Then we can enjoy this. I can't give you everything you're used to, but I believe that I can make you happy, and that's more important."

Surprised by the frankness of his words, she let them sink in. Apparently, he saw her as the strong woman she so desperately wanted to be. And that's when anxiety stepped in.

*Could she?*

They shared the house specialty for dessert, a feather-light raspberry meringue gateau.

Later, as he drove the dark and winding road back to Glenshee, both were mellow from the meal.

"I hope my friends don't try to play any tricks on us. They know where we are and might get some funny ideas, since we didn't go to the party. I had to tell them. Someone must know where I am at all times. Guess I haven't told you yet, but I'm always on call and could be sent away at any time."

She thought of another James. Bond. James Bond. He came and went.

There were no messages. No pranksters appeared to be lurking about. Still mellow, they went to their room.

This time, they slowly undressed, tenderly touching here, kissing there. Then, eagerly, his hands explored her body.

She felt nothing tentative about his gentleness, rather it was so provocative and sweet at the same time that she fell away, as if in a dream of love. It was real but it was also dreamlike, as if she were swimming in some strange, evanescent sea where she was entirely weightless. At one point she protested, but he begged her. "Don't worry, I won't leave a mark on you." She had a feeling that he knew her limit was perhaps reached. But his touch was that of a feather falling from illimitable space. And when they joined again, their dance was without motion. It was the deepest, most fulfilling holding and embrasure she'd ever known.

And it was a night that would never end.

Finally, in contentment and exhaustion, they fell asleep in each other's arms. Ginny awakened intermittently, watching him sleep.

*I am so lucky. This man is so very special.*

He slept peacefully, but occasionally, when he woke it was with a reassuring smile. "There's no tomorrow, you know," he whispered.

A gray morning dawned as light snow fell silently in the glen. Their morning kiss was long and satisfying. They looked at the bed and laughed. The covers were hopelessly tangled.

For a long time, they didn't speak.

Then, at last, she asked, "What are your plans?"

"For the day ... or for the rest of my life?"

This answer surprised her, so she quickly said, "I have to get back to Edinburgh and get on with my research."

"I'm planning to come down to Edinburgh and stay with you for the rest of the week," he said.

"But it's your holiday and you wanted to ski."

"That's okay. I really just wanted to get out of London and away from the pressure. There sure isn't much snow, and I want to be with you. You can do your work in the day and I'll amuse myself. I love Edinburgh and can always find things to do. Then we'll have the nights together. There are some nice places that I can show you, and wonderful places to eat. It will be a lot more fun than being here."

"I'm surprised that you'd want to leave the skiing and your friends to be with me, whether there is snow or not. It's too wonderful... I'm flattered."

Then she remembered, "But you must know that I've arranged to meet a very married friend. He's a Scottish colleague, a PhD anthropologist, and I called him from London to confirm our meeting. We made plans to get together at the end of the week."

"I don't want to hinder your work," he said. "What's his name?"

"His name is Malcolm McIntosh. He directs a small textile museum up here, and as part of his 'act,' wears a kilt all the time. He's an expert on the tartans. It was my job for the museum to entertain him during his four days in Miami while on an American speaking tour. He's been researching the same thing I'm working on, from a Scottish perspective. He was sitting over here and wondering about the Indians, if you can believe that. At any rate, he has museum business in London and was taking the train to Edinburgh and we were to go to London together to compare notes. He's quite an interesting character, and somehow you can't help but like him."

"Oh, no, not two of you!" he joked. "That'll be okay, and I won't get in the way. But I have some things I have to do here before I can leave. Got to check on that call to London and square away with my friends. There's a ten o'clock train that I'll put you on. I'll finish up here and then get to Edinburgh around six. Just for looks, book a room for me at your hotel. Rothesay, is it? I'll meet you there at six."

They dressed, packed, said little; there was so much to think about. As Jim paid the bill, Ginny stood at the door of the inn, watching the soundless fall of snow. She reflected on their time together. It had been magic.

Had been? So soon gone?

*Was it real or will I wake up and find it's just a dream?*

*No, it was real.*

She could still taste it on her lips.

Very real, too real.

And strange as it seemed, they had each found their little patch of heaven together. Two foundlings in the Highlands. And the Highlands had cast its spell on them.

Too good to be true?

Jim took her arm and they stepped into the snow and ran to the car door. As always, Ginny headed for the wrong side of the car, an act Jim could not let go without comment.

Ginny replied, "Why do the British do everything backwards? Sit on the wrong side of the car, drive on the wrong side of the road, eat upside down, or is it more American rebellion that makes us opposites?" But she had just fallen very much in love with the British. At least with one.

Jim loaded the car and they began the journey to Perth. Passing through Blairgowrie in the daylight, she noticed a sign pointing to Balmoral. *Balmoral and Balmorality*, Ginny thought. The very name smacked of romance, that hideaway of Queen Victoria. The popular theory that after Albert's death, her Highland servant became her secret lover.

"I've always wanted to see Balmoral, " she said. "Maybe next time."

There was little to say on the trip. Jim was beyond quiet.

"You're not talking," she said with a tinge of insecurity. "Is everything okay?"

"Umm. Silent and deep. That's me."

She tried to imagine the face of Jim on the train. Yes, it was a little like this. Deep in a world of his own.

"Are you sure everything's okay?"

He nodded. "Yes. Oh, I forget that women need reassurance. I've never been better. Did you see that Land Rover we just passed? Do you watch *MASH* on television? We love MASH in the British army. It's our favorite show. The guy driving the Land Rover is one of my men, Barry Wells, and I call him 'Radar,' like Radar O'Reilly. He's my paymaster, and a radio man."

He lapsed into silence once more and Ginny could only wonder what thoughts were in his head. Would she want to know?

Too soon, they were at the train station in Perth and Jim was opening the car door. He checked the train schedule in the terminal.

"Take the train to Stirling and then change to the one to Edinburgh," he advised. "You'll get there faster. Let's get some coffee."

Sipping from their cups, Jim suddenly seemed serious, saying, "Maybe I'd better give an address to you, just so you'll have it. I never know what can happen." He wrote an address on her notepad. It was in England. "This is always my home base. If I'm not here, my mail is sent to me from this address to wherever I am. Let's put you on that train now, and I'll make that call to London from here."

Her train was ready for boarding as they reached the gate.

"I won't go beyond here, Ginny. It was wonderful. Thank you for coming. I'll see you tonight at six in Edinburgh."

"Thank you for everything, Jim. It truly was wonderful. Not to be missed. Six at the Rothesay."

He gave her a long, passionate goodbye kiss, then handed her bag to her. She turned to walk the long platform to her train, not daring to look back. *Did life have more to offer?*

# 3
# Edinburgh / London

Ginny followed his instructions, got off the train at Stirling, and waited for her connection. When the train to Edinburgh was announced, she quickly got aboard, stopped in the washroom, and splashed cool water on her face. Looking in the mirror, she perceived a change.

She had broken the shackles and for once felt completely in control. Refreshed and secure on the right train, she relaxed, feeling warm, wonderful, and very satisfied. Honestly, she hadn't felt so good in years. She curled up in her seat and slept so she would be fresh for her appointment that afternoon.

Edinburgh was windy, gray, cold, and alternating between sleet and snow. The Rothesay seemed as empty as when she left. It would be nice to have company there. She rang the bell to call the manager.

"I need to reserve another room for this evening." She told him. "A friend will be checking in around six."

"No problem. We certainly have rooms."

That was the understatement of the year.

Ginny stowed her bag and glanced in the mirror. A trip to the hairdresser would be a good idea. The American hair dryer adapter didn't work in the outlet in her room, so it was impossible to do her hair herself. She had noticed a unisex salon around the corner from the hotel when she had passed it on Monday. It was on an interesting street, crowded with boutiques, meat markets, fruit and vegetable stands, bakeries, liquor and wine, and cheese stores. A perfect place to shop for a welcoming party for Jim.

The salon was bustling but there was one stylist available, and he took her to his chair immediately. The warm shampoo and blow-dry felt terrific, and she reveled in a bit of self-indulgence. Her hairstyle was easy, and she was back out on the street again in a half hour.

Ginny turned onto Princes Street, making way to her appointment at the National Gallery. Walking along, a perfume ad in a department store window caught her eye, and she went inside. Perfume was not on her packing list, but now she wanted to both look and smell great for the evening with Jim. She selected a small spray bottle of her favorite, Chloe, sultry and very expensive. She then bought a black nightgown with lace in the lingerie department and put it in her bag.

The Keeper at the museum was awaiting Ginny's visit. The museum collection was outstanding. There were only a few paintings and drawings relating to the period in question. It took a little over an hour to photograph the artworks and make notes. After seeing the paintings of Scots, she devoted the rest of her stay to sheer artistic pleasure, absorbed in the glory of the Degas and Rodin, Constable, and Gainsborough.

By four-thirty, Ginny had covered as much territory as possible, her feet giving out before the eyes. She bought a catalog of the museum collection and left. It was starting to get dark — and much colder — as she hurried through the streets, returning to the wine and cheese shops. She had decent knowledge of California wines, but knew little about European wines. The wine merchant helped her select a good one, and even gave her a bottle opener. At the cheese shop two doors down, she bought a nice wedge of Brie, crackers, a cheese knife, and colorful cocktail napkins. Grapes and apples from a nearby fruit stand completed the welcome party

There were no messages when she checked in with the manager at the Rothesay. She took the lift to her floor and went to her room, which was no warmer than before. The wine would quickly chill on the windowsill.

She filled the tub with hot water, stretched out, and soaked her aching feet and legs. The excitement began to build as she thought of seeing Jim again. Had it all been a dream, a mirage? She would know soon, as six o'clock was rapidly approaching.

The saving grace of the Rothesay was the warm towel rack, which was offset by the shock of the cold tile bathroom floor. Ginny quickly dried off and dressed. Her best gray tweed suit and a simple black silk blouse with faux pearls seemed right for the occasion. She brushed her clean hair, put on a simple selection of makeup and lightly sprayed on the Chloe.

Taking the black nightgown out of the bag, she held it up to her, looking in the mirror.

"Not bad," she said as she fluffed the gown and set it by the bed.

Ginny hummed as she arranged her party spread on the only table in the room. Two water glasses would have to serve as crystal, but the wine was well chilled. The cheese, crackers, and fruit looked attractive, spread on a cocktail napkin. Seemed now, there was nothing left to do but wait for Jim's call.

As the minutes slipped by, Ginny began to pace. *Will our closeness be the same, or will there be awkward moments? No, everything will be fine,* she assured herself.

She had known Jim for such a short time, but he said they were comfortable, as if they had known each other forever. He was so polite, considerate, caring, and charming. His stories, both serious and funny, had enraptured her for hours in the Highlands. They shared a warmth and intimacy that wouldn't end just because they were in Edinburgh. After all, Edinburgh had its own charm. The more these thoughts ran through her mind, the more her apprehensions melted away

Six-fifteen. The shrill ring of the phone in the cold silent room jolted Ginny.

"Is this Ginny Thomas?" asked the unfamiliar voice on the other end of the line.

Her heart skipped a beat. "Yes," she could barely reply.

"I'm Sergeant Wells," the voice said. "Lieutenant Evans asked me to call. I'm calling from Glenshee. James won't be able to meet you. He was called back to London unexpectedly. There's some sort of crisis and they called him back. He said he has your number and address in America, and you'll hear from him as soon as he gets a chance. He said he's sorry, but it can't be helped."

"Thank you for the call," Ginny said, as she hung up the phone in disbelief. The old rule of thumb still applied; expect the unexpected and it will happen. *Blast it!* Tears softly rolled down her cheeks. From the highest of expectations to the lowest of disappointment. With a sense of defeat, she picked up the phone and cancelled Jim's reservation.

She opened the bottle of wine, drank a glass, and cut some of the cheese. Stifling cries of bitter disappointment and frustration. *Why did this happen? What kind of crisis could be so swift and important? Who had the nerve to call him away from a holiday he so desperately needed?*

A thousand thoughts raced through her mind. *Was I a fool? Was that all there was to it, a one-night stand? Was it a lie?* No, for once she felt confident enough that there must be a genuine reason for Jim to not be there. Jim was honest and had been sincerely moved by the emotions they so openly shared. She didn't know what the problem was, but knew it must be a big one. Besides, he had warned her that he could be called away at any time, night or day.

She undressed, put her pretty gown into *Liberator*, and pulled on her thermal underwear. Certainly not the evening she had planned.

The room suddenly seemed colder than ever. She tried to concentrate on her notes from the museum and plan the next day's schedule, but it was useless. She turned the lights off and stared into the quiet darkness of the room until she finally fell asleep.

Fortunately, the following days were busy. Ginny was able to shake off the numbness of the big letdown and forced all of her concentration into the project at hand. After all, she was there for research, and the trip would be a success on that score.

She met her scheduled Thursday appointment for another try at the men at the castle. This time, they greeted her with enthusiasm, and showed her the rare prints and drawings she had traveled so far to see.

Ginny took endless photographs and made pages and pages of notes, describing military dress worn by the regiments in North America, men's names, clans, and where they were from.

Her theories were being substantiated. Similarities in clothing styles could not be denied. Even Mr Ross and Mr Graham were becoming interested in her work. Mr Ross personally took her through the Scottish United Services Museum, pointing out details of officer's uniforms she might have missed. She saw her first real silver gorget, a crescent-shaped neck piece worn to protect an officer's throat. The only others she had seen were in portraits.

After a full day of study in the castle, she thanked the gentlemen for their kindnesses and cooperation, and promised to send them a copy of her paper. They suggested a trip to the Register House, said it might be useful, and called and made an appointment for her for the next morning.

The long walk down the hill from the castle was invigorating, but she was sad to have finished her work there. She found a pub, had a dark beer with fish and chips, and took time to reflect on the day.

Back at the hotel she checked with the desk to see if there were any messages. Nothing. No word from Jim, nor from anyone else, for that matter. Now it was a true solo flight. She climbed into bed with her books and notes.

On Friday she awoke in a fit of frustration. *Where in God's name is Jim? This is so unfair!*

Once more gripped by anger, she decided to call the Glenshee number to see if it was all a bad joke. The phone gave three funny rings before it was answered.

"Lieutenant Evans, please."

"Sorry. He's not here. He's been called away."

"Okay, I know that. I just thought I'd check to see if he had come back yet."

"No, he won't be coming back. He went up to London and then off somewhere. I don't rightly know where."

"I was told that he would contact me when he could. Will that be in the next day or so? I leave here on Saturday and fly back to the States on Monday."

"I'm afraid that I have no idea. You'll just have to wait and see. He could be gone for a long time."

"Well, thanks," Ginny said. "I'm sorry to have bothered you. I was just worried about him. Goodbye."

*That was fruitless,* she thought. *Best to get over to the Register House, which is hopefully less frustrating.*

Ginny bought *The Scotsman,* the morning Edinburgh newspaper, and searched it for a clue. *Whatever happened that was so important that the "body snatchers" could whisk Jim away?*

She climbed the steps to the Register House, a treasury of Scottish documents.

Ironically, an exhibition of documents and letters from Highlanders in America was featured. There was frequent mention of activities with the Indians, both battles with them and joint cooperative ventures. Inventory lists of trade goods taken to the New World provided valuable information. The Keeper, Miss McGregor, was interested in Ginny's work, very knowledgeable about the subject, and arranged for her to see anything she requested.

That final day in Edinburgh was the icing on the cake. Her paper would stand up to any test now. All she had to do was to go back to Miami and write it.

She finished the day walking down the Royal Mile, poking in the fine shops. She bought a brown plaid kilt and scarf.

The tartan was similar to the one used by Burberry and very popular. *Must be Tourist Clan*, she thought. *I'll have Malcolm identify it tomorrow.*

At the end of the Mile, she finished her tour of Edinburgh with a visit to the royal palace, Holyrood, and listened to the guide describe its long and often tragic history.

Ginny became increasingly more depressed. The work had gone exceptionally well, but she had never experienced such loneliness before. What might have been a wonderful week of work balanced with fun was now all work and evening isolation.

March weather, not known to be the best in Scotland, was holding true to form, incredibly changeable. An hour of sun during the cool day was followed by rain, sleet, or snow flurries, and not necessarily in that order. She was beginning to long for the continuous warm Florida sun.

Since this was her last evening in Edinburgh, she decided to do something special. Something to create a fond memory of the fair city. She took a taxi to the Rothesay, determined to make the evening pleasant.

As the taxi driver let her out in front of the hotel, he said in his thick Scottish accent. "Your hotel will sure be full this evenin'."

"Not likely. There hasn't been a soul here but me and the manager this whole week," she said.

"Ah, you'll see, ma'am. It'll fill up!"

Ginny checked at the desk to see if there was a message. There was nothing. The manager must be tired of her asking, but it was her last night anyway.

As she headed for the lift, he stopped her. "By the way, he said. I've taken the liberty of moving your room. We'll be havin' a lot of guests and you'll be more comfortable. It'll be quieter." He gave her the key and told her to go to the top floor.

*Well, it also might be warmer. I can't imagine what the penthouse will be like at the Rothesay. And whatever happened to Jim? He seemed so happy. No, he was so happy. I'm sure of it. Why on earth did he vanish?* Their storybook romance had come to an abrupt halt. *Wasn't that what Jim called it, a storybook romance? It seemed unreal and funny at the time. But …what would be the end of the story?*

Ginny remembered he had actually asked, "Does our romance have to end sadly? Do I have to die in the end for it to be a bestseller?"

Ginny shuddered at the memory.

The new room was warmer, and larger. Why didn't she ask to move before? She had been too pre-occupied with work to push. Besides, the freezing room kept her awake and alert longer, and she got more work done in the evenings. Always putting up with an intolerable situation -- was this just another survival mechanism she'd picked up dealing with Wayne? She supposed so.

Then she remembered that she was to meet Malcolm the next morning, and was eager to see if he agreed with her findings. She searched her notes and found the number that he sent in his last letter and picked up the phone. There was a quick response to the ring, and she recognized his voice.

"Hi, Malcolm. This is Ginny Thomas.

"Hello! I was afraid that I wasn't going to hear from you. Where are you?"

"Edinburgh. I guess that I got sidetracked. Are we meeting tomorrow as planned?"

"Yes, but there's a slight change. I have to go to my sister's birthday party in Kent, and then I have a lot of things to bring for my business in London, so I'm going to drive. Take the morning train to Stirling and I'll meet you at the station. We can talk while I drive. I've booked a room for you at the hotel where I'm staying, and I'll leave you there and drive on to the party. It'll be something of a family reunion, a meeting of the McIntosh clan. So, I must be there for a while, but I'll meet you in the afternoon and we can see some American Indian things in a small museum that you might not know about."

"Sounds fine, Malcolm. It'll be great to see you again. I'm getting a bit stir-crazy being alone. I'm about to start talking to the walls. I want your opinion on some interesting news, both about work and something more personal, if that's all right. I'll take the train at Waverly and meet you at Stirling. I've been there once already. See you there."

"Fine. See you tomorrow. Don't worry! I'll be there. Just sit tight."

Ginny hoped he was more reliable than the last Brit she was supposed to meet.

The bathroom was warm and she took a long bath. The full days of study had been tiring, but her research was wrapping up pretty well. She couldn't wait to exchange ideas with Malcolm. Not many people in the world were quite as enthusiastic about their mutual interest, and their conversations were lively when they were together. Maybe he could give her some insight into the British army and the SAS, whatever that was.

She dressed slowly and decided to return to Rosie's for her private celebration of the last night in Edinburgh. It was an excellent choice. The restaurant was cozy, flower-filled, and the Italian food was always better than she had expected. She needed the comfort food and lingered over a glass of red wine and a steaming pot of tea. It was shortly after nine when she left and the taxi delivered her to the Rothesay.

All was quiet. There did not seem to be the crowd of guests the manager had anticipated. Ginny went to her room and packed up *Liberator* for her early morning departure, then climbed into bed, turned out the light, and fell asleep.

She awoke to bedlam. Stomping down the halls, bodies crashing into walls, big, raucous male voices shouting and singing.

Afraid to turn on the light, she checked the luminous dial of her travel clock. One o'clock. The noise was deafening. Terrified but listening carefully, Ginny had been in Scotland long enough to detect the difference in accents. The hotel was suddenly full of drunken Irishmen.

Not knowing what to do, she grabbed her bag and found her container of Mace. She had no opportunity to test it and could only pray it would be strong enough to deal with drunks if she needed it.

The crashing and thrashing continued. Ginny could hear her heart beating over the uproar, but sat quietly in the dark, hoping no one would know she was there.

Then a body thumped against her door. A knock, a slurred voice, "Le' me in!"

Ginny swallowed hard and shouted back,"Go away! I've got a gun pointed at the door and I'm not afraid to use it!"

A moment of silence outside. Then a subdued and sobered voice answered, "Please don't shoot me. I was only looking for me mate. I'll go away."

Fading footsteps. Ginny let out a sigh and laughed to herself. Enough was enough. She had been terrified for as long as she could stand, and it was now three-thirty. Needing some rest, she fumbled for the phone in the dark and picked up the receiver. The manager answered immediately, probably expecting her call.

"What the devil's going on here? Please come rescue me! Where did they all come from?"

"Soccer match, ma'am. They're Irish and their team just beat Edinburgh. I'm awfully sorry for the disturbance. I keep trying to quiet them down. I'll be right up and try again."

In no time, Ginny could hear the manager outside of her door.

"Everyone to bed now. If you don't cooperate, I'll call the police again!"

*Again?*

The last of the revelers lumbered to their rooms and within five minutes the hotel was quiet as a tomb. She sensed her adrenaline still pumping and her heart racing, but she took several deep breaths. Then she concentrated on falling asleep and finally, being exhausted, got there.

Next morning, she checked out of the Rothesay. The manager apologized again for the chaos in the wee hours of morning, and Ginny thanked him for his concern. She was relieved when she boarded the taxi to Waverley station.

Ginny bought *The Scotsman* at the terminal newsstand. *Liberator* seemed heavier than ever that morning, filled with even more books she'd purchased in Edinburgh. The train to Stirling was waiting on track 12. She was becoming more of a veteran on the BritRail system and confidently found a Second-Class car and selected a window seat.

As the train jolted to a start, she fixed her eyes on her newspaper, searching for a clue to the whereabouts of her missing officer. She had little contact with the news of the world, lacking a television in her room. A small article on the front page did catch her eye, however.

*BALMORAL VISIT*, the headline read. *The Prince of Wales and his fiancé, Lady Diana Spencer, arrived by train in Aberdeen to spend a private weekend on the Balmoral estate.*

"That must be it," she said, both excited and relieved. It seemed strange that Jim was on holiday with his men and staying so close to Balmoral. He'd said he had been guarding the royals. They must have been sent there to maintain the security and privacy of the courting royal couple. The photographers and reporters hounded them enough. Maybe all of those soldiers were on standby for the visit, and Jim had been called back to London to ride the train to Aberdeen. It seemed like a logical answer. *How romantic. But the nerve of them to ruin our brief time together. Yet, imagine, meeting and parting with Jim because of the going and coming of the famous lovers, Charles and Diana. What a nice confection of an ending to our sweet story. Jim won't have to die after all! Maybe I'll talk to him before I leave for the States and our story can have a happy ending.*

Satisfied, Ginny turned to the window to see that the weather outside had grown nasty. Heavy wind and hard driving rain and sleet pounded against the train window.

There was no sign of Malcolm when she disembarked at the Stirling station.

She bought a cup of tea in the restaurant and settled in a seat overlooking the terminal parking lot. It wasn't long before a small red car pulled into a parking space and Malcolm emerged from the driver's seat. He dramatically tossed his wool cape over his shoulders and ran into the terminal.

Ginny waved and he spotted her immediately, quickly sliding into the seat next to her and giving her a friendly peck on the cheek.

There he was, just as she remembered him, the Scotsman's Scot. He took off his cap and shook away the raindrops. He wore a kilt in the McIntosh clan tartan, held by a wide black leather belt with a large silver buckle and leather sporran. His knee-high wool stockings probably held a small knife that Scots traditionally carried. It was always fun to be with Malcolm and watch people's reaction to this living fossil. He was aware of their curiosity too and delighted in the role he lived to the hilt in his kilt.

"Bloody nasty weather out there! We'd better hurry if I'm going to make it to the party on time tonight. It'll be like this the whole way, so we'd better get going. If you need a trip to the loo, why don't you run along and I'll buy some sandwiches and scones, so we can eat in the car and won't have to stop."

The horrible weather was obviously getting worse. Gales of rain and sleet pounded the little car as he sped along the motorway. The torrents flooded the gullies and groups of sheep huddled together in the pastures.

"March. In like a lion, out like a lamb! I doubt if there'll be any lambs left after this storm," Malcom said.

Malcolm put a cassette of Highland music into the car stereo and they soon forgot about the weather outside as they became absorbed in conversation. Ginny brought Malcolm up to date on her week. He was very familiar with the keepers she worked with in Edinburgh, and had many rounds with the men in the castle himself. He could well imagine the hard time they'd given her. Malcolm's rich guffaw rang out as she described her skirmishes and ultimate truce with the two scholars. When Ginny finally exhausted her tales of scholarly pursuits, she said, "There's more. Remember that I said I have personal news, too?"

"How could I forget? I figured that you were saving the best for last!"

"Where to begin? It's all so strange. I met the most charming and handsome British army officer on the train from London to Edinburgh last Sunday. He's a paratrooper, and said he's in the Special Air Services, or something like that. We had coffee in the station and talked. I mentioned my interest in the Highlands on the train. He said he was going up there, and in no time, he invited me up for the day. He was to ski near Glenshee, and said he could show me around.

"At first the thought scared me to death. You know I've rarely ventured away alone, much less running off to meet a handsome officer!"

"Right! I'm astounded that you escaped from that husband of yours and got over here at all."

"Unfortunately, ending that is the first thing I have to do when I get back. Anyway, my hotel was awfully lonely, and the thought became more appealing by the hour. Besides, you know how curious I am about the Highlands. So, I called him on Monday, and he said to take the train on Tuesday morning to Stirling and then to Perth, and he met me at the train station in Perth. Probably near you and didn't know it. He showed me around Glenshee and we had a wonderful time. Absolutely magic. Glenshee — that place that's so rich in faery lore. Right up my alley. We could not have been happier. When he put me on the train on Wednesday morning, he said he would meet me in Edinburgh at six in the evening and stay the week with me. You would have met him.

"The strange thing is that then he vanished. I got a phone call from a sergeant saying that a crisis had come up and he had been called back to London. Said he'd get in touch with me eventually. I can't imagine what came up."

Ginny told Malcolm the story about Charles and Diana in *The Scotsman* and they agreed that might be the answer.

"Made love among the heather, eh?" Malcolm teased.

Ginny blushed. "Of course not! He was an officer and a gentleman." But she knew the glint in her eye and smile on her face belied her answer.

"Well, I'll be gentleman enough to pretend to be gullible enough to believe that," Malcolm said, and laughed.

The trip was long and tiring. At times visibility was ten feet or less, and the storm was relentless. But the conversation was lively and the time went fast. They talked about his small but prestigious museum, nestled in an eighteenth-century merchant's home. The museum was internationally known because Malcolm worked tirelessly and enthusiastically to promote and support it. Ginny had actually been close in Perth, but hadn't realized it, being so preoccupied with Jim.

The countryside gave way to villages and then to the outskirts of London with its row houses and small yards. Soon they were in the bustling heart of the city. Malcolm knew his way around London well, and even though the roads were congested and the weather was abominable, in no time they were at the Hogarth Hotel, where Malcolm had booked rooms.

Ginny registered and Malcolm helped her wrestle *Liberator* to her room. He made a quick phone call to assure his wife that he was safe and leaving immediately for the party.

"Check with me in my room tomorrow at two, and we can decide where to meet from there. The collection that I want to show you is in an obscure museum and I'll have to take you there. Have a nice evening. Bye." Malcolm made a hasty exit.

Ginny looked around the room. The hotel was nicer than any she had stayed in on previous trips to London. In the lobby, she noticed that young Middle Easterners, probably Saudi students, mostly staffed the hotel. The room was freshly redecorated, clean, and modern, even with a color TV, a step up for sure. There was an electric teakettle, as well as cups, spoons, coffee, and tea for the morning.

Alone in London on a stormy night. She could hear the wind howl outside, and sleet continued to beat against the window. In an unfamiliar area of London, it seemed to her like a good night to nestle in and use up the emergency provisions she brought from Miami. She filled the teakettle, made tea and instant pea soup, and opened her can of tuna and box of crackers. Not a feast, but it would suffice.

She settled down with her meal and flipped the TV on to the news, the weather was the lead story. The storm was widespread and causing a considerable amount of damage throughout the United Kingdom. There was loss of both property and the danger of losing an entire crop of spring lambs. The good news was that the storm would probably wear out during the night, and the next day was expected to be cold but sunny.

The next story was about the fighting that had started again in Northern Ireland. This time they were rioting over some hunger strikers in prison in Belfast.

*Such nonsense,* Ginny thought. She could neither understand, nor had she bothered to consider the plight of that war-torn country, with its conflict called The Troubles. Although she had a considerable amount of Irish blood coursing through her veins, this problem was not hers. America had its own share of problems.

The fighting looked intense and ugly. The rioters were throwing rocks, bricks, and they were burning vehicles. She could only wonder why they couldn't straighten out that situation.

She switched the channel to a movie, a comedy about the romantic escapades of a nineteenth century British army officer, which seemed more appropriate. Ginny positioned the screen so she could see it from the bathtub, filled the tub with hot water and took a long, luxurious bath in the warm, comfortable room. It was amazing that her greatest comfort and luxury on the trip had been warm baths. She washed her hair for the first time in days.

The movie was amusing, but the officer reminded her of Jim. She remembered that she told him she had stayed at the Green Park Hotel in London before she left for Edinburgh. What if he tried to call her there? Should she call the Green Park and leave a message that she was at the Hogarth? No, why bother? They probably wouldn't pass the message along anyway.

She searched in her bag for the address Jim had given her before he said goodbye in Perth. Looking at the address, she had no idea where it was, but noticed that he also wrote down a phone number.

Why not give that a try? Nothing to lose, really. She picked up the phone and dialed the operator, asking her to ring the number.

Another operator answered and Ginny gave her the extension number for the Officers Mess. The phone rang a long time before it was finally answered.

"Lieutenant Evans, please," Ginny said.

A stranger laughed on the other end of the line, "Never heard of him. But then, I'm newly arrived here."

She realized that she was wasting both her time and money, so she thanked the officer and put down the receiver.

The situation seemed hopeless. Turning off the light, she fell asleep listening to the howling gale. And woke to a sunny Sunday morning in London, the sky clear and a brilliant blue. The air was cool, invigorating, and clean, as if London had a cleansing bath and everything was new once more. Ginny walked to the Victoria and Albert Museum, finding that it did not open until noon. There was time to look in the windows of the bookstores and shops that lined the street.

She found a Russian tearoom where the aroma lured her inside. Checking around the tables to see what the other diners were eating, she asked a few questions and ordered. The hearty food was perfect for the chilly day, and Ginny felt less alone in the small crowded restaurant. After enough time, she paid her bill and walked back to the Victoria and Albert.

The collections of the museum were outstanding, and even though she didn't have long, she relished the opportunity to enjoy it alone. The costume and textile collections held her attention for the better part of an hour, until she remembered to check her watch and call Malcolm. He answered immediately and arranged their meeting.

The remainder of the afternoon was spent with Malcolm, visiting the small museum on the outskirts of London that had a little-known gem of a Native American art collection. Back at the Hogarth, they each ordered Scotch and water at a small table in the bar and made dinner plans. Ginny returned to her room to dress and called Miami to tell Wayne when she would be coming home ... and to check his reaction.

"You can just stay, for all I care," Wayne said. "I'll be in Washington again for a few days anyway. Then we have some things to talk about."

"Yes, I know," said Ginny, dreading the encounter. "See you when you get back."

She decided to cheer herself up and that it would be a good time to break in her new kilt. Why not wear it if she was dining with a Scottish gentleman in a kilt? They met in the lobby and walked in the crisp starry night to an Indian restaurant which was Malcolm's favorite. It was down a narrow alley lined with several pubs and restaurants. As they walked, Malcolm explained that he had a loft nearby. The same one from when he was an anthropology student at the University of London. The area was his old stomping-grounds seemed to welcome him, and he was always glad to get back to it.

The restaurant was small and crowded. The prices were all right and the food was superb but for some reason, Ginny couldn't eat.

"You're picking at your food," Malcolm said. "I think you might be in love with your *troopy*."

"You may be right," Ginny said. "But what do you know about *troopies*?"

"My son was a paratrooper. He served in Northern Ireland for a tour in Belfast. An awful place. It reeks of fear, distrust, and hatred. He loved the army, but was damn glad to get out of there. By the way, if your officer is in the SAS, that's pretty impressive. 'Who Dares Wins.' They're the best."

"My troopy was in Northern Ireland, too. He served in Bloody Sunday in '72. Two tours there, a real glutton for punishment, as if he had a choice."

As they walked back to the hotel, they laughed and carried on, with Malcolm humming a tune and dancing a jig on the now empty street. It felt good to have someone to share a laugh with again, and to talk of common interests, not just law, as it would be with Wayne.

In her room, she made tea, and spread her photographs and notes on the bed. Malcolm agreed that she was on the right track, and she made a point to tape his comments. The tape would jog her memory when she finally settled down to finish writing her paper. They finished up finally and said goodnight.

She woke with mixed emotions, packed *Liberator* for the return trip home. Malcolm was in the lobby, they had a quick breakfast after which he called for a taxi.

As the taxi driver put *Liberator* in the front seat, Malcolm gave her a casual brotherly hug and said, "Good luck with your paper. As you say in America, knock 'em dead." Then the taxi sped off to deliver her to Victoria Station for the train to Gatwick.

The Laker Skytrain was full. Ginny had a snug window seat. As the jumbo jet roared down the runway to begin the long flight to Miami, she reflected on her stay in England and Scotland. It had been an incredible time.

She had embarked on the trip emotionally more like a schoolgirl on a Study Abroad Program escaping from a dictatorial dad. Now she was returning more self-assured, with a better understanding of herself, life, and the world. She would never be the same after all that she had experienced in those few days. But could that courage last?

Looking back at England as the plane headed homeward, she remembered Jim and the Highlands. He was right. Their story should be written. Fate brought them together and, just as suddenly, tore them apart. She knew that she should begin to document their passionate romance as it unfolded. Who could tell how it would end?

Or had it?

There was plenty of time to write on the long trip across the pond. She pulled a yellow legal pad out of her bag. She wrote, shed tears, and continued writing until she had filled fifteen long pages with her every memory of making "love among the heather," as Malcolm so correctly called it. When every last word was spent, she slept. She had to be rested and ready for the ordeal of returning to reality.

# 4
# Miami/Memories

Ginny worked on readjusting to the scenery during the thirty-minute taxi ride from the airport to her home. She appreciated Miami's warm sunshine more than ever after her stay in cold and gloomy Great Britain. As always, the house looked beautiful. The housekeeper had been in that day, and the smell of lemon furniture polish lingered in the air. The thought of ever leaving this house saddened her. It was only a mile by bicycle from Biscayne Bay with a favorite beach nearby. This was her anchor and had been her home, a vital part of her life for so long, for better or worse. Sometimes you can wander lonely through a home, loving it more than the person you share it with.

An angry note from Wayne waited in the foyer stating that he would be back the next evening, and deal with her then. Ginny rolled *Liberator* down the hall to the guest bedroom where she now decided to stay the course. She poured a glass of wine and roamed from room to room, glass in hand, like a guest at a gallery opening, viewing the art she treasured. She lingered in the large family room, sitting in a black leather chair, sipping wine.

*This is where it all started ...*

Looking out at the pool through the large sliding glass doors, she remembered the last night she was there — and why she so quickly left. But so much had happened since then, an ocean away.

She went back to that last night in the house when she left.

The sliding glass doors were opened onto the pool deck and a fresh breeze from Biscayne Bay floated through the sprawling South Florida home. The pool shimmered as a turquoise pond, and golden twinkling Japanese stone lanterns in the garden added atmosphere. The main attraction, however, was the moon, peeking from behind the tall palm trees, ready to make an entrance.

*More memories ...*

In the kitchen, she arranged twenty candles in the creamy icing of the birthday cake, with "Happy Birthday Eric" spelled in blue icing. It seemed impossible that she could have a son that old. Laughter and happy chatter resonated from the room where the family gathered and Eric opened his presents. It was Spring Break and she could tell he was enjoying being home from college.

But the sound ringing in her head, the bitter and foolish argument with Wayne before the guests arrived. There had been so many senseless fights recently that she couldn't even recall what this one was really about, but the ultimate struggle was over Wayne's control of her. She believed he now equated marriage to ownership. The fights had gone on for years, but recently had become more frequent and dangerous.

Tall and distinguished-looking, with streaks of gray in his dark hair, Wayne was meticulously dressed, wearing his Gucci shoes and Rolex watch. His success always a constant reminder of her own lost opportunities. He walked into the kitchen and glared at her. Ignoring the look, she cheerfully called to him, "Wayne, would you please open the champagne?"

Her mask was in place, but her insides were quivering.

"About time you knocked the rust off the stove and cooked a decent meal," he said, emptying my plate of uneaten food in the garbage. "You're usually at that damn museum or out on the Indian reservation."

"I love going out to the reservation, talking to people, and I learn so much there. That's my research. The museum's my job, and it's only part-time."

"You call that a job? Paralegals make a lot more than you."

"Not everyone is interested in law, Wayne."

"Well, you'd better be interested in law, Babe. It feeds you."

"Please, please, Wayne. Not tonight. It's Eric's twentieth birthday, for God's sake." His constant humiliation, the remarks, and put-downs drained her.

She carried the cake into the family room where they always gathered to celebrate birthdays, holidays and rites of passage. She was so proud that she worked with the architect to design the room with the stunning high open-beamed wood ceiling, joined at the point with a dramatic skylight. Guests liked to gather at the well-stocked wet bar with a granite countertop and black leather barstools. The unique art collection reflected her love of Native American and African art, including masks, pottery, baskets, and signed prints. A bookcase spanning one wall was filled with a large TV, art and travel books and photos.

As the family organizer and cheerleader, she always did her best to make family events as perfect and pleasant as possible, but her heart wasn't in it. She looked at the celebrants on the sectional sofa. Wayne's parents, Mattie and Henry, were seated in their usual spot. As always, Henry clung to Mattie's hand like a tethered balloon that would drift to the skylight if Mattie turned him loose.

She looked at her younger sister, Kathy, sitting with their mother, Anne, who was widowed at thirty-three, when their father suffered and died from a malignant brain tumor. Never enough morphine to kill the pain. She was almost thirteen and it emotionally scarred her, but went unnoticed. The trauma filled their mother with a deep-seated fear of life's sudden drastic changes. She passed that burden of anxiety on to Ginny and her sister. Kathy was hopelessly caught up in the web of their mother's fears. Ginny had the good sense to flee the trap and went to college, but the ingrained anxiety remained steadfast.

She met Wayne in high school and they married soon after she graduated. But she remembered that the arrogant Wayne of today was not the Wayne she married when they were young students, poor, and so much in love. He was once a good man, husband, and father, caring, kind, and considerate. They spent many great years together, full of hope, dreams, friends, fun, and travel. She treasured those days, reflecting, "Whatever went wrong?" she would ask herself, and still did. As he became a more successful attorney, he asserted more control and spent less time at home. His sense of wealth and power went to his head.

Ginny took a sip of wine and tried to shake off the thoughts of her sad little family.

She remembered again the party of the last night, lighting the candles. They all joined in an off-key singing of "Happy Birthday." She sliced the cake and said to Eric, "This one's for you, Birthday Boy," handing him the biggest piece. His appetite had subsided little since the days when he played football in high school.

"Here, Mom," she had said, passing cake to her and to Kathy.

Wayne picked up two Waterford crystal flutes and poured champagne for his parents. He was in his element, talking finances with Henry, sharing their obsession with stocks and bonds. Mattie's gnarled and rough hands reflected her efforts to maintain their rental properties, and her life had not been easy. Wayne's doting parents worked hard for his indulgences as a spoiled only child. Looking around the room at the forced smiles, resentment twisted her stomach and the long arguments left her feeling empty. She hoped that no one noticed her eyes were slightly red and puffy, in spite of all of the makeup she put on.

Ginny remembered the lull in the conversation, when suddenly she spoke up. She didn't know where it came from; maybe it was the champagne talking. More likely it was from all of the years of frustration.

"Everyone should know that the house of Thomas is falling down around us," she heard herself announce.

Mouths dropped open and there were sudden gasps as all pretenses stopped. She realized what she said and put her fingers to her lips, holding back any other words.

"Now look what you've done!" Wayne shouted.

Unexplained courage surfaced, forcing her to stand her ground. "Wayne, I just wanted to clear the air, let everyone know that things are not as they seem."

Then it happened. She was the first to notice. There was a flutter as a large Great Horned Owl flew through the opened glass doors and into the room. It landed and perched on top of the bookcase, with unblinking eyes latched firmly on her.

There was a stunned silence.

She turned to the shocked faces staring at the big bird. "Does everyone see this?" she calmly asked. "Everyone here sees this and I'm not the only one. No one here can say I imagined this and that I'm crazy."

"Jeez, we see it. You aren't crazy, Ginny," Kathy said, in awe.

*But do they understand?* she wondered. Not wanting to alarm the family, and she wasn't superstitious, but a respected Indian elder once cautioned her that the unexpected visit of an owl must be taken seriously. A messenger.

A warning of change or death. The probability of this occurrence itself was bizarre enough. Western logic made her skeptical of the danger, but her work gave her new respect for other ways of thinking. Owl or no owl, she wasn't ready for death yet, but if anyone was ripe for change, she was. Her concern was then for the winged messenger. She turned as the owl swooped though the open doors to freedom as strangely as it had arrived.

The party was over. The confused guests made a hasty exit, not lingering for long goodbyes. Eric wisely decided to spend the night with a friend. The astonishing visitor even caught Wayne off guard. Silently, they cleaned up the party dishes and turned out the kitchen lights.

Fearful of what Wayne might do, while he was in the bathroom, she went to her closet, quickly changed to her nightgown, and slipped under the covers on her side of the bed. Wayne had an early flight in the morning to Washington to take a deposition with an important client. He didn't read, as usual, and turned out the light as he got in bed without a word.

She couldn't forget how she tossed and turned that restless night, planning her escape. A research trip had been on her agenda for a long time, and that time had come. She knew she would never get Wayne's approval for the trip. After all of the trouble that he gave her, his approval was no longer necessary, and off she would go. Fear subsided and the excitement built.

The next morning, she was buried under the covers while Wayne silently dressed. As soon as she heard the garage door shut, she threw off the covers and raced to the storage closet. Pulling out her big black suitcase on wheels, she started filling it with warm clothes. During March, England and Scotland would be very cold. She called Laker Airways and made a reservation on the six o'clock evening flight from Miami to London.

Quick phone calls were next, first to the museum to cancel her few appointments and let them know that I would be away for twelve days. She only told a few close friends of her sudden plans. Then she called Dr. Johnson, the psychologist and marriage counselor who was her private consultant in all things concerning herself, her marriage, and Wayne.

Ginny left a message on his answering machine to cancel her next visit. Her final calls were to her sister, then her mother. She dreaded the unending words of caution.

After messaging she withdrew most of the money from her museum salary – her hidden account -- and purchased Traveler's checks. Lastly she picked up her airline ticket from the travel agent who arranged her London BritRail pass for the train trip to Edinburgh.

At home Ginny gathered the notes, names, and contact information of the people she'd corresponded with over the years. These were librarians and archivists in London and Edinburgh. She put her personal notes and addresses into her travel bag along with passport, camera, and film.

Her son Eric walked in the front door just as she moved her suitcase and carry-on bag to the foyer. His look of surprise was tinged with admiration.

"Can't take it anymore, eh, Mom?" he asked.

She told him, "No, I can't." She felt so bad for him, and took his hands in hers, tears running down her cheeks. "Eric, I'm so sorry. I never wanted our lives to come to this. Are you okay?"

"Sure, Mom. I live here too and know about the arguments. Other than that, Dad's always at work or away, he's never around, never bonds with me."

"You'll be back in college soon. The positive thing is that I'm finally going to take the research trip I've wanted to make for so long."

Eric raised his hands in protest. "Hey, I don't want to know the details, so leave me out of it. But if you need a ride to the airport, I can give you a lift."

She'd forgotten that her good-looking son had grown so tall – in fact taller than she was. Now she reached up to give him a hug and a kiss on the cheek. Her little boy wasn't little anymore, and then after the airport ride and goodbye, Ginny was all alone.

While waiting to board her flight, she made the call she most dreaded, to Wayne's hotel in Washington, hoping to just leave a message. Unfortunately, he was in his room.

"Wayne, I think it would be best if I get away for while so things can cool down a bit. No need to worry."

Loud and angry shouts of protest were still crackling across the wire as she gave him details and then hung up.

She was exhilarated.

There would be plenty of time for reflection on the long flight across the Atlantic. But as soon as the huge 747 rumbled down the runway and was safely in the air, she was faced with the enormity of that giant step she had just taken. She chuckled unexpectedly at the thought.

She closed her eyes, oblivious to the other passengers in the crowded aircraft and became absorbed in the motion and sound of the engines. She turned her head into the hum, listening until thoughts again crowded out sounds., reminding her of where she was and why. The arrival of that owl focused her attention on what she knew for so long: change was a must. She took brief ventures into the frightening but creative "real world," finishing graduate school and then getting a small job. Yet, like a trembling little girl overcome by the fear her mother taught her, she fell back into the familiar nightmare of hearth and home.

However, her survival methods were deafness and detachment.

She knew, deep down, that the only safe haven was deep within herself. That was her real journey.

She knew that she was an artist. But she never thought of herself as a writer, much less a scholar. But then, she never had a chance before to think of herself as anything except daughter, wife, and mother.

Wayne was always the main attraction, the wealthy attorney with the large law practice headed by his name. Relegated to a supporting role as the party planner, she entertained his business associates and their wives who were caught in the same trap she was.

❧❦

Ginny had lingered long enough on those memories of the day she defiantly and bravely left her home. She sighed and took a last goodnight sip of wine. It was unanswerable, she knew, but she asked herself …

*What is life?*
*What am I afraid of?*
*What am I doing?*

# 5
# Miami

She opened her study door and the red light on the machine was blinking, calling her to rewind the tape. She turned up the volume, sank in her desk chair, and only listened, not yet ready to think. There were many messages, some important, some not so important, and the usual hang-ups.

The last message stunned her. It was the only person she wanted to hear from. That was the good news. Jim had told her that he hated answering machines, but there he was.

The bad news was unthinkable.

He cleared his throat. "Hi. It's me. Hope you had a good trip back. There's a letter on the way to you. Unfortunately, I'm calling from Belfast, where I'm likely to remain until September or October. Perhaps I'll get a week of leave in between. I don't know. I'll write you this week and let you know what's happening. I'll give you a phone number where you can call me. Anyway. I'll explain everything when I talk to you later. Ciao!"

Shocked, she stared at the machine in disbelief, thinking, *No, it can't be. Belfast? Northern Ireland?* She suddenly realized that she was very much in love with someone in a vortex of military maneuvers.

She smashed her fist on the desk. "This is so unfair!" She shouted to the empty room. Angry and confused, she'd never known such frustration and helplessness. Tears stung her eyes as she headed for the bedroom. The only blessing was that Wayne wasn't here to witness her agony. How could she explain this to anyone?

Through her tears, she wrote a letter to Jim. She tried to keep it light, to be cheerful, to tell him how much their time together meant to her.

> *The trip home was fine. There was plenty of time to write fifteen long pages of our story on the plane, and I'll send a copy to you once I've edited it. I hope you're safe and will be careful. From what I've read and seen on TV, the situation looks very nasty in Belfast. How and when will I hear from you again?*

She addressed the letter to his UK address and could only hope that it would get to him. She would mail it the next morning. Between the neither here nor there blur of jet lag and the incredible circumstances, Ginny just tried to hang on to what was left of her sanity until she could sort things out.

At some point, she wrote Jim another letter, although there was little left to say.

She went to the post office to mail both.

Somehow it felt good to write to Jim; it eased the torment. Wayne was due to fly back from Washington that afternoon and she needed a handle on herself for that event.

Ginny called her psychologist, Dr. Johnson, for an appointment, and he agreed to see her on Friday. Thank God for Dr. Johnson. Hopefully he could help her figure out her next step.

She had seen two marriage counselors alone because Wayne refused to go with her. (One hand clapping). Both were psychologists, and each continued therapy with her alone to help strengthen her sense of self-esteem.

How Wayne hated that! He demanded that she quit seeing the first psychologist because she was a woman. Wayne refused to pay for her treatment and insisted she must be having the "menopausal crazies," though she had no real health issues in that department.

Fortunately, Dr. Johnson was excellent. He said very little to Ginny, listening to her talk and leaving her in the position of figuring things out for herself, which she ultimately had to do anyway. She was totally open with him and learned to analyze her situation more or less objectively,and make her own decisions. But now she was in one hell of a jam.

Wayne entered the house and dumped his briefcase and luggage on the floor, then frowned at her. "I hope you had yourself a good time. You've got of a lot of nerve."

Calling on all of the defense mechanisms she so carefully learned over the years, Ginny put on a smile, forced enthusiasm, and offered wine. Lots of white wine always was a saving grace. It never failed to dull the senses and ease the pain, at least for a while. She poured two glasses of their favorite California Chardonnay.

"Cut it out," she said, handing him a glass. "Let's sit by the pool and I'll tell you about my trip."

Ginny wore her happy face and told Wayne all that she could about her trip and work, adding any funny stories she could remember. As an attorney, Wayne had a knack for knowing when to back off and cool the hottest of situations. They somehow got through the evening.

The next morning Wayne left for his office early.

Ginny tried to put her thoughts back together. She went into her book-lined studio, her refuge and place of comfort. Reading over her notes, she tried to organize the many pieces she had amassed, more information than she realized. Too much to focus on yet. England and Scotland became more like a dream as she stared at the warm Florida sunlight streaming through the sky-light in her studio.

Eleven-thirty. The phone rang and she answered it absently, in anoth-er world. There was a little *beep* that she quickly learned to recognize as the sound of a satellite beaming an international call.

"Ginny?" Her name echoed. "Is that you or your bloody machine?"

"Me, Jim. Me. Really." She turned on the recorder to catch his every word, the sound of his voice. "I was so glad to get your message on my ma-chine. I was so worried."

"Yes?"

"Yes. I had no idea what could have happened. I made up a million stories for myself. I tried to figure out where you went."

"Didn't you get a message?"

"They said you went back to London."

"Yes. When I phoned London, they said I was required back immediately."

"That's awful. You weren't supposed to go to a hot spot, were you?"

"I go where I'm sent."

"I have trouble understanding that mentality."

"It's not very bad. In fact, it's pretty quiet at the moment, but that won't last long."

"My last night in London, I saw a spot on BBC-TV news about the situation with Bobby Sands and the other hunger strikers and the fighting in Belfast. This's all new to me. I know so little about British and Northern Ireland history and politics. But I do have Irish blood. My grandmother's family came to America from Dublin, but I know even less about that as well. Belfast sure didn't look like anywhere I'd want to be. I had no idea that you were there."

"No, you wouldn't."

"They were throwing rocks and burning things. It looked awful."

"We're completely confined in the camp. Our only movement is by helicopter anyway."

"Well, that will keep you out of trouble."

"Oh yeah, keep me out of mischief. Save a few pennies as well."

Ginny laughed. "To go somewhere?"

At that point their voices overlapped. "Will you write to me and keep in touch? I thought we had such a nice time."

"Yes, we did."

"And then you vanished."

"You have to get used to that sort of thing with the army, I'm afraid."

"I know. I kept — and keep — telling myself that. Remember, I've been married to an army officer, but it was nothing like this. Strictly nine to five with JAG on an army post."

"Yes, but it could be worse. It's not as if it's the Far East or Middle East. It's still part of Great Britain."

"Not the best part."

"No. I'd like to simply find a good time when I can phone and talk to you."

"This is a pretty good time, almost twelve in the morning here. If we set up a day, I'd be here, under all circumstances. Since I work part-time in the museum, I don't have an office there and I frequently work at home. I wouldn't miss your call."

"I'll do that then. What about Sunday?"

"No. Weekends are impossible, at least until I figure out what I'm going to do."

Ginny was still a married woman, no matter how bad the circumstances, she'd be living a double life until she could decide how to handle paying an attorney, and the trauma of a divorce. When Wayne wasn't playing tennis or golf with his buddies on the weekends, he was close to home, tanning by the pool and reading the *Wall Street Journal.*

"Okay, Monday evening I'll call you at eight my time, so that's about three your time."

"Can I write to you there?"

"Write to the address I gave you and my mail comes over to me."

"I read an article on the train from Edinburgh to London that said Prince Charles and Diana were at Balmoral and I made up this ending to our story that you were called there. A super ending. Much better than the truth."

"No, I wasn't there."

"I see that now. I'm working on the paper I'm presenting in May. I'll send a copy to you when I'm through."

"I've sent you a little present. Look for a little parcel. I sent it to your other address, your post office box," Jim said.

"Great! I'm writing our story and I'll send it when I'm through with it. I wrote fifteen pages while on the plane the other day."

"Listen, where did you stay last Saturday night?" he asked.

"Saturday night? I was in London at the Hogarth Hotel."

"Well, because I phoned you up at the Green Park Hotel, where you said you stayed before."

"Did you? Saturday night was an awful and lonely night at the Hogarth."

"They said at the Green Park, that they had no person by that name. They had a Mr Thomas staying there. Funny, I thought. Where the hell is she staying then?"

"I'll explain. Remember I mentioned my colleague, Malcolm McIntosh, whom I was meeting? He had museum business in London and was also going to a family party at his sister's house in Kent that night, so he needed his car. He made our plans and met me at the Stirling train station. Instead of taking the train, he drove us into London. It was a long trip in horrible weather. He made room reservations for each of us at the hotel where he was staying, the Hogarth. He left me there and went to the party. It was such an awful night that I didn't even go out for dinner. I made tea and instant soup in my room. I know the soup sounds terrible to you. And we could have been together."

Jim gave a wicked little laugh. "No, I was phoning from Belfast. Look, I'll phone Monday afternoon, three your time. In the meantime, I'll write a letter to you and send some things."

"And photograph?" I asked.

"Okay, I will — until then. Ciao."

Ginny played the tape over and over, hanging on each word. It was difficult to talk on an international call, with the echo and delay. In carefully studying the tape, she wondered in retrospect if she had missed something important. Where their voices overlapped, his words were barely audible, but sounded like "Save some money to get married." Maybe she was too nervous or excited to catch it at the time. Was it wishful thinking? It couldn't happen soon. She would never be sure of what he said. It was a question she would never dare to ask.

Their conversation sounded stilted, and halting, but at least they were in contact. His accent sounded more lilting and nicer than she had remembered. It was frustrating that they had so little time together and now had to talk on phone calls beamed by satellite in order to build some kind of relationship. Their brief time together was so tender and meaningful, their needs so deep, that they couldn't just let it end there.

The distance seemed insurmountable. Whatever could come from this? That tape, with hesitant and sometimes overlapping conversation, was all that she had to convince herself that both the Highlands and Jim were real.

❧❧

It was a relief to slide into the arms of the brown leather chair in the semi-dark office of Dr. Johnson. The ever-present Kleenex box was in position. She knew she would probably need a lot for this session.

"How was your trip? I got the message that you were going away. Then you sounded upset when you rescheduled your appointment. Didn't it go as well as expected?"

"You can't imagine! After a horrible argument, I finally just took off to London on the research trip I've been saying I needed to make. Just like that. My work went better than I ever dreamed. Everyone was so cooperative in the museums in London and Edinburgh. The scenery was beautiful. Edinburgh Castle is magnificent. But that isn't the hitch. If I thought I had problems before, I've really got them now."

Ginny told him the story of how on the train she met the charming and handsome officer in the elite British Army Special Air Services, and their incredible time together.

"His name is James to his British friends, but I call him Jim. Our time together was the first peace and happiness I've known in a long time. We were destined to meet it seems like. He is someone who listens to me, really seems to care and encourages my independence.

"We had a day and night together in the Scottish Highlands and he was going to Edinburgh to stay with me for the week. He was suddenly called back to London and turned up in the middle of the Bobby Sands hunger strike riots in Northern Ireland. Have you heard about that in the news? I never wanted to get in a situation like this. In fact, I've always run from them. I only wanted a supposedly safe relationship, a nine to five type of guy for me. But that hasn't worked out too well with Wayne either."

"How do you think this will affect your life? You've got enough crises for ten people."

"I sure didn't ask for this one. I guess I had no idea what I was getting into. I keep thinking this is like Alice following the rabbit down the hole and ending up in Wonderland. But this is no Wonderland. I know nothing about British politics and The Troubles in Northern Ireland. The situation changed so fast and I was in love before I knew it. For the first in a long time, I felt special to someone, and he was to me. Is that love? Love at first sight? Whatever love is!"

"How can you be sure?"

"It won't be easy to figure that out. Now I guess I will just have to wait and see what happens. The strange thing is that I feel absolutely no guilt about this, after all of the guilt trips I've had pulled on me."

Dr. Johnson nodded.

"One thing that I've learned from these long hours with you is that now I'm acutely aware of things that are going on in my life. I've had a taste of freedom for the first time. I see that I can pick or choose if I want to participate or not. Before I only let life happen to me. It rolled before my eyes like a soap opera, a victim, not a participant. Now I have to take charge of my life, be in control, and make my own decisions.

"I guess the first big decision I made was to go to Britain. It took more courage than I'd ever known to just buy a ticket, pack up, get on that plane and fly to London. But getting on the train from Edinburgh to the Highlands to meet Jim really pushed me over the edge. It was the first decision I ever made thinking just of me. Do you know what I found out? I like me, and also like the way other people see me. Excluding Wayne, of course.

"So there I was in the Scottish Highlands, with an exciting, handsome man, encouraging me just to be myself. For once I felt like a real woman, not 'Daddy's bad little girl' if I didn't jump through hoops. When I was with Jim, I was someone else, the strong confident Ginny who hides inside. I was surprised how much out time together meant to him, too. He has seen so much of life. I was so vulnerable. With all that Wayne has put me through, the passion and pleasure seemed justified. Is that wrong?"

Dr. Johnson looked up from his notes. "No, but go slow. There's no hurry, with him stuck in Northern Ireland. You don't want to make any hasty moves and lose everything. Do you think you're ready to go ahead with a divorce now?"

"Will I ever be ready? Why can't I break free of the hold Wayne has on me? He has control of all of the money. He was once my rock, but all that has changed. I just don't know."

"You'll be okay. Have you seen a lawyer?"

"Not yet. I have talked to a woman attorney before who is very understanding of situations like mine."

"See her right away. She can protect you and see that you'll be taken care of financially. Don't worry about that."

It was amazing how fast the fifty minutes went with Dr. Johnson. But despite what he told her, Ginny did worry. She knew that Wayne would call in the legal sharks.

On Monday at three, she waited by the phone. It never rang. She checked her box at the post office every day. When she opened the little door, all that she ever got was a cool draft from the empty hole. She also wrote to Jim daily. It was the only way to ease the pain, and she rarely remembered what she had written.

That precious time in the Highlands was too important to forget. Yet their heaven in the Highlands became a hell on earth. Life seemed to play a cruel, nasty trick on two people whose only mistake was to share a few hours of happiness and love.

The news from Northern Ireland was bad and getting worse. Each day Ginny checked the morning paper on the deteriorating condition of hunger striker Bobby Sands. Other prisoners in H-Block at Maze Prison in Belfast were refusing food.

Ginny studied the stories with serious interest, trying to understand the messy situation that suddenly impacted her life as well. As she told Jim, she had little interest in world politics. Recognizing that there were situations she couldn't change, she simply ignored them, but suddenly she felt very involved in this one.

By Friday, Ginny's frustration reached a new level. She was not working on her paper as she should have been, and had trouble getting her work done while at the museum. She went home early, and her concentration turned to the short Highland story. She edited, polished, and refined the text to send it to Jim. As she wrote, she re-lived each beautiful moment.

The ring of the phone broke her chain of thought.

The clipped accent of a British woman asked, "Is this Virginia Thomas?"

"Yes," she said.

"I'm calling from London. James Evans asked me to call you and have you call him today. He can't call the States from where he is. He said for you to call at two-thirty, your time." She recited long phone and extension numbers. "You'll have to get the operator to assist you with the call. Did you get that? I can repeat it."

"I got it. And, might I ask, who are you?"

"I'm just an old friend he could depend on."

"Thanks very much. I'll be sure to call him on time. Goodbye."

At 2:25 she called the operator to place the call. Jim answered when the operator rang the extension.

"Jim, where are you?"

"I'm in England, in an army camp about forty miles north of London."

"How did you get back? I thought that you'd be in Belfast for a long time."

"Didn't you get a letter?"

"No letter, nothing."

"I posted a letter on Monday."

"I may have given you the wrong number." She read out her box number.

"Yes, that's the right number. I'm sure it will arrive."

"What's going on? What are you doing?"

"What am I doing? Nothing much."

"Nothing much? I've been sick with worry. I've been up at night wondering where you were."

"There are no phones here where I can make calls out of the United Kingdom."

"And you're stuck there. Will you be there long?"

"I'll be going back to Northern Ireland in July for four months. In my letter I suggested that I might come over to see you the end of June."

"June? Great! I think you'll like it here. I've thought about you so much."

"I must have had seven letters so far."

"I know that I've written a lot. It helps ease the frustration. This is the most agonizing situation I've ever known. I still haven't received anything from you."

"I've sent a package," he said. "It's only a book, but something I think you'll enjoy. It's just a little something from me to you."

"You'll come at the end of June? Will you be in England until then? What kind of base is it? A training area?"

"It's something like that. Nothing I can talk about."

Ginny was learning that there were lots of things he couldn't talk about.

"Where are you phoning from?" he asked.

"My personal phone and the bills are all mine. My husband has lots of money but he sure doesn't share it with me."

"Figure out the time when the rates drop and phone me then," he said.

"I'll call at eleven at night, your time."

"Okay. Call me tomorrow night."

"Okay, 'til then."

"Ciao."

As Ginny hung up the phone, she realized that if there was love at first sight, or at least lust at first sight, they had a bad case of it. But would that be enough? Could it span an ocean and survive a conflict? Maybe it was all a big mistake and not supposed to happen. Star-crossed lovers. But it did happen and they were suddenly stuck with more grief than they bargained for. The cruelest joke of all was the mail. The package and letters Jim said he sent never arrived. Were they keeping his mail as well? The frustration of the empty mailbox grew oppressive.

Then one wonderful day, a letter was waiting in her box. Strangely, it was dated long before the postmark. Had it been held somewhere?

*Dear Ginny,*

*I have thought a lot about our meeting and one day (and night) in the Highlands and even now, after analyzing what happened, I am still in a daze. I don't usually chat-up girls on trains, least of all invite them to spend the day (and night) with me after ten minutes of talk. Still, I did and you came, and it was heaven. But where do we go from here?"*

That became the million-dollar question. She finished reading the letter that was signed *Love, Jim, OXOX.* Hugs and kisses, no less. She folded back the blue envelope with a stamp of the Queen.

*I'm not just imagining things. He was knocked off his feet as much as I was!*

At least they still had the phone. She called him the next night and twice the next week.

"Bad news, Ginny. I'm off to Northern Ireland again, sooner than planned," Then he said, "Look, I just can't predict when or where I'll turn up next. Try to understand that."

She was beginning to get the picture, but it was a new way of thinking for her, totally unpredictable. His plans changed like the wind. But then, no one could have predicted the violence unfolding. On March 30th, John Hinkley made a daring assassination attempt on President Ronald Reagan before the eyes of a shocked nation. The whole world seemed haywire.

They talked again on the 5th of April.

"I'll call you from Ireland next week," Jim said. "I'll just say I'm going out to have a look around and find a phone. I've written twelve pages to you."

"Good," she said. "This is so confusing. I've finally received just one let-ter from you, and no package. What's going on? Do body-snatchers keep your outgoing mail, too? Have I written too much? I don't even remember what I've written. I must sound like a crazy lady. Or maybe I've become one."

"No. I don't get many letters."

"All I get is a cold draft from opening my little mail box. Hopefully that will change and the mail will all get here, right? Will you be safe where you're going?"

"Oh, no problem but you can get run over crossing the road there."

"That's true. Look at the problems we're having in Miami. Recently a married couple, British tourists, were badly beaten while their young children watched. It was awful!"

"I've been reading that you're having a big crime wave there. I'm probably safer in Northern Ireland. You're a bit of a lawless country. So many gunmen running around."

He was certainly right on that point. Things had become very tough in Miami with an unprecedented wave of crimes committed by desperate young men since the Cuban Mariel refugee influx took available jobs. In February, just before she went to England, Ginny and Wayne were robbed at gunpoint in the parking garage of his office building, a mere six blocks from the police station. Three wild-eyed, drugged-up thugs drove away in Wayne's Mercedes, shouting and waving guns at them as they stood against the wall with their hands in the air. Her jewelry, their money, and his car were stolen. Ginny shuddered, remembering the incident.

"True. Are you still coming over here?" I asked.

"Yes. I'm also trying to come over in October, bringing a team to run in the New York marathon. We'll stay seven to ten days."

"Could I come up and see you in New York? I love New York."

"I hoped that you would do just that."

"We'll put that on the list. Let's see how June goes first."

"Right. Play it by ear. How's your President?"

"Fine today. Coming along nicely."

"If for some reason I can't phone you on the 12th, call me on Monday the 20th. I'll be back in England."

" I worry about you. Suddenly I care for someone doing very dangerous things and I don't like it."

"Right. I'd better go. Keep writing, same address and it'll get to me. I will talk to you on the 12th or 20th. Ciao."

Leave it to the Irish to celebrate Easter Sunday with rioting to mark the Easter Rebellion.

Somehow, Jim was able to phone from Belfast.

"Can't talk long. Just wanted you to know that I'm safe. We're on alert and thousands of rioters are gathering."

Wayne was reading the Sunday *Wall Street Journal* on a chaise lounge by the pool. Ginny and Wayne had established a truce, giving each other a lot of latitude. She watched him nervously through the glass door, however.

"I'm at least glad you're okay, but I can't talk too long either. Too dangerous here, too."

"I understand," he said. "Call me in England on the twentieth. Looks like I'll be back then."

Ginny began working on her paper in earnest, hard as it was to concentrate. Fortunately, she had gathered enough information on her trip, and it was simply a task of putting it all together, editing the final draft, organizing her slides, and practicing her speech timing.

After two more days of hard work, she was ready to call Margie and give the presentation a trial run. It also was the first opportunity she had to fill Margie in on the events in the Highlands. Hadn't Jim asked if she had a confidant? Margie agreed to meet for lunch after she finished teaching her class at noon on Thursday.

Margie was winding down her lecture when Ginny entered the dark classroom. Slides projected on the screen were of a Navajo woman, seated at her upright loom weaving a rug under a tree in front of her *hogan* home. Margie had spent three months on the Navajo reservation, patiently watching the weaver work and they had become good friends.

"I'll tell you what the Navajo weaver thinks as she is finishing her rug," Margie said to her class, but directing her gaze to Ginny. "Finish with *Hozho*, beauty, balance, and harmony. As you are agonizing on finishing, look forward. Focus and go forth."

Focus and go forth. That was the only way she could go, Ginny realized. There was no going back. Her course was set - but how?

"Hi! What's up? You look like you've seen a ghost," Margie said, as the last of her students left the classroom.

"I hope not! Wait until I explain. There's so much to tell you. First let me do my Dog and Pony Show."

Ginny slipped the tray of slides on the projector and gave her full presentation for Margie. The new photo portraits of Highland officers she had taken in Edinburgh dramatically proved her theories. The timing was perfect and filled the allotted half hour. Margie made only a few simple suggestions, then she locked up the classroom and they went to their favorite off-campus lunch spot.

Seated at a corner table, Ginny told Margie the whole story of her trip, the museums and their keepers. Finally, she told Margie the other story, of meeting Jim on the train to Edinburgh and her trip to the Highlands, and of his sudden departure to Northern Ireland.

"And now the news from Northern Ireland is worse than ever, with the hunger strikers closer to death. As if I didn't have enough troubles, now this. What's a nice American woman like me doing worrying about Northern Ireland anyway? It's not my war. I just don't understand."

"I've got to hand it to you; you've really done it this time. What're you going to do? You have every reason to get a divorce over with as quickly as possible. After this, surely you can see what Wayne has done to you. All of his mind trips. How many times have we hashed this over? Now go do something about it. Go for it!"

She was right. They had agonized together for long hours over the situation many times before.

Margie said, "Maybe it's just a test. You'll see how strong you really are now. You'll be surprised, I bet. But you've got other things to finish first. Remember what I said, 'finish with *Hozho*'. And for God's sake, don't forget dignity. I saw you there and you know that bit was for you, don't you? But now, focus and go forth."

"First things first," Ginny said. "Who knows what will happen with Jim? This Northern Ireland situation doesn't help. First I'll go to my meeting in Arizona and then come back and figure out how to get my life on the right track."

On the 20th, she called Jim as planned.

"Sorry, he's not here," said the officer who answered. "He's still in Northern Ireland and I have no idea when he'll return."

As always, his plans changed with the wind.

Her post office box was empty, as usual. Concerned, she boarded the plane for connecting flights to Tucson. Last time she'd made many friends at the conference, colleagues from museums and universities across America who shared her interest in Native American art, and she looked forward to seeing them again. But she could not totally forget about Northern Ireland with the situation getting worse as Bobby Sands' condition deteriorated daily. How the Irish love a martyr. The meeting was a much-needed distraction.

In the middle of the night, in the quiet of the dark hotel room, she again came face to face with herself, as she had in London and Edinburgh. Just being out of Miami cleared her head. She struggled to find out what was going on in her life, looking close at her mistakes. She was in a trap of her own making. But there had been many small successes with bright possibilities for the future.

Alone in distant cities, far from the domination and the clutter of her everyday life, she was able to drop her mask, all false pretenses of happiness. She focused on her struggle to *become*, to understand whatever that was. The inner force, The Voice, had once told her the next step was to complete graduate school, combining her love of art and other cultures. That goal long accomplished, it now was relentless in pushing her on to new challenges.

*Is this the final stage of letting go?* she wondered. *I sure hope so, for everyone concerned. But there are no crutches, not Wayne, Dr. Johnson, or Jim. Certainly not Jim. This is a real solo flight on a high wire without a net.*

Ginny tossed and turned through the night. Sleep was impossible. As dawn approached, she knew that she would have to find a way to end the home-front nightmare.

Despite the sleepless night, her presentation was flawless. Her theory was well received and the research was considered thorough and innovative. Several colleagues came to the rostrum after her talk to discuss her ideas, and many asked for copies of her paper.

The next morning, Ginny bought the Tucson morning newspaper after she checked out. The news from Northern Ireland was worse than usual. As Bobby Sands came closer to death, more intense rioting erupted throughout the country. The worst of the violence was in Londonderry, and began after the emotion-packed funeral of two teenage girls run over by a British army vehicle. The mother of one of the girls collapsed on the grave of her daughter at the funeral, and grieving relatives of the other girl had to be carried from the gravesite. Several hours after, a mob smashed into a new car showroom and drove six cars into the street and ignited them. The trouble soon spread to other areas.

Ginny frowned. She remembered the sight of the burning vehicles on the TV screen in London that last night. She read on:

*In Belfast, stone-throwing Catholic youths attacked security patrols, hijacked four vehicles, and set one on fire. British troops fired plastic bullets at the mob and the demonstrators responded with gasoline bombs. One British soldier, hit by a petrol bomb, leaped from his armored personnel carrier, his uniform blazing, and extinguished the flames in the street.*

It was beyond Ginny's comprehension. Fear gripped her stomach as she thought how it could have been Jim, or that he might have been involved. The story said that the Pope expressed concern over the hunger strikes and was considering intervention.

She put the newspaper aside, gathering her flight bag. The taxi was waiting to take her to the airport for her connecting flights from Tucson to Miami.

When delivered to the front door of her home by taxi, Ginny felt a deep sense of relief. She was glad that Wayne was away again. She could think about getting on with the business at hand. But how could she ever have the nerve to tell Wayne what was really going on in her life? Could she face that day? The charade had now gone on for so long.

She went into her studio and the red light on her machine was flashing. Ginny closed the door, turned on the light, crossed the room, rewound the tape, and listened to the messages. A few friends, her mother, a journal editor wanting a copy of her paper for publication. Then suddenly, there he was.

"Hello, Machine. It's me. When you get back, I hope, A, you had a safe trip; and B, your presentation went well. And I hope you have my letters. Regretfully, I don't think we're going to speak on the phone until next weekend, on Sunday, when I'll call you. If I haven't called you between two or three your time, will you call me ten or eleven at night, UK time? I do hope I'll be able to call you before then."

There was the mournful sound of seagulls crying in the background. *Hadn't news stories mentioned the seagulls circling Maze prison?* Ginny thought.

He continued, "Not a lot of news. I've written you several letters. The situation's pretty quiet in Ireland at the moment, except for Londonderry, where I'm not, fortunately. So don't worry about that. Although it's very boring, being stuck in this God forsaken place."

Again, the cry of seagulls.

"Anyway, I'll close now, Ginny, and talk to you Sunday. I don't even know what the damn date is. I haven't got a diary with me. I think you know when I mean. Take care and I'll talk to you then. Ciao." There was a *beep* and click as the message ended.

Ginny felt tears rolling down her face. How miserable he sounded. He said that the British army really didn't want to be in Northern Ireland any more than they were wanted there. Margaret Thatcher put them there. They just had a job to do, alternately as boring, dangerous, and unpleasant as it was. The IRA terrorists were well-trained and armed, and associated with and learned their skills with other terrorist groups. It was a menacing and growing worldwide threat. At least he was safe for the moment.

She went to bed for another fitful night with little sleep. The only blessing was that Wayne was out of town so often.

The next morning, she was at the post office as soon as the doors opened. She put the key in the lock of her box and cautiously opened the door, as if something might pop out at her. She thought of the old trick with a fake peanut brittle can that has a spring in it. To her surprise and delight, there was a blue envelope inside the box, a "bluey." British Forces Mail Service, she now knew. The two stamps were silver profiles of the Queen, and it was addressed in Jim's handwriting.

There was so much more to know about him. She realized that they had just touched the tip of the iceberg in their brief encounter. She wondered how anyone could ever make a career out of the army. It had to be for the sheer love of combat, the pomp and circumstance. Jim was a warrior, a true nineteenth century British adventurer type. The British viewed a military career with great respect, and many Royals and the wealthy served.

The army was Jim's life. His letter helped explain how he felt about it.

*The week has been uneventful, with the prospect of more violence in the weeks ahead if Bobby Sands dies. I have always lived my life according to the following maxim, expressed so well in this version of a poem you may have read at some time.*

The poem included the lines,

*A man who has lived well...*
*Who leaves the world better than he found it ...*
*And gave the best he had...*

Ginny knew those were his goals. He continued:

*I know that hardly seems to fit the bill of a soldier of the Queen, but I do need an ideal to fall back on in times of stress and troubles. I freely admit that I am not proud of a lot of the things that I have done over the years, and indeed do have sleepless nights haunted by them.*

*But I console myself that I was only carrying out the duties assigned to me, and if it was not me, it would be someone else who might not do as good a job.*

*You seem to be discovering yourself now. Please, though, do be careful. Don't throw away lightly all that you have built up over the years. You've come out of your shell and realized how self-confident you can be. Don't go back into the shell.*

*Where do we go from here? I really don't know. God willing (and the British Army) I will be over in June. We must not expect the same as the Highlands, for that was special and possibly a once in a lifetime experience. But a different relationship should be sought. I have no idea how; time will tell. Perhaps the ocean may prove too big a barrier. I just don't know . . .*

Poetry, no less. She was familiar with the poem and had been required to learn it in school. In this context it took on real meaning. Ginny put the letter back in the envelope The letter must have been very hard to write, and was so formal, as if from another time and place, yet terribly sensitive and appropriate.

She wondered if he had sleepless nights or ever cried out in his sleep. It must have been difficult to try to explain that. His beautiful eyes were often so sad, yet at times hard and cruel. What must it be like to look down a gun sight and have to pull the trigger, to kill someone even in the line of duty. Kill or be killed. He told her that he was a damn good soldier and an excellent marksman, a highly skilled sniper.

She had no desire to know the details of how he used those skills. That didn't fit the image of the Jim she knew, and Ginny couldn't imagine taking another's life. She had trouble disposing of pesky spiders, cockroaches, and other critters, especially since she had learned from her Indian friends to respect all of God's creatures.

*Where do we go from here?* she wondered. *That's a big ocean between us.*

The phone was their major line of communication. For some unexplained reason the many letters and the package he said he sent never arrived. Ginny couldn't help wondering if they had been confiscated. They talked as often as possible. She would call when he was in England, and he called when in Ireland.

One day at the end of April, he finished his call with, "I'll call you tomorrow at three o' clock."

At three, Ginny waited by her phone. She was considered the museum expert in discussing stories found in Native American art, and had been asked to do a guest appearance on a local PBS live television talk show that evening. She would be showing and talking about stories in the designs of beautiful Pueblo pottery from the desert Southwest. She looked over some notes to pass the time.

3:30. 4:00. 4:30; time dragged by. The phone never rang and finally she had to leave for the TV station.

Each day, Ginny went through the frustrating ritual of checking her post office box, but it was always empty. She was on a first-name basis with Madge, the woman who put the mail in the boxes.

"Whoever he is, forget him, Honey," Madge said. "No one's worth this."

Ginny was used to getting the things she wanted immediately, if not sooner, but now she was learning the ultimate lesson: life just isn't that way.

May. On the fifth of May, Bobby Sands, the twenty-seven year- old pris-oner now elected a Parliament member, died in Maze prison. All eyes were on Northern Ireland as rumors persisted that the country would erupt into wide scale civil war. Tens of thousands of marchers joined in the funeral procession behind Sands' casket, draped with the tricolor flag of the Irish Republic. News coverage was heavy, even in America. Angry mobs hurled rocks and petrol bombs at the police and soldiers. Ginny searched the television screen, afraid she would get a glimpse of Jim in the midst of the violence. She tried to calm herself, but began to have anxiety attacks in the middle of the night.

In mid-May, Ginny stood in line in a crowded supermarket. The custom-er ahead was paying the cashier and said, "Did you hear that the Pope got shot?"

Ginny waited for the punch line. There wasn't one. The Pope actually had been shot. She put her groceries in the car and hurried home to watch with horror the special coverage on television. It was another act of insanity in an increasingly dangerous world she could no longer ignore. She suddenly was tuned into the implications of worldwide terrorism, and other forms of craziness.

Three more hunger strikers died of self-starvation in the H-Block that May: Francis Hughes, Patsy O'Hara, and Raymond McCreesh. Each mass funeral captured international attention and the imprisoned young Irishmen became martyrs. Their deaths turned worldwide sympathy against Margaret

Thatcher's policies and the British presence in Northern Ireland. The IRA played the situation to the hilt. Realizing that they could not win militarily, they recognized more than ever that they could gain public sympathy through the media. Always hungry for a good story, the world press stood by with ready cameras, filming every uprising. The incidents were emotional, angry, and very photogenic. Ginny watched the TV and read the papers with increasing alarm, until she finally accepted the fact that there was little she could do about it, and worked to put it out of her mind. Forgetting about it, however was impossible.

She might never know why or where Jim had gone again so suddenly. In all honesty, she knew very little about the man who so swiftly had stolen her heart.

# PART TWO

# 6
# Northern Ireland /
# IRA Bandit Country

*Dear Jim,*

*When I fall asleep and during my dreams I hear your voice, when, in reality, it is your letters that sit at my bedside. I have no need of them now for they are inscribed in my heart. I hear, so distinct, the voices of those around you, dear.*

*I hear the twinkle sometimes of birds, sometimes of other things like beer bottles. It is all a maze, a jumble, but believe me because you have written it in your hand, to me, it is mine. I transcribe it the way you said it. Maybe, in this writing, in my telling your story, you will be here.*

*Love always,*
*Ginny*

am now firmly entrenched in South Armagh, IRA Bandit Country, the most dangerous place in the world for a British soldier. I am now in the right place for someone who thrives on action. Since the Irish Republican Army had heated up their activities in the region, using it as a convenient staging point for distribution of arms brought across the border, the British decided to strengthen their presence. They had deployed a SAS Sabre Squadron, the one unit that intimidated the IRA.

The closely-knit population in the small sprawling farming community was strongly anti-British. The people weren't necessarily pro-IRA, but they were controlled by the IRA's most effective terrorist weapon of all, fear. IRA methods of dealing with locals who mingled with British soldiers brought terror to the people's hearts. Young girls who committed minor offenses, such as getting friendly with a soldier, suffered the humiliation of having their head shaved, were tarred and feathered, and tied to a lamp post with a warning note. Kneecappings were for more serious offenses.

Fear and stress were the norm for the soldiers as well. A soldier could never let down his guard: a tour in Northern Ireland was a terrifying new way of life for the young soldiers, the least desirable tour of duty the British Army had to offer. Soldiers were always anxious, trained never to dare to stand still, to keep their eyes always moving with their guns cocked, usually with the safety catches off. They never knew where that bullet with their name on it might come from, if there was a bomb behind the next hedgerow or in a near-by dustbin. Even rosy-cheeked, freckle-faced, blue-eyed little children were threats, harbingers of death.

All soldiers were confined to their camps in South Armagh. When not on patrol, they were only allowed two beers a day and no spirits, so there was no solace even in the stupor produced by alcohol. As I have said, it was a great place to save a few coins; there's nothing to spend money on.

Boredom is an epidemic and watching video or gambling is the only entertainment. The men sleep with their uniforms and boots on, always on alert. A soldier's tour is usually about four months long, with just a four-day respite. The only relief is when the tour ends.

The British government, in its determination to end IRA domination in South Armagh strengthened the police stations in Crosmaglen and Forkhill, turning them into armed fortresses similar to the old forts in the American Wild West. Surrounding the morose station in the center of Crosmaglen were walls twenty feet high, with watchtowers in the corners topped by mortar-proof netting. Homemade mortars had proven very effective weapons for the IRA. They could install four or five mortars on the back of a lorry, park it some two hundred yards away from a target, and fire into the site by remote control, creating havoc and destruction. The netting offered only a tenuous form of determent.

Eyes are always watching, and no one could approach within twenty yards of the police station without coming under surveillance by eerie closed circuit television cameras, or by soldiers on guard. Helicopter normally was the only way in or out. Even the garbage is flown out by helicopter.

Foot patrols leave by the front door, but only after careful checking. Large rumbling armored vehicles are used less often than they once were because of the danger of land mines. Their route is predictable and they are ready targets. The IRA have become masters of the use of land mines and car bombs starting out in the 1970s. Later, they learned to make more powerful bombs in stronger housings and became sophisticated in methods of hiding the bombs and detonating them. It was decided that the use of foot and helicopter patrols with less predictable routes would eliminate some loss of life. It also gave the soldiers more of an opportunity to get out and talk to the locals. The British learned that the only way they could make progress in Northern Ireland was through a "hearts and mind" campaign, an effort to isolate the terrorists and convince the locals that the Army was there to help.

The life of an officer was little better, and in some ways worse than that of an enlisted man. Their tour of duty was longer, and their responsibilities were greater. James shared cramped quarters and emotional strain with many other officers. They slept in sleeping bags on a bunk bed. An old *Playboy* center-fold Playmate hung on the wall over the bed of James's bunkmate, left by the officer who used the bed before him. It was a sad reminder of the world they left behind. Perhaps the Playmate kept hope alive, but lust led only to frustration.

The major concern was stopping shipments of arms to the IRA. Sufficient funds to keep the terrorists well supplied were raised by sources such as NORAID, the Irish Northern Aid Committee. These well-meaning but misguided Americans who sent money were ignorant of the fact that the funds provided arms and explosives not only for the IRA, but also for other international terrorist groups as well. Many lives would be saved anytime a shipment could be aborted or destroyed.

I spend part of my time leading patrols in the field, and most the rest of my time in camp, planning operations. This schedule was broken only by trips to the Army headquarters just outside of Belfast. The tour in South Armagh differs from my other tours in Derry and Belfast, crowded poverty-stricken cities where urban guerilla warfare was the name of the game.

The border district of South Armagh is a region of large expanses of green fields divided by hedgerows. The hedgerows were useful for conceal-ment, for both sides. The border also served as an easy escape route. A patrol in hot pursuit of suspects had to successfully prevent passage across the border into the safe territory, because the British Army could not operate on the oth-er side of the border. Several SAS patrols had chased terrorists over the border, with resounding repercussions. Once in the south, a suspect was virtually home free, although relations with the Irish Gardai had improved considerably and there was a bit more cooperation.

Northern Ireland was particularly frustrating to the highly skilled pro-fessionals of the SAS. Their role had been restricted primarily to surveillance and intelligence gathering. Frequently, with the suspect in their grasp, closure was impossible because their hands were tied by lack of authority to act. The necessary go-ahead had to come from leaders who feared for their political skins. Taking out a group of gunmen in a region with strong family ties was not considered a popular thing to do, no matter how violent the culprit's crime had been.

Information from a mole who was working deep within the IRA in South Armagh was passed on to me. As you well know I am a great admirer of the source, Captain John Morgan. The thirty-two-year old Morgan is the well-ed-ucated son of a doctor who could have settled for a quiet ceremonial military career with cushy appointments. Instead, he opted for the most dangerous of undercover espionage assignments. Morgan was a member of the Mobile Reaction Force, the plain-clothes squads working in pairs or singly. The more qualified men work alone with carefully developed new identities.

Morgan, though, was trained by both SAS and M16. To cover his Oxford accent, he labored side by side with construction workers in London and became "one of the boys," drinking with them in the seedy pubs of Kilburn. Morgan picking up the appropriate dialect for his next assignment, South Armagh.

Morgan's likeable nature and true concern for people led to his ready acceptance in the community. He regularly drank and sang with the men in a dark, smoke-filled Forkhill pub and always had a sympathetic ear for every-one's problems. Thus Morgan inspired trust and soon developed contacts close to the inner workings of the IRA. Most of all, he picked up informed gossip about arms shipment and explosives smuggled into Ulster from the Irish Republic. I'll now give you a clear picture of Morgan's method. It may sound like fiction but it's completely true. If I rendered it in diary form or any other way than this sort of fictitious-sounding style, I could be in trouble. But as a story it sort of holds as a truthful untruth, if you know what I mean. Anyway, reading it you will understand, Ginny.

Huddled at a table over a beer one evening, Morgan could tell that his two friends were agitated. It didn't take long to find the source of their irritation.

"So much killin'," said the first, taking a long drag from his cigarette and watching the smoke as it slowly rose as a circle in the air. "Will we never see the end of it?"

"Aye. Well, now they'll have more fuel for their fire."

Silently, Morgan listened, sipping the mocha-colored foam that topped his dark pint of Guinness. The two men continued, filling in the details.

"There's talk of a big shipment from the south for the IRA boys," one of the men said.

"Bigger than most. There'll be a meetin' soon, I think in a deserted farm. I accidentally overheard me brother-in-law talking on the phone about the meetin', but I didn't hear when the get-together would be. Guess I didn't really want to know. Think it'll be within the next couple of days. Me poor sister and the girls, if anything goes wrong."

Morgan listened intently, had one more stout for the road, then told his friends he was calling it a night. On his way home, he stopped by a phone booth and made a quick call to headquarters at Hereford.

The message was sent along immediately to me, James, in Crosmaglen. I noted the source and studied the detail of the message passed on from Morgan. A cell meeting appeared imminent and quick action was needed. I was ordered to command the operation.

I called together his four best men for a surveillance patrol and briefed them on the information he needed. Corporal Price led the patrol, backed up by radioman Sergeant Saunders, another corporal, and a trooper. They had an afternoon to prepare their kit, gather their weapons, equipment, cameras, night sights, and high powered listening devices. Messages describing any activity around the farm were to be sent by rapid transmission to ears in Crossmaglen; their radio frequency would be monitored at all times.

That night they were inserted in the darkness, flown by helicopter to a spot some three miles from the farm. Logic said that the meeting was to take place in the empty barn and the men set up their sophisticated electronics, microphones, and miniature transmitters inside the target area. Cameras were aimed at the entrance. Satisfied with their bugging job, the men secured their positions long before dawn.

They blended into a hedgerow some thirty yards from the barn itself. Incredibly, the four soldiers were absolutely concealed even though close to the barn. A soldier must be well disciplined to handle the lonely vigil of surveillance in the rain and windswept hedgerows of Northern Ireland. The drizzle or rain can be incessant and the weather varies between rotten and miserable. The soldier is soaked to the skin for days, frequently in freezing weather, with only cold food to eat.

No movement; he must carry out normal bodily functions without moving. Living rough in the field for ten days, the soldier is unwashed, unshaven, unsung, and unheard of, just performing his duty.

The patrol checked their equipment. The listening devices, powerful directional mikes, were operational. Sergeant Saunders tested his high-speed radio, sending the message, "Zero, Indian One in position. Out." The words only had to be mouthed into his throat mike.

There was an affirmative response that the transmission was picked up in Crosmaglen and the waiting began.

Day one. Nothing.

Day two. Nothing.

On the night of day three, eerie yellow fog-lights beamed through the low mist that hung on the black lonely road leading up to the farm. A car with Belfast plates stopped near the deserted barn and two men got out to cautiously circle the wooden building. Satisfied that all was well, they went inside. "Hello, Zero. This is Indian One, Zero. We've got some action out here," transmitted Saunders.

Ears at Crosmaglen were now alert.

A half hour later, another car pulled up, this time with plates from the south. Two more men hurried into the barn. The men spoke in hushed voices as the suppliers from the south explained the details of the drop to the Northern Ireland contacts. The mikes picked up every word, and the information was recorded in Crosmaglen. Within an hour, the plans were set and the men from the south returned to their car, heading back across the border. Soon the other two men walked out of the barn, took another look around, got in their car, and sped away.

Saunders fired the information back to headquarters. The surveillance team closed up shop and arranged for a helicopter pick-up the next night.

From the descriptions, the IRA carried out their charade quite well, with no leading characters participating in the meeting, just messenger boys.

You see, I now knew the date, time, and method of delivery of the arms, which were in Dundalk, just over the border. The big shipment of arms, ammunition, and explosives were earmarked not only for the Belfast Brigade, but for the South Armagh Brigade as well, and would be delivered in one week. I set about planning the proper military operation, the aim being to catch not only those receiving the shipment, but those making the drop as well. I determined it might be necessary to let the weapons carry forward, bringing more terrorists into the net.

At this stage, no names had been mentioned and the IRA security felt confident that they had done a pretty good job, except for the fact that they had no idea they were under surveillance.

So I carried on with the operation, unaware of who would be involved in the drop and the pickup. Although I was to control the operation, it was still out of my hands. The three to four hundred needed to supply the manpower to carry it out had to be called in from several other agencies, the RUC, Special Branch, and regular British army units. The men involved were briefed and rehearsed the operation in a similar farm far from the target.

One week later, all is ready. The surveillance teams were again in position and it was just a question of waiting.

Two A.M. An old lorry trundled over the border and now made its way to the barn. Four carloads of men descended from nowhere and began unloading cargo. Working quietly in the darkness, they were confident that their labor was unobserved.

Saunders radioed back to Crosmaglen, "Hello, Zero. This is Indian One, Zero."

The wheels of the operation were turning.

The weapons and ammunition were transferred and the four cars disappeared as quickly as they arrived. The men were unaware that they were under discreet but comprehensive watch from squads of undercover soldiers and regular troops along the route. At this point, descriptions were being flashed back to the base in Crosmaglen. Again, most of the participants were thought to be unknown messenger boys. However, the description of one of three men in an older model dark blue Mercedes struck a chord in my mind, taking me back to Londonderry in 1971 and '72, reminding me of a young IRA gunman, name of O'Hara. I flashed a message back to his surveillance squad for confirmation.

"Run that last description by me again," he told me.

"Approximately 5'10", husky build, about 12 1/2 stones, black hair, blue eyes. Distinguishing marks: deep scar over right eye. That's all, sir."

"That's enough. Good work. Thanks, Saunders, "

*More than enough!* My suspicions were confirmed. I knew that we had one of the most wanted gunmen in Northern Ireland in our grasp.

Sean O'Hara. He left a trail of death, destruction, and havoc wherever he went. The British Army had been hunting him since 1972 for the murder of at least five British soldiers, including two undercover men. I actually seethed with bitter hatred at the thought of the name of O'Hara, without a doubt the deadliest and evilest bastard I've ever known. Here is some info on that bastard.

O'Hara was born in 1948, to Irish parents who immigrated to London in wartime, seeking jobs that were unavailable in Ireland. After the war, they settled in a section of northern London, Kilburn, and Sean went to a Roman Catholic school there. His friends were among the many London Irish or Irish-born children in the school, and he readily identified with his Irish heritage.

Young Sean was very close to his mother, a kind-hearted, religious woman, who did her best to keep a neat house for Sean and his older sister, though there was little money. When his father was sober enough to find work, which wasn't often, he spent most of the money on drinking bouts at the pubs, stumbling home, senseless. Sean's mother fervently believed that drink was the work of the devil, and gave her husband harsh tongue-lashings. After the screaming and shouting, the brawls began. The arguments were long and heated, and even the sturdy Mrs O'Hara was no match for her brute of a husband.

As small children, Sean and his sister watched the fights, trembling under their bed. As he got older and bigger, Sean began to defend his mother, slugging it out with his old man in earnest. The violent arguments continued until Mr O'Hara passed out from drunkenness or Sean fled the house in fear.

Mrs O'Hara's health deteriorated. The doctors were not sure if she was actually sick or just sick at heart, but on the day she was laid to rest, a part of Sean O'Hara was buried with her. The one thing that remained alive in him was her love for Ireland.

His father quickly married again, this time to the shrew he so deserved. One day when Sean was sixteen, in a fit of disgust with the whole scene, he beat the living daylights out of his father. He gathered his few belongings worth taking with him, and left the house of misery forever.

He took a few odd jobs just to survive until he could join the British Army. It was there he learned the military tactics that would become so useful to him in the future. He mastered the basics of weaponry, explosives, and mounting an operation. He had a stint in Borneo in 1966, which introduced him to the art of guerilla warfare. He also developed a strong distaste for the lingering policy of British colonialism and became interested in the other side of the coin, revolutionary activities.

Because of his frequent rebellion to the strict military discipline and his open disapproval of colonialism, Sean was often in hot water. When his regiment returned to England, he was discharged from the army. With an increasing deep-seated hatred of Britain, he left for Northern Ireland to find his mother's family roots in the barricades of the Bogside and Creegan of Londonderry.

The grinding poverty of Catholic Londonderry was a fine festering place for Sean's hatred of the British rule. He learned the Gaelic language and immediately joined the IRA, becoming a dedicated revolutionary, and a talented urban guerilla. With his military skill and zeal, he was a welcomed addition to the local organization. He quickly earned respect for his work and brandished a deep scar over his right eye to prove it. The scar was acquired in a skirmish with two undercover British soldiers at a dance in the Creggan Community Centre.

I, Staff Sergeant James Evans, was one of those two soldiers, on special assignment from the First Parachute Regiment to the Mobile Response Force. I let my hair grow long and dressed out of uniform, in a casual shirt, sweater, and trousers. I worked well with my partner, Mick Gardiner, and we became close friends. We had to be. Our lives depended on each other. We roamed the streets of Londonderry or cruised in the unmarked car assigned to us. It was my first tour in Northern Ireland and I was selected for undercover work because of my knack for learning languages, particularly the rough dialects of the district.

We learned the quickest way to pick up information was to chat with locals in the public houses or to attend community dances. I suppose we were good-looking enough to have a winning way with the girls. Not a bad way to gain a few tips.

It was a cold winter evening and the dance hall was crowded. Over the loud music, we were chatting up two pretty girls. The dance hall manager suddenly ran up to us.

"Excuse me, gentlemen, but you should know that there's a bomb in the gent's toilet."

They hadn't fooled anyone.

We raced upstairs to the toilet. Sure enough, there was a package wrapped in brown paper in the toilet.

I got the pistol under my left armpit, ran to the stage, grabbed the mike from the band and ordered, "Everybody clear out! Clear the hall immediately! Only use this side door and be bloody quick about it!"

Mick put in a call for "Felix," code name for the bomb disposal boys. After making sure everyone had evacuated, they ran across the dance floor to join the anxious crowd in the cold outside. Just as they passed through the light of the open door, a sniper's fire rang out.

Stunned, I looked at Mick who slumped to the ground beside me, blood gushing from an open chest wound. I turned and saw the gunman ready to take another shot, this time at me. I ducked in time to hear the bullet fly over my head, then fired at the gunman, and the bullet slashed across his forehead.

Half-blinded by the blood flowing into his eyes, the gunman fled.

I turned to my downed partner and held him in my arms as he took his last breath, his blood soaking both of us. The tragedy of the moment hardened me and strengthened my determination and mission to rid the earth of filthy terrorists everywhere.

I was able to give a good description of the young gunman and the new wound he received. He was identified as Sean O'Hara. Sean wore the scar like a badge of courage and soon became one of the most wanted gunmen in Northern Ireland.

"Bloody Sunday" in Londonderry, the 30th of January 1972, brought me and Sean O'Hara face to face once more.

Fifteen thousand demonstrators were scheduled to march in an anti-interment demonstration on that sunny, crisp Sunday afternoon. I had rejoined my parachute regiment to help identify known IRA gunmen.

The regiment was brought into Derry to control the crowd and prevent violence. The IRA would not miss that opportunity to stir up trouble and the paras were briefed on the most dangerous gunmen in the region, including O'Hara. They were given strict orders not to fire unless fired on. The mood of the crowd changed as the day grew gray and dismal. I never forgot when the rock throwing first began, pounding the paras. No one knows for sure when the shooting actually started, but stray shots were fired and in the confusion that followed, two soldiers opened fire on a man who was set to light a nail bomb on Williams Street. He fell to the ground and the shooting match was on. I scuffled with hooligans, took several into custody and then raced to a nearby Catholic church with two other paras, where a sniper was reported to be firing on the crowd. As I reached the steps, a shot rang out and the bullet whizzed by one of my companions. I spotted the assailant, positioned in the corner of the church. The gunman, dressed in a brown coat, looked menacing with the deep scar over his right eye, as he stared down a rifle sight aimed directly at me.

It was O'Hara!

O'Hara fired again, narrowly missing me. I ran at him. O'Hara fled into the church and was quickly lost among the women and children sheltered inside. Another close call, and I could never forget that face.

And since that day, I followed O'Hara with an eye on his every action. From 1972 to '73, O'Hara commanded the Creegan Brigade of Provisional

Irish Republic Army. He was an Army Council member from 1975 to '80. Moving quickly up the ladder, he had been the leader of PIRA since 1980.

O'Hara's horizon had expanded and he was now a full-blown deadly international terrorist.

His global involvement was confirmed by his sightings: Berlin, 1975. He was working with German terrorists' groups, sharing expertise in the use of explosives. They were developing skills in dealing with sophisticated and powerful bombs. I was stationed in Berlin at the time and picked up on the mention of the name of a known IRA terrorist in Germany, Sean O'Hara.

Lebanon, 1976: O'Hara was said to be training with PLO terrorist groups. I learned that nasty bit of news while he was on an exchange visit to the Israeli Defense Force at that time.

Northern Spain, 1979: While touring Spain on holiday, I was told of an IRA terrorist named O'Hara known to be operating with Basque Separatists. They were fine-tuning the art of political assassination, killing several high ranking military figures, including the military governor of Madrid.

During the summer, they continued their terrorist activities, raising havoc with the vital tourist industry by setting off bombs at numerous vacation beaches.

London, 1980: The most recent sighting of O'Hara reported that he was on home turf, holed up in Kilburn. Since I was the recognized specialist on O'Hara, the information led him to work deep again, this time as a taxi driver, combing the streets of the region for nearly six months. The operation successfully broke up two IRA active service units. As for taking O'Hara, the exercise was fruitless, and the big fish once more slipped through the net into obscurity.

O'Hara got around. But in 1981, he was in South Armagh, putting all of his sinister knowledge to use on behalf of his beloved Ireland.

I put aside thoughts of revenge and came back to the reality of the operation at hand. I had no choice but to make the decision that the operation must be changed. O'Hara was a shrewd character and it wouldn't be long before he realized he was under intense surveillance. It would be too risky to hold out and follow the car much longer. The trap must be sprung as quick as possible. I gave the order to proceed with the ambush immediately.

How damn frustrating to be operating from a command position in Crosmaglen. Had I any warning that O'Hara was involved, I would have never missed an opportunity to take him out myself.

With the original plan scrapped, the troops on duty at the vehicle checkpoint were alerted that the blue Mercedes was headed their way. Spikes were quickly positioned across the road. Machine guns were set up on either side of the road and soldiers with rifles lined up off of the road.

The men didn't have long to wait.

The Mercedes roared through the checkpoint. The tires ripped apart. The driver lost control as the car went into a skid, and the soldiers fired into it. A direct hit caused the Mercedes to explode in a hot red ball of flames.

Once the flames were extinguished, the charred remains of two victims were pulled from the wreckage. A trail of blood indicated that the third gunman had skillfully escaped in the confusion, having the presence of mind to open the door and roll out of the car into the darkness before it exploded. Descriptions of the two bodies were flashed back to me in Crosmaglen. Both were the wrong height and build to be O'Hara. He had slipped the net again.

All border-crossing points were closed. A hot pursuit operation was mounted. Helicopters were brought in, droning across the region as the powerful night-sun searchlights scoured the landscape. Tracker dogs sniffed the countryside, with the same negative results. The next day, the pursuit was aborted. A pounding rain had mixed blood with mud, dissolving the scent, and the tracker dogs were called off. Extra troops were rushed to the area to continue the search for three more days. Sadly, the results were the same. No trace of O'Hara.

"Slippery bastard!" I said, when I heard that O'Hara had escaped my grasp yet again. I was sure though that, as I kept saying, *His day will come, even if I have to kill him with my bare hands! What a pleasure that would be!* In spite of that, I knew personal revenge should not be motive enough. Taking out a dangerous IRA operative was motive enough. But personal is personal. You can't take that out of the equation.

I was credited with the overall success of the operation that netted the other cars, the lorry, and the large shipment of arms. Most of the gunmen were just messenger boys, as I suspected. The two who were killed were better known for their talents with explosives.

For me, the success was outweighed by the fact the big catch got away and I could not forget that. The vendetta deepened.

John Morgan made his usual rounds, hoping to pick up information on the whereabouts of O'Hara. He pulled his MG into the parking lot of the pub to meet his friends. His made a routine call on his car radio, giving his location to his base. The standard precautionary checks were made by the undercover agent on a job every ninety minutes after that. The call was his last.

Morgan had grabbed a pint of dark stout, looked around the bar and found the men at their usual table. The pair was gloomy when he joined them. They had reason to be; one of the chaps now had a sister whose husband was being held in custody. Morgan quietly listened as the two men talked.

"He was never good for anything. I only worry about my sister and those three wee girls. We can do without the likes of him."

"Aye, but one got away, the big one, in fact. Now where might he be? There was enough of a ruckus to find him."

Morgan's curiosity intensified, but the two would never have suspected it. He sat there, unflinching and staring into his Guinness, as they speculated on where O'Hara might have found refuge. Many suggestions were offered, some maybe worth pursuing. Finally, giving a big yawn, Morgan excused himself.

"The day's been a bit much, lads. Tomorrow's only more of the same. Good evenin' to ya."

He left the pub, totally unaware that he was being followed. Two checks on his whereabouts were made before his base became alarmed. An agent could easily miss one call, but two meant trouble.

A car was quickly dispatched to the pub.

Morgan's car was in the yard where he parked it. A dent in the hood with blood and strands of human hair reaffirmed the reason for alarm. The trickling path of blood led to tire tracks, and then disappeared.

Again all borders were closed and the hunt was on. And again the wall tightly closed around the IRA. No one had seen or heard anything that would have been of use to the authorities. Laboratory tests proved that the blood on the car was the same rare type as Morgan's.

The IRA scored again and the next day had the audacity to announce they had killed an SAS operative in South Armagh. The British government denied Morgan was a member of the SAS. Rumors reported that he died fighting bravely. Although he was savagely tortured and beaten in the parking lot, he struggled vainly until his head was smashed against his own car, knocking him unconscious. He was clubbed again, and then dragged away. His body never found.

Hearing the story, I was once more sickened by the problem that was Northern Ireland. It was mine to live with, but how could I explain it to someone like you, Ginny? If I can't quite understand it, how can I expect you to?

Ciao,
Your very own ...

# 7
# Miami

S ome days, Ginny would make the beautiful drive through the Everglades
to the reservation, alone as always, which was best. Wayne was so often
away, fortunately. He found the flatness of the landscape boring, missing what
lay beneath and the drama of the clouds. The sunny brilliant blue sky was
calming, with bright green sawgrass swaying in the breeze. Gators or turtles
swam in the dark water or sunned on rocks. Flocks of white ibis circled and
flew above the grass, landing in distant trees. A lone heron waded along the
canal, here and there. The trip was a peaceful distraction.

Ginny could as easily be in a foreign country as in Florida. She met
with her Indian friends in their *chickees*, huts with a palmetto-thatched roof
once used as a home, now used as a place to sew, cook, or eat. She watched the
women work while as they talked of family life, their clans and beliefs, sewing,
new patchwork designs, and clothing competitions. She found listening to
their stories very soul satisfying. The smell of smoke from a cooking fire filled
the air, a comforting reminder that food was always ready for their families.

The men would tell her legends and historical tales, stories of wars their
people had to fight against American soldiers to stay in their homeland, and
pressing more current political problems. Oral stories, passed down through
generations. Now, however, they wanted the stories written down in English,
never to be lost. Often Ginny would tape and transcribe them, passing along
typed copies she would share on her next visit.

One day in mid-August, she was listening to a good friend, a respected elder who was telling her a story. Suddenly, he stopped and said, "Ginny, I see you. I don't mean I see as you are on the outside. I mean I see the inside. I'm not religious and don't go to church or anything. I'm spiritual and I see that you are too. You don't come out here to tell us what you want to hear. You listen and respect and understand what I say. I trust you. That's why I like talking with you."

That was the kindest thing he'd ever said to her. Ginny's hard work was rewarded, just by knowing that it was meaningful to the people. That was something Wayne would never understand, because money wasn't involved. After years of visiting her friends, bit by bit, they'd opened up and told her more, a trust she cherished.

Pleased with the visit and the information she gathered, she planned to use it in a book she intended to write someday, whenever she got around to it. Her work, as it evolved, was becoming more diverse, interesting, perhaps opening more doors of opportunity. She sorted it out in her head on the drive back to Miami and reality.

Ginny went straight to the post office. There was a pink notice in her box — her package had arrived. Her heart pounded as she stood in line, waiting her turn. A large brown envelope was handed to her, with two Diana and Charles wedding portrait stamps on it, marked "Photographs: Do Not Bend." She hurried to her car and opened it.

Inside was a black and white photograph of Jim wearing fatigues, leaning against a military vehicle. The photograph was taken in some sort of a compound, an area with high walls topped by barbed wire. His dark hair curled on his forehead and his eyes looked straight into the camera, sad and serious. Tall and handsome as she remembered him, he was in one piece, but very grim. Ginny was thrilled to finally have a picture of him, but found the photo saddened her. A letter accompanied it. In the letter there was a new address in the heading, this time in Northern Ireland.

> *As you can see from the address, I'm firmly entrenched in the wild hills of South Armagh in Northern Ireland, straddling the border with the Irish Republic. Situation here is pretty grim with the hunger strikers starving themselves off every day, the daily rioting, bombings, shootings. Still, life is not so pleasant on the mainland with rioting in*

*major cities. How long before the army gets involved at home? Even so, we managed the wedding. Did you see any of it? I'm told it was pretty impressive.*

*My plans, as such, are still fluid. I expect to remain in Northern Ireland for some six months and then move on to Belize, although I never take anything for granted anymore. I expect I could just as easily finish up in Saudi Arabia or Iran.*

*I've enclosed a photograph of me. It's not very good, I'm afraid, but the best available.*

It had been months since she had heard from him. There was not a word of explanation. It was as if that time simply did not exist. What a crazy way to live. Could she handle this kind of existence on a long-term basis? She remembered her frustration of the last three months. Was that over or was there more to come? She drove home in a daze. What two different worlds, from the peaceful Florida Everglades to war-torn Northern Ireland.

The next day, while working in her study, transcribing the taped interviews she made on the reservation the day before, Ginny turned from her work to the photograph of Jim, and studied the details with a magnifying glass.

*He has no idea how good-looking he is. Hollywood couldn't typecast a more perfect person for the role he is living. But who will play me?*

She read the letter over and over. He was suddenly in touch, but for how long?

The phone rang and she absently answered it. There was silence on the other end, and then she heard Jim's voice.

"Hi. Remember me?"

"Jim! I just got a letter from you yesterday, and after so many months. Is this really you on the phone? Where've you been? I've been so worried, and frustrated. I haven't known what to think."

"I can't really tell you where I've been or what I've been up to. I'm settled. Unfortunately, I'll be here for a while. But at least I have a phone and can call you, and we can write. Did you get my new address?"

"Yes. And a great photograph. I had all but given up. What a surprise. I love it."

"Do you? I really haven't had a reason to get a photo taken until now.

I've had a lot of letters from you. They did get to me and help my morale. And thanks for your photograph. Very nice."

Ginny imagined a mountain of mail if he'd gotten it all at once. They talked for the better part of an hour.

Finally, Jim said, "Enough for today. I'll call you tomorrow."

"Will you really? It won't be another three months, will it?"

"No, I promise. Same time, 'til then. Ciao."

Ginny slowly put down the phone and stared at it for a long time. At least, Jim was in touch again. Was the nightmare finally over?

Busy with her work and confused by the long silence, she made no effort toward a divorce, lingering in limbo. Wayne was gone so much, and she was busy, too. Not the best of all possible worlds, but they basically had lived like this for years. Ships passing in the night. Jim being back in the picture changed things.

This began a routine of daily phone calls from Jim, sometimes there were two or three calls in a day. There was no way she could call him. His phone bills must have been outrageous. She jokingly wondered if he had robbed a bank, or was using a military line, but didn't really want to know the answer. She was just glad to hear from him, no matter what.

Bluey envelopes finally began to fill her box. He was trying to establish some kind of a relationship, difficult as it was under the circumstances. Letters between them were questioning; wanting to know everything about each other, simple facts, background information, the kinds of things lovers thirst to know. Their questions and answers were like many that contestants exchanged on the television show, *The Dating Game*. This was new to her. Married at eighteen, Ginny had never dated as an adult before. He did his best to fill her in about his interests, hobbies, and travels.

> *I don't really have much time for hobbies, but I do enjoy music, reading, and theater, but not cinema. I used to enjoy dancing but don't seem to have much time for that now. I spend a lot of time with sports: skiing, swimming, parachuting, football, rugby, cricket. I love athletics.*
>
> *I've told you that I traveled a lot. All of Europe, of course, and more interesting spots beyond: Libya, Israel, Jordan, Lebanon, Turkey, Kuwait, Congo, Rhodesia, Cyprus, Greece, Singapore, Borneo, Brunei,*

*Malaysia, Vietnam, Hong Kong, Thailand, India, Iran, and Ceylon.*
*I'm grateful to the army for the opportunity to see the world, even if*
*most of it was through the sight of a rifle.*

His list seemed to grow as he remembered his adventures. He hadn't missed much, it seemed to her. As she read the list of the many places he had been, she thought about her own life and the few places she had seen, often in the confines of a tour group. She read on.

*Are you religious? I'm afraid I'm not. Don't get me wrong; I do*
*believe in God, but purely in my own way, without having to go to*
*church or subscribing to views I disagree with. Especially since religion*
*has caused more death than war, disease, or natural disasters.*

They sure agreed there. She thought the problems in Northern Ireland, caused by religion, were insane. She remembered her decision when she was sixteen to join a church and a Christian youth group, seeking a way to fill a void in her life that her family never filled. She'd actually thought she wanted to be a missionary, to travel to faraway places, meeting exotic people. She hadn't heard of Margaret Mead yet. It wasn't until college that she realized she really was more interested in anthropology, learning about and appreciating the ways of different people, not trying to change them. All of her research about tribal cultures in graduate school anthropology courses had strengthened those views, and led to her current work. What her Native American friend said was right; she was spiritual.

How difficult it would be to relate to each other by letters. Something wonderful had happened in the Highlands and neither one wanted to let go of the magic. It had been so much more than just a day and night together. It had been an instant recognition of kindred spirits. They'd tapped unknown levels of passion, and found a powerful, unexpected love. At all costs, they had to follow it to find out what it meant, and where it would lead them.

Ginny wrote cheerful letters every day, telling Jim what she was doing, her trips out to the Everglades and the people she visited, and the news from the States. She sent articles about Northern Ireland from *The Miami Herald*, letting Jim know that the American press was basically unkind to the British presence there.

Jim wrote all he could about the ongoing crisis.

*Thanks for the two letters I received today; our helicopter re-supply brought them in . . . Rioting continues, more soldiers shot. I think it would have been better if the USA could have had the Irish problem and we could have had Vietnam. At least there you knew who your enemy was.*

*Is it really five months since we met and parted? I would like to see you again dearly, but it will not be for some time. I am truly stuck in this hell-hole of war. But Belize beckons early next year, and I'm told it's fairly easy to get weekends off there (a quick flight to Miami). Shall we see how things develop?*

*I won't promise to write every day, and there may be periods when you will not hear from me for weeks or more, but I'll do my best.*

It only took four days to a week for a letter to cross the ocean. With the phone and letters, their tenuous line of communication was open. They did their best to keep their spirits up and put frustration out of their minds. They could only speculate how it might eventually end. What kind of life could they ever have together?

*I'm totally obligated to the Queen until 1985. I can resign my commission before then but I'd lose a lot of money. There's the problem of what to do. I suppose I could be a mercenary in Africa. I have plenty of contacts, but there must be something better.*

*I still think about you a lot. I can shut my mind off completely to relax and you're there. The memory of our night is etched in my mind. It was an experience, no matter what else happens, I'll never forget. I have no idea how it would be living together for a period longer than a day. We're both strong willed, and I usually get what I want. At least there's one arena we have no problems with, though I do like to get some sleep now and then.*

Ginny laughed. Each letter was interesting, sad, a flashback of love. She couldn't invent such a situation in her wildest imagination. This was storybook quality. She had never met anyone like him and was vicariously experiencing more of the world than she had ever known. The real world is not all sunshine and parties. There are no easy answers and things don't always turn out the way you want them to. She was finding out the true meaning of Yin and Yang, of opposites, and also the significance of the saying "How can you know pleasure without knowing pain?" Agony and ecstasy. Their relationship was the ultimate of highs and lows, pleasure and pain.

Jim brought up a very important fact in that letter. She had seen him as an army officer forever, and now he was looking forward to getting out of the army in 1985. The date was set and he planned to start a very different life. He went so far as to speculate if that life could include her, and how they would get along.

Ginny had never expected him to contemplate all of this. This was another ballgame, and now he was singing another song, one beyond her wildest dreams. Often, she wondered if their relationship would survive the humdrum of daily life together. Would it just become another struggle over who was in charge? She had done that once, and it had been a big mistake. Would she risk it again? Would he risk it at all?

September. Somehow the phone calls continued and he also continued to write

> It's Sunday morning in South Armagh, very quiet and peaceful. This afternoon, after a session in the local pubs, they will start on us, first with the stones and bricks, then moving on to the petrol bombs. Perhaps an IRA gunman will chance his arm and try for a couple of shots. So our day goes on.
>
> I'm taking the boys up to Scotland in January for two weeks of warfare training. It just won't be the same as my last visit.
>
> Someday I fancy settling down on a small Greek island with a boat; do a bit of charter work, fish, contemplate my life, what was and what wasn't, and grow old in a nice relaxed atmosphere, with none of the troubles of the world bothering me. Reports are coming in that a crowd in four columns and about seven-thousand strong is approaching our Security Force base, so I must go.

He shared his dreams and anxieties so easily. From dreaming about settling down on a boat on a Greek Island to suddenly facing an angry mob of militants. A boat on a Greek Island. It was a very romantic thought, but unimaginable. Was she still part of the picture? Would she want to be? She loved

Miami, and couldn't imagine living permanently elsewhere.

The letters came with more black and white photographs, evidently taken at the same time as the first one she'd received. Just looking at them broke her heart. There were several pictures inside the base. One was taken from a helicopter. Another photo was a shot of the patrol as it moved along the street, rifles ready. There was a shot of Jim, just picked up from days in the field and inside a vehicle. He looked more like he had been run over by it, dark circles under his hollow, empty eyes. There was a notation on the back saying that it was taken after three nights without sleep. The last was a picture someone had taken of Jim sound asleep on a bench with the sign "Forkhill" behind him. On the back he had written: "You catch forty winks when you can!" The photos would have lost the dramatic impact if they had been in color.

*"A soldier's life is terrible hard." Alice was right.*

She could not imagine what his life was like, and afraid to ask too much. He told her what he could, but explained he was limited to what he could say for security reasons.

In another letter:

> *Thought I'd tell you a little bit about my men and Northern Ireland. I command a unit composed of five sections, each of six men plus my sergeant and radio-man. Each section specializes in different aspects of our work. We are based at a place called Castledillon (not on the map), but spend most of our time in Crosmaglen or Forkhill, (small towns dominated by the IRA). We also operate in other areas of South Armagh that are in border areas with Eire.*
>
> *To my lads, I'm mother, father, brother, priest, and bank manager. I'm responsible for their training, welfare, and most important, morale. In addition to my own operational tasks, looking after my boys means I have very little time to myself. After a patrol lasting three or four days, my kit has to be cleaned, weapons looked after, some sleep, hot food. But before I can do my own, I have to be sure my boys have no problems. They're a great bunch though.*
>
> *It was very sad about two young lads shot last week after being lured to a flat by two girls. One of my lads was killed five weeks ago, not by an IRA gunman, but by an overzealous sentry. Fancy if you spent four months here and then were shot and killed by one of your own!*

*I can't see an end to the troubles in Ireland. The two factions are poles apart — plus it's always raining here!*

She put the letter down. This was his real life, not a novel she was reading. He was deeply concerned about his men, and locked into his work. She understood that his work had kept him from having relationships. He was wise, far from naive, but Ginny sensed an unexplained openness and innocence, judging from his response to a book on love that she sent to him:

*I'm not sure I agree with the definition of love. Mind you, I've not experienced much in the way of love anyway. I was madly in love with a girl (or so I thought) back in 1964. Since then, a bit of lust, a few friends, and the army. I never did think of myself as a romantic.*

*Also, you never comment on the sexual part of our relationship. What do you like doing, sexually, and what do you not?*

Did she even know? She'd never been asked that before, and yet they were swept away in a most romantic adventure.

Was this love? How could she be sure? She was keenly aware of the drama of it all, though it was nothing she could explain to anyone, or anything they would understand, anyway. She lived in two worlds and was very much alone in both.

Dr Johnson witnessed her anguish weekly but didn't discourage her, not that it would have done any good. She was intent on living this to the hilt, both the agony and the ecstasy. It was a story she was driven to see to the end. Perhaps write. She was becoming more of a writer than an artist. This story was a gift she couldn't cut out of her life. Dr Johnson noticed real growth; she was experiencing life in a most difficult set of circumstances, and squarely dealing with real issues.

He worked with her fears; he knew them well. Her biggest fear was financial, a deep-seated insecurity from seeing her mother left as a young widow with no money and two children. So the family moved in with her parents.

Ginny could never kick her own fear of being a bag lady. Wayne knew those fears intimately and used money to manipulate her whenever possible. It was all clear now. Some of her demons were real and therapy wasn't just amusement. It was crucial, and working. Ginny, gaining courage, could recognize many of her problems, and was beginning to deal with them.

The only other person she could talk to was Margie. Margie did her best to understand and wanted to see Ginny out of her misery, no matter what it took. But Margie was single, had never been married, of course didn't have children, and didn't grasp the depth of the dilemma and its complexities. She had no idea of the strength of the ties to home that kept Ginny from making a clean break. She couldn't just move out. She had little money of her own, and nowhere to go. Margie could only listen, sympathize, and encourage, distressed whenever she saw Ginny waiver.

The phone calls were the saving grace. Jim was frequently out in the field on patrols, but he called whenever he was at base, sometimes two or three time a day. The calls were often interrupted, but he called back as soon as possible. In early September, he made a surprise request.

"Is it possible for you to get to London? One of my lads has to be in court on November 27th, and I have to testify on his behalf. I know I'll be there then, and it's the only time I can get out of this place. Could you meet me? I'm dying to see you again."

This was not what she'd expected, and it took her breath away. "Sure. I don't know how, but I'll work it out somehow. I'll be there."

"We'll only have a long weekend, but that's better than nothing, far as I'm concerned. I'll have to come back here right after, but I'd love to show you around London."

She realized that November 26th would be Thanksgiving. Eric would be home from college, and the family would ritually gather for a big dinner at her house. Could she forget about her son — and where would she be?

"Is that date firm? Can't it be any other time? I just realized that's Thanksgiving, and my son will be home from college. That's a problem."

"I'm sorry, Ginny, but that's it. I don't see any other time when I'll be able to get out of here. Please try to come."

"Okay. I'll be there. If that's it, then that's it. I'll work it out. Nothing's more important than seeing you again. It's a date."

They talked about all of the things they would do and only hinted at the things they couldn't talk about. The phone line could have ears, so conversations were always discreet.

Ginny hung up in disbelief. They dared to think about getting together again? That was the one thing she wanted to do more than anything in the world, but it was on an important holiday. She wondered which was really more important. But now what?

The problems a meeting would create were enormous. Her double life had to end as fast as possible. Unhappy as she was, she had never even thought of having an affair before, and realized that she couldn't keep this deceit going on for much longer. She was too honest for that. After their brief romantic day and night in the Highlands, it had just been phone calls and letters. She had followed Dr Johnson's suggestions and played her cards close to her chest.

Wayne had no idea of what was going on. It wasn't as if he expressed deep love for her or love at all. She simply was supposed to be *his,* a possession. She was not to be with someone who was caring and exciting. He would go ballistic if he found out. But then, she had no idea what he might be doing when he was away so much. Did he have affairs? At this point, she neither knew nor cared.

The third element in their marriage, ever since he was in law school, had always been Law, with a capital L. When he got his class ring from law school, he took off his wedding ring and never wore it again. Law was like a mistress, demanding all of his time. Then there were the many business trips away from Miami and the frequent night meetings when he was in town. After so much neglect, she really didn't care anymore, She couldn't. They were more like housemates, at best, sharing a lonely house.

She had to see an attorney as soon as possible. Wasn't a divorce what she wanted anyway? Or did she? It was time to put everyone out of their misery, just as Jim said. She called her attorney and made an appointment for the following week. She had saved just enough that there would be money for a retainer fee and for the trip to England.

What would she do when she returned from England? She would have to come back to Miami, no doubt about that. But where would she go?

Those old fears filled her, and she felt the butterflies fluttering in her stomach as the full impact of the decision sunk in. Her funds would be limited and she was going out on a limb and sawing it off behind her.

She was so hesitant and afraid when she agreed to meet Jim in the Highlands, but she dared to go. Dare. That was the key. Look how that turned out a once in a lifetime experience. WHO DARES WINS. Wasn't that the SAS motto, a war cry?

There was no way she could even consider missing an opportunity to see Jim again. Best she could, she pushed the fear out of her mind, refused to think about the "what ifs," and concentrated on how wonderful it would be to be with him. The anticipation built as she planned her escape.

Ginny studied the colorful Laker Airways brochure in the travel agency. Sir Freddie Laker had incredible airfares and hotel packages. The rate included airport transfers and was far cheaper than her booking the hotel. The agent recommended the Hyde Park Towers, in a convenient Bayswater location. The Laker planes were always full, so she advised Ginny to book as soon as possible.

Determined, Ginny had the agent make the reservation for a ten-day package in London, departing Miami on Wednesday, November 25th. When Jim called the next day, she excitedly gave the details to him. Once her course was set, serious concerns developed. How in the devil would she pull this off? She was glad when the day to meet with her attorney finally rolled around.

Evelyn Singer was an excellent attorney specializing in family law. She was the same age as Ginny and had been divorced for many years. She had seen a lot of scared women like Ginny come through her door. Devoting their lives to their families was okay, but when they tried to just have their own life or careers, all hell broke loose. The situation had become almost epidemic in America, inspired by the women's movement. Evelyn admired the clients who were making the effort to stand on their own feet and applauded their successes. She also knew how vulnerable they were and did everything she could to protect them. She understood Ginny's situation very clearly, ever since that first day she came into her office a year ago, crying and confused by Wayne's explosive responses and badgering.

On this day, Evelyn greeted Ginny with, "What's up? Is Wayne still driving you crazy?"

Ginny laughed. "Of course. But the plot's thickened. I'm in a real mess this time."

She told Evelyn about her trip to England and Scotland, and how she had met Jim. When she told her of the wonderful time they had in the Highlands, Evelyn, always a romantic, cheered, "Good for you!"

"But there's more. He was immediately sent to Northern Ireland, and that's where he is now. A real nightmare. He's going to be in London to go to court for one of his soldiers around Thanksgiving, and asked me to meet him there. Just for a few days and then he has to return to Northern Ireland.

I booked my flight and I'm going, but I'm terrified. Looks like I must file for divorce before I take off this time."

"Why?"

"What do you mean, 'Why?' I'm not kidding about this."

"I know you aren't. But why file? You don't know how things will work out in London. You may learn to hate each other really quick. He hasn't offered you any reassurances. Let Wayne file if he wants to. You have nothing to lose, and that way he'll have to pay the fee to file."

That seemed to make sense to Ginny. She trusted Evelyn's judgment, even though it sounded risky.

"Look, have a wonderful time and don't worry about a thing. You've earned this after all of the grief Wayne's given you. Call me when you get back from England and we'll see what has to be done."

Ginny thanked her and left, relieved. The relief was temporary, however, as she lapsed into moments ranging from anxiety to sheer panic. The pressure was taking its toll, but she also was sick and tired of the foolish fights and Wayne's childish demands.

That evening, the two of them sat drinking wine on their veranda, with candles flickering. They looked out over the turquoise water dancing in the pool lights, the Japanese lanterns glowing. In spite of the serene atmosphere, an argument flared from nowhere, and they fought for an hour over her lack of desire to cook gourmet meals for just the two of them. Then the fight turned against her research and her work at the museum.

Getting her fill of bickering, Ginny finally exploded.

"I've had it with you and your constant complaining and the way you treat me with lack of respect! There's a big world out there. It can be an awful place or a wonderful place. Lately, I've experienced a bit of hell as well as a patch of paradise that made me question my very existence. I'm on my way to see if that paradise was real."

Ginny became very determined as she continued. "You might as well know. I met a fascinating British army officer in Britain. He serves in the SAS, Special Air Services. He is deep, intelligent, and found both me and the work I do interesting. We spent very little time together, and he's unfortunately in Northern Ireland now, but he's asked me to meet him in London. I won't say when. That can be the big surprise, but I've made my plans, and I'm going."

A direct hit. Wayne was stunned. He had been too preoccupied to notice that his castle was crumbling. She had maintained the double life quite well to that point. Now her patience was exhausted, and furthermore, she was off to London.

Regaining his composure after that sobering bit of news, Wayne set down his wine glass and, in a calm voice, said "Tell me about it."

She told him how she met Jim on the train, and eventually decided to accept his offer to spend the day with him in the Highlands because of her interest in Highlanders. She spared Wayne the details and said it was only for a day, and then he was suddenly swooped away, turning up on duty in Northern Ireland.

Wayne astonished Ginny with his response. He softened, and for the first time suggested that they go to a marriage counselor together, one selected by her gynecologist, as if that was an issue.

She had his attention at last. In both her mind and heart, Ginny knew it was already too late. She was too disgusted with Wayne, and too much in love with Jim. She told him she would think about it, and another round in their bitter battle was over.

There are no sure things in life. If she was insecure before, she now had a genuine reason to be. Dr Johnson was pleased with her progress, and she, no matter what, decided to continue seeing him alone as well.

# 8
# Northern Ireland /
# IRA Bandit Country

*Dear Ginny,*

*Here I am in Bandit Country, as we say . I have no way of writing this to you except as a story. I am not supposed to be writing this, but no one reads "stories" attached to letters, especially if they sound like fiction, and clearly this one does, so I am typing this as if I were you . I mean to say, dear girl, you are the writer, I am the soldier, let's leave it at that. Here goes. But I must warn you, this story is for strong stomachs. I may be flip about writing it but there were real tears in my Cockney eyes when writing. I think I know, can't be sure, but I think this may be why you like writing. It's like the guys who write on the walls in Belfast for all to see, then they vanish in the night. But please don't let this sad story keep you awake, Ginny. It's bad enough that it happened. But I had to share it with my Secret Sharer.*

*All for now,*
*Jim/James*

## STANDARD OPERATING PROCEDURE

James settled down at his desk for paperwork, his least favorite job; personnel records and reports always to bring up to date. He much preferred being out on the ground than dealing with this stuff.

"Excuse me, Boss," said a voice from the open door. "Got a minute to spare?

James looked up and saw one of his young soldiers, Corporal Robert Williams. James did his best to always be available for his men, and had a genuine sympathetic ear for their problems. His men respected him, and he had earned their confidence, but there had to be a pretty big need for a soldier to come forth like this.

"No problem, Williams. Take a pew. What's on your mind?

"Well, it's about my leave, Sir."

"That's coming up, is it? When are you scheduled to go?"

"In two weeks."

"I know you must be itching to get out of here. What are your plans?"

"That's just it. If it's okay with you, I'd like to stay here."

"Stay here? You must be mad!"

"Well, I'm an orphan. I have no family or friends to visit, really. But the main reason, there's this girl. Here. I thought I might get to see a bit more of her if I just, you know, hang around."

"Now that's bloody lunacy. You know what could happen if you see her here. How did you meet her anyway?"

"Well, her name's Mary O'Connor. I've been doing town patrols and she just seemed to be there, at the same place, every week. We talk. This has been going on for a while, two months or more, and I'm pretty fond of her. Always being there herself, she must take a fancy to me, too. I'd like to see more of her."

"Well, you sure don't want to do it here. Listen, I've got a friend with a small hotel in Malta. That's a nice safe place, and it's pretty cheap too. Have you saved any money?"

"Sure, sir. There's not much to spend it on here. I've saved quite a bit."

"Why don't I ring up this chap and see if he has room for you two to stay with him? He's an old friend and I don't think there'll be any problems. Do you think she'd go away with you? "

"I hadn't thought of that, but I hope so. I'll see her tomorrow, and let you know after that. Thanks again, Boss!"

"For God's sake, be careful!"

James understood. He was now keenly aware of how it felt to be passionately in love with someone, longing to spend time with them, and getting to know them. He called his friend and there was no problem making the arrangements. The hotel just had a cancellation, a very private guest room. The soldier and girl would be welcome. James even worked out flight arrangements for them. Better to have them safely out of Northern Ireland.

Williams reported back to James as soon as he returned from his patrol. "She'll go, Sir."

James laughed. "I sort of thought she would. She's probably never been out of Crosmaglen, let alone Northern Ireland. And you're a nice looking soldier. I've made your flight arrangements and you'll be met in Malta."

"This's bloody kind of you, Sir. Very understanding. Thank you."

"Good luck, Williams. Let me know how it went when you get back."

"You'll be the first to know."

James was too preoccupied with patrols to think too much about his story of the soldier and his girl. He had enough problems of his own. The pressure was on to scour the countryside and round up as many gunmen as possible.

The mop-up was going quite well, and the army was making progress, but at great expense to the men involved. They were exhausted.

James's only distraction were the letters from Ginny and his calls to her. She was his main stronghold, his link to the outside world. In those rare moments when he could rest, he closed his eyes and she was there. He had his vivid memories of that night they shared and he fantasized about their upcoming meeting in London.

No wonder he was so sympathetic with young Robert Williams. He knew what it was to long to be with someone. But a lot of water had to go over the dam before he could get to London. For the moment, she had to be the farthest thing from his mind.

There was a two-week operation that would hopefully clean house, and the arrests would break a vital link in the supply chain of arms from the south. This time James would not only plan the patrol, he would participate. It would be mean and grueling. In the meantime, planning the operation and maintaining daily routines occupied his thoughts.

Time passed quickly, and before he knew it, Williams had left and returned from his holiday with Mary.

He appeared at James's desk. "I just want to thank you again, Sir."

"Oh, how did it go? Malta's not bad, is it?"

"It was wonderful. I've asked her to marry me when I leave here and she said 'Yes.' We can make a fine life for ourselves out of Northern Ireland, and she'd sure have no regrets about leaving. I wish you could meet her, dark brown hair and shiny blue eyes. Good figure, too, if I say so myself. Too good to spend the rest of her life in this place. Here's a picture I took of her in Malta." He handed James the photograph.

"Great, Williams. You're right; she is good looking. I'm happy for you. Glad I could help out. You don't have much longer here. I checked your record, only a month or so and then back to Hereford."

"Right, sir. We'll get married in Hereford."

"Until then, make sure no one sees you with her. A month isn't long."

Williams left, but James had a concern for the girl's safety.

Four days later, Williams was back in his office.

"I'm worried, Sir. She didn't meet me. I've been out for a look around twice now, our usual spot, and she just hasn't been there. We got along so well, all the talk about us, about getting married. There must be some reason why she hasn't been out to see me.

"Relax, Williams. Maybe she just had things to catch up on. You know how work piles up when you've been away. Give her a day or two. When do you go out again?"

"Tomorrow."

"Fine. Let me know what happens. I'm sure she'll reappear. Maybe she's sewing her wedding dress."

The next evening Williams came in from his patrol and headed straight for James's office.

"Something's wrong. I know it. No sign of her. This isn't like Mary."

James didn't want Williams to know how concerned he was. He knew the consequences if the IRA suspected the girl was involved with a Brit. It would serve no purpose to let him know, and only panic the young man.

"Get a good night's sleep and I'll look into this tomorrow. Try not to think about it. We'll figure out how to get in touch with her."

They didn't have to. The next day a message was phoned into the

Ops room. "You might tell those paras of yours to go have a look at the old Doherty farm. Not much has been happenin' there for years, but I think you'd find somethin' quite interestin' in that empty farmhouse."

The caller hung up.

The message was immediately brought to James's attention. The first thought was that it was a come-on. Ordinarily it was nothing to rush into, but for some gnawing reason, James felt they better check it out. He followed standard operating procedure, and organized a patrol that included an explosives expert and a medic, just in case. Dispatching the men as soon as they were assembled, James joined them.

The road to the Doherty farm was blocked, the farmhouse cordoned off.

The explosives man made a slow approach to the crumbling building. There was no sign of life around anywhere. They blew the door off and the men waited for a response. After the explosion, there was absolute silence. Nothing.

Cautiously, "Felix" and the patrol commander entered the house, disgusted by what they found. It was enough to make even hardened soldiers cry. They called James in.

He looked at the lovely girl, unconscious and spread eagle on the floor. Immediately he recognized her from the photograph Williams had shown him.

Mary O'Connor!

He fought the urge to vomit.

Her kneecaps were a bloody mess, with a Black and Decker power drill on the floor, left beside her as a reminder. The IRA had a particularly ugly way of using the tool on victims, at a very slow speed. The cruelest form of torture imaginable.

Mary had lost a lot of blood and was in shock, but she was still alive and mercifully unconscious.

"Fucking Hell! Get the medic in here! And get on the radio to Crosmaglen! I want a chopper in here now!"

The medic gave her a shot of morphine and started a saline drip on the girl. James held her hand until the chopper arrived to airlift her to the hospital in Belfast.

Back in base, James went straight to find Williams, who sensed a problem when he saw James approaching. He grabbed his rifle as his worst suspicions became a reality when told what happened.

"Mary! Oh, God, no! I'll kill every one of those bastards!"

It took three soldiers to wrestle the hysterical soldier to the ground and twist the rifle he was holding from his hands. They pinned him there while the medic gave him an injection to knock him out.

Another chopper took Williams to the mental ward of the hospital, where he would be sedated for days. Sickened, James knew that Mary would recover but never walk again.

# 9
# Miami

So far Ginny had kept her letters and phone conversations with Jim quietly under control. That, too, was how she usually presented herself to the world. She wanted more than anything to be a strong and confident woman. But on receiving Jim's story, she broke down uncontrollably. She reverted to a terrified little girl. She was also afraid that Wayne would know just how to manipulate her fear to his advantage. He would have her in the palm of his hand.

So far, too, Jim had not seen Ginny's fear and trepidation side. The tidal wave of emotion that could sweep her away like one of those out of season hurricanes Miami was heir to, when the calm of seaside air became lightning and thunder and merciless wind storm.

For a little while Ginny didn't know what to say about Jim's story. Should she say it was well-written? No, that would be inappropriate. Should she tell him that she broke down reading it? No, she couldn't allow herself that luxury either, he wouldn't understand.

While she was waiting to respond, he wrote her …

> Sometimes I find you difficult to understand, like you are two
> different people, one strong and the other insecure, and the two don't
> compute. Still, perhaps someday I'll get to know the two of you. As
> long as I'm able, I'll write and telephone.

*Providing all goes according to plan, I'll see you in November. Though until then, Ginny, keep an open mind (and heart) about how you feel about me. Don't let me become too important to you, because as you know only too well, I can step out of your life, vanish, for long periods with you not knowing what is going on. The action is heating up here, so I may not spend as much time in base as I have these last couple of weeks, which means less time on the phone.*

*You asked if I could ever live in America. Could I ask you what America has to offer me? But then again, what could I offer America? I do admit that Britain is going downhill and is not the great empire it once was. Two world wars have cost us dearly, but that's old hat now.*

*It's a wild night outside, cold, wet, and windy, not really the right climate to go out stomping around in the countryside. Better close as I leave for my patrol.*

They had talked on the phone the day the letter was written, and talk concentrated on their meeting. The time would arrive before they knew it, and the thought of it put Ginny in alternating states of panic and joy. In closing the phone conversation, Jim said he would call her in five days, just to assure her that he was safely back from his patrol.

She had enough to worry about. The stormy sessions were beginning with Wayne and the new marriage counselor they selected, Rhoda Levy.

Ginny drove down the tree-lined street, checked the number and parked in front of a large Spanish-style house in Coral Gables, Rhoda's home office. Arriving before Wayne gave Ginny some time to size up the situation. The office was in the back of the house and the door was open.

She pulled on the cord of the bell with a sign "Ring me," and Rhoda promptly walked through a bead curtain to greet her. She wore large-framed eyeglasses on her beak nose, and was a plump owl-like woman, with a wise and pleasant face.

Ginny sat down on the sofa, noticing that the room was full of owls. Every nook and cranny in her arena was crammed with owls; ceramic owls, carved wood and stone owls, paintings of owls. A macramé owl hung on the wall over the sofa, giving Ginny an uneasy feeling.

They reminded Ginny of the crucial night when the large owl flew in through the open glass doors of their family room during Eric's birthday celebration. That changed everything.

Wayne entered the room and after a short introduction, joined Ginny on the sofa. They began at the beginning, the good years turned sour, sorting out the bits and pieces of their many years together.

Having no idea how bitter Ginny was, Wayne was shocked when confronted with the depths of her resentment. It was the first time he had to listen, to hear her agony. He thought he had been so good to her, cared for her, had given her everything. Why wasn't that enough? It just wasn't what she wanted and needed. Each session was wrenching, and left Ginny a basket case for days.

After one particularly stormy session, she raced to her studio for the call she expected from Jim. The phone rang on time and she grabbed it, relieved.

"Ginny Thomas?"

"Yes."

"James Evans, my commanding officer, asked me to call. He's had to go out on the ground again. He'll be back on the 22nd and call you then."

"Will he be okay?" *A silly question, why did she ask it?*

"Oh, yeah. He'll be fine."

She thanked him for the call and hung up, her stomach in knots. The mission was longer than most, and it thrust him deeper into the countryside, although she had no knowledge of the situation. She received a letter addressed in an unfamiliar handwriting and feared the worst. But inside was a letter from Jim, written in pencil and not under the best of circumstances.

> *Please excuse the pencil, but I'm writing in the field on an operation, and I'll give this to our helicopter pilot to post when he brings our supplies in. It doesn't look as if I'll be able to speak to you until we finish this operation on the 22nd. The weather is lousy. It hasn't stopped raining for three days and there is no worse feeling than being soaked to the skin all the time. Must go now. Hear the chopper coming.*

Ginny put the letter aside and stared into space. It always was as if she was watching an old war movie, or worse yet, living in one. And in a way she was.

He called as planned, but there was little he could say about his patrol.

"Well, it looks like the hunger strike aftermath may soon be over.

Only problem then, of course, is seeing what tactics the IRA will use next. Probably more car bombs and attacks against Security Force base, or even off duty personnel."

"I'm dealing with problems here as well. Nothing like yours, of course. My life's chaos and I can't wait until London."

"I've no definite news there. I've asked for a couple of extra days, but it really depends on the security situation at the time. I can't wait to get out of here. Even London would be an improvement. I don't think I've ever known weather as bad as what we're going through now. It's worse than the monsoons of Borneo. We were out on patrol last night and I came back soaked to the skin, and there was no hot water in the shower. Still, at least there was water."

Ginny shivered and looked out at the continuous warm Florida sunshine. Northern Ireland was unimaginable.

"How horrible. I know you'll appreciate Florida when you get here someday. Guess things could be much worse here."

"By the way, are there any drug users in your circle of friends? That may be a strange question, but we hear so much of the drug problem in the United States that I wondered how close you are to it. I've known a lot of U.S. servicemen who take drugs, but none in the British Army.

"Drugs never interested me, and I must admit I don't drink that much, as you know, the odd gin and tonic or a glass or two of white wine with dinner. I used to smoke but gave it up."

Ginny considered his questions about drugs and her split personality. Was he vetting her out? She realized that sometimes her letters with all of her insecurities certainly must sound goofy. She continued to elaborate on his question: "No, no one I know, and certainly not me. Of course, as you must have heard, Miami is the cocaine distribution capital of the world, rampant with cocaine cowboys killing each other off. There are huge drug busts. I heard on the news that there was a big one yesterday, just a block from my house, in a very nice neighborhood. The participants were Colombian drug runners, certainly an unwanted element in our community. Thinking about it, my friends drink alcohol and extravagant cocktail parties are the norm. I used to drink rum or bourbon, but now pretty much only drink white wine. But I know nothing about other drugs. Never tried them."

*And less about war, she thought.* She was learning more about combat than she wanted to.

Talking with Jim eased the agony of the marriage that was being carefully dissected by Rhoda.

There were several weeks with many intense calls from Jim. During his call on October 5th, he told her of the places he wanted to show her in London, which helped buoy her spirits. They talked twice that day, and at the end of the second call, he said he would call the next day at 11:30.

October 6th. Ginny caught up on some work she had brought home from the museum. The phone in her study did not ring all day, and the silence was unnerving. She flipped on the television to catch the noon news and found a horrified world was watching the gunning down of Egyptian president Anwar Sadat by his own troops. Sadat was an acknowledged peacemaker.

Would the madness ever end? Who next? The Queen? Margaret Thatcher? She didn't dwell on the unthinkable.

Special coverage showed the assassination over and over. Ginny sat, repulsed by the terrorism and craziness that again gripped the world media. She had never paid much attention before meeting Jim. Now she was aware, concerned, and emotionally involved. And where in the devil was Jim, anyway?

October 7th. She returned to her studio in tears. The session with Rhoda was merciless. In an effort to win Wayne's confidence and keep him in therapy, she tore at Ginny. "Unnecessary roughness!" she shouted, as she left the room, tears blinding her eyes. She wasn't sure how she was able to drive home.

The light was blinking on Machine. The message was hard to understand because of the caller's thick accent. After playing the tape several times, she understood

"My name is Lieutenant Simon McBain. James Evans asked me to call you. He won't be here anymore, at least for a while. The army has deployed him elsewhere. He couldn't say where, but I have a feelin' it has somethin' to do with Sadat and the Middle East. You can't return my call, but James said he'd get in touch with you as soon as he can. I'm sorry. That's all. Bye."

"Damn them all!" Ginny shouted in fury to an empty room. "The world's full of scumbags!"

*How in God's name did I ever get myself in such a mess? But then, the whole world is in a mess, so why should I be an exception?*

*'He was deployed elsewhere by the army!' I thought only machines were "deployed." But then, he's treated like a robot, just an effective military machine, a tool for an uncaring, unfeeling army. An automaton they plug into a terminal to brainwash and then send off to kill the enemy. 'I go where I'm sent.' he said.*

By now, Ginny knew what that meant, too.

*What are they doing with him this time? Or worse, what will he have to do to someone else? That was a thought she was not ready to deal with yet. Love a soldier, yes? Love a highly skilled killer? A lot to handle. Danger to him was everywhere. What about revenge?*

That wasn't the sensitive Jim she knew.

The lengthy therapy sessions continued. Visits with Wayne and Rhoda left Ginny in a shambles, but it was up to Dr Johnson to put the pieces back together again. Now with Rhoda giving the appearance of siding with Wayne, he had new fuel to throw on the flames of their already heated battles.

"Don't you know guilt anymore? Have you no conscience? How could you think of walking out on your entire family?" Wayne said.

There could have been no one more fractured than Ginny, with her world falling apart on all fronts. She had long lunches with Margie, who tried to console her, but there was little else that could be done. Margie asked if Ginny was masochistic or if it just seemed that way. Who in their right mind would want to live with all of this grief at once?

October 13th. Ginny returned to her study after an argumentative lunch with Margie, whose understanding and patience were obviously wearing thin. Exasperated, she sat down at her desk and the phone rang.

There was a familiar *beep.*

"Hi. It's me."

"I give up. Where are you this time?"

"I'm unfortunately back here in Northern Ireland. To stay, I might add."

"Where have you been? By the way, thanks for the phone call to let me know that you'd been called away. Your friend left a message on my machine, so I didn't get to talk to him. But he said something about Sadat and the Middle East. Is that where you went?"

"I'm not at liberty to say. At least it was warm, for a change."

She wondered if that was a clue or an affirmation.

"I didn't know if I should cancel my reservation or what to do. I've never been so up in the air in my life!"

"No, don't cancel. I'll be there. But you shouldn't worry so much. This is just the way my life is. I've tried to tell you that, many times. That's why the army's been my life. I can't share this kind of life. I can't have someone worrying about me all the time. With my job, you just never know when I could vanish, for how long, where I could turn up, or even if I will turn up, for that matter."

There was plenty to be concerned about, both on the home front and abroad. Although the phone calls continued, surprises never ended. Jim composed a very strange letter on October 14th:

*I've given a lot of thought to you over the past few weeks and I've spent a lot of time composing this letter. The type of relationship that you are after is not one that I can give you. You really want someone who is warm, loving, and kind. I just don't fit that bill. By the very nature of my occupation, I'm cold and hard. I suppose there are times when I think I have feelings for someone, but it always goes back to 'no feelings.' It goes with the training.*

*I don't think now that I could ever settle down to a permanent relationship. I'm too used to my own company, to looking after myself, sleeping in a single bed, doing my own washing and ironing. Sometimes I don't even like myself, so how could anyone else like me?"*

Ginny stopped reading for a moment and allowed herself to take a deep breath. She wondered who in hell wrote such a letter. Then she read on…

*I would like to continue as a friend, if that's what you want, but I can understand if you don't. I've really made a bit of a mess of this letter. I wanted it to be much kinder, but the words aren't there. Please think fondly of me, and try to understand how I feel.*

*You're a super woman, someone I'll never forget. But you deserve someone better, and I'm sure you'll meet the right person. Please try to understand.*

Ginny was stunned. She could not believe this was her Jim.

Did he wake up one day terrified because he really felt something for someone? How did she fall for the hero from a spy thriller when she knew that the plot and ending was always the same? A real life James Bond, a breed to himself, the elusive lone gunman. *Love 'em and leave 'em.* That's the most Bond ever wanted from a relationship. And he never stayed long enough to give a job description to his confused lover of the moment.

Relationship? They weren't supposed to get that far. She and Jim just didn't know what they were getting into.

*Was this all a big mistake for him?* she wondered.

*I guess so. For me, this is something I couldn't keep from happening no matter how hard I tried. There's too much to learn from it. Didn't I want to experience the world? Well, I guess I am. Big-time. He is so brave. He's tries to warn me about his life. How dare I complain?*

How he must have struggled with that letter. Yes, this was all a big mistake for him. He wasn't supposed to fall in love. This was not in his script. It seemed to her that he had done just that. Now that he knew it, he was scared to death and trying to squirm out of it the only way he knew how. He really didn't want to hurt Ginny, but was honestly telling her something she just couldn't understand. *Who knows,* she thought. *Maybe this is his form letter for getting out of tight spots.*

Her jumbled and painful thoughts were interrupted by the ringing of the phone, and there he was, friendly as ever.

"Perfect timing, right on cue," she said.

"Oh, you must have gotten my letter. Care to talk about it?"

"You better believe I do. What do you mean, you aren't the man for me? I need someone sweet, loving, and kind. Let me decide what kind of man I need. Whether you know it or not, you can be sweet, loving, and kind. In fact, that's the only way I think of you."

"No, no. I'm trying to tell you something, Ginny. You really don't understand me or know what I do. I'm trying to be honest. Listen to me. The army's my life. I can't get involved; my work won't let me. As you've seen, I can get called away at any time, and never know when I'm coming back, or even if I'm coming back. You don't want that."

The sad truth was that he *was* telling her the truth, and she just couldn't accept it.

"Like I told you, let me decide what I want and need."

"But I'm a loner, Ginny. I have to be. Can't you accept that?"

"No. Was I with someone else in the Highlands? Don't you remember what you felt there? Why are you calling me all of the time? You must feel the same way I do Can't you just admit it?"

"You're right. It would be cheaper to adopt you. I just got a £750 phone bill. That's almost $1500 in American money at today's rate. I could come over for that, but I can't get away."

"What about London? Call the whole thing off? You can't imagine the problems I have here, not anything like yours, but we each have our battlefronts."

"Only if you want to, but I hope you don't want to cancel."

"Of course I don't want to. I want to see you more than anything else in the world. Your letter changes things, though. It makes me more afraid and cautious than ever. Can you imagine my deep-seated insecurity? The thing I need most is a sense of security, and you offer me nothing. I'm really out on a limb and sawing it off behind me faster than you can believe.

"Look, you have enough to deal with, so I haven't told you everything. I'm always very honest and up front; too honest for my own good and this has been very hard for me. In a bad moment, I told Wayne about the British army officer I met in England. Not all of the details, of course. But I said I spent a day with you and it meant a lot to me. I also said that on one unannounced day I'm leaving for a meeting with you. Last warning, I guess. I hate surprising people."

"What did he say?"

"It got his attention. He finally agreed to see a marriage counselor. That's a joke. Why now, when I'm walking out the door? After all of the years and having a son, I felt it only fair to give it a try, so we have been seeing this woman, Rhoda, and it's been devastating. They both take cracks at me. If it weren't for my psychologist, Dr Johnson, I think I'd have been committed. He keeps encouraging me to be strong."

"Good advice. You'll have to be. I had no idea things were this rough for you. You haven't said anything about this. But understand that I still won't promise you anything. I can't. And I told you that after London, I have to come back here. What'll you do?"

"I haven't a clue. That's what terrifies me. I only want to be with you. I'll figure the rest out later."

"But you've got to make some plans. How's your divorce coming? Have you done anything about that yet? I've wondered why you haven't mentioned it lately."

"I saw my attorney and I'm following her advice. She told me to go to London, have a wonderful time, and figure out what to do next when I get home. I guess I'm playing my whole life by ear right now."

"But that's so risky. Can you handle that?"

"I honestly don't know. Sometimes I feel like I'm cracking up and it certainly must show, especially in my letters. I see no other way for now. She's a very smart attorney, one of the best for women in my situation."

"Okay. London's on. There are no promises for the future though. And listen, I'm going to have to be out in the field a lot. I'll write and call all I can, but there's going to be a point when I'll be out for three weeks, and the next time you hear from me is when I knock at your hotel room door in London. That's just the way it's got to be."

"Okay" she said with a sigh. "I understand."

"Got to run. Call you tomorrow. Take care."

The countdown was on. As each day passed, Ginny grew more afraid, but more determined. Which would win out, fear or determination? Time would tell. After all, she had everything to gain and nothing to lose. Or was it the other way around?

"Risk taking," she told Dr Johnson one day. "Isn't that the new psychology buzzword? If you don't take risks, or give yourself a chance, you'll never know your potential. Dare. That's great in theory, but often a disaster in practice. Then come the learning experiences. God knows I've had my share of those. How many times have I picked myself up, dusted myself off, put on a smile, and gone blundering forth?"

Dr Johnson smiled and nodded. "Well, here we go again. The old moth after that flame," she said with a wink.

Yet the deck was stacked against her. Rhoda was relentless in trying to save the marriage, at all costs. That was her job, wasn't it?

The session started.

"Your marriage is like glue, Elmer's glue. You two have been married too long to become unstuck," she said.

And she was right. She hit a tender nerve there. *It would be like divorcing my father. Oh, God, not him again.*

Rhoda continued. "Look at the history you've shared. You married so young and you've been married most of your lives, all of your adult lives. Who else knows as much about you as each other?"

The tears started to flow.

"You've shared a son. He's grown now, but that's something that you did together. He'll always be yours together."

*Please have mercy,* Ginny thought, wiping tears. *But she's right again.*

"Even if you're able to make the legal break, I don't think you can make the emotional one."

Ginny had tried to break up with Wayne before, but never could. He was the mainstay of her life, her rock, right or wrong, once her savior and now her captor.

*What's his hang-up? Is he really crazy about me or just crazy to stick around? He figures I'm his property and he'll fight to the death to keep me. What other reason could there be? There's something sick about this, or we wouldn't be here.*

Rhoda turned again to the topic of guilt. Rhoda and Wayne were both masterful guilt merchants. It was their favorite tool, like a lion tamer with a whip and a chair.

Ginny said, "I remember guilt. It's a word I put out of my life long ago. One day Wayne yelled at me that I should do this and I shouldn't do that, and I decided that was enough. I follow my own *shoulds* and dance to my own beat." She had often talked to Dr Johnson about Wayne's preoccupation with "Thou shalt not." His parents raised him with a Bible-belt background mentality. He could only see black and white, and there was no room for grey. It made him right, good, smug. It gave him credibility, and Ginny had conceded that if he was good, then she must be bad. That was the dangerous game of cat and mouse they had been playing for years, until one day she woke up and said to herself, "I won't play anymore. I'm okay. You're okay. Nobody's bad here. We're just different, and *viva la difference!*"

The game was over.

Their marriage had become a symbiosis of two neurotics clinging to the sinking raft of marriage to survive. That was the glue. When Ginny decided that she neither wanted to be neurotic nor symbiotic anymore, Wayne became totally confused. She had changed the rules of the game without telling him, and the jig was up. He could no longer control her if she wouldn't play the "guilty bad little girl" anymore. Yet still, he could always play on her insecurity by withholding money, and he resorted to that whenever he saw the control slipping away.

But guilt was the topic of this session.

"Are you really going to meet someone in London? What will your friends think?"

"Who cares? They know about all of this and the bad relationship with Wayne. They say 'Go for it.'"

"Most of all, what'll your son think? What kind of role model are you?" Rhoda whittled away at Ginny, like a sculptor with a chisel.

*Touché! That did smart.* Ginny sniffled. *Rhoda found a tender spot there. She didn't spare a trick.*

Eric already knew and understood.

"Outrageous! Your behavior is outrageous!" Rhoda hammered home her final blow.

Wayne loved it. "See? Surely you feel guilty now! You heard what Rhoda said. You're outrageous!"

"Give me a break, " Ginny said, stinging from the blow. "If this is outrageous, I wouldn't have missed a minute of it." She learned to love the word outrageous; she even began to aspire to it.

She sat through the sessions and tried to roll with the punches, but that wasn't easy. Rhoda had gone overboard to win Wayne's trust in order to be able to work with him. Any kind of therapy for him was better than none; Ginny kept reminding herself of that.

But Rhoda was too heavy on the guilt trip, and Ginny knew she was wasting her time. Anything that could be recognized as guilt or remorse had to come from within, and related to her personal understanding of right and wrong. That was a step to personal freedom.

A big step.

November. As the day of departure drew closer, the pressures, internal and external, grew stronger. The doubts became monumental. Tossing through sleepless nights in the guest room, she asked herself over and over if she knew what she was doing.

"Does a day and night together justify changing a lifetime?" she asked Margie one day at lunch. "As much as I think I love Jim, he's given me nothing to hang my hopes on. I'm flying without a net here."

Margie was encouraging. "What the heck? How could things get worse? In case you haven't figured it out, this really isn't about Jim anyway. It's about getting out of the stalemate you're stuck in."

"What will I come home to? My clothes will probably be thrown in the street or the swimming pool. And I just can't look for a better job or an apartment right now."

"Get an apartment when you come back. And you could wait tables if you really have to. I'm only kidding, of course. What're you so afraid of?"

"I guess I could think of a thousand demons, if I tried. That's my problem. Dr Johnson's right. My head is crowded with unrealistic fears. If you worry about demons, they become real, and it's difficult or even impossible to convince yourself that they're just smoke and mirrors."

"Look, you'll be fine. Don't you know that jobs will have a way of finding you? You're talented. You could always stay with me for a little while if you have to. I have a spare room. Now I'm planning to put you on that plane, no matter what, for my sanity as much as yours. I'm tired of hearing about all of this. When do you leave?"

"Wednesday, November 25th. That's another big problem. It's the day before Thanksgiving. Eric will be home from college. What will he think of my leaving? "

"Oh, come on. He's a grown up. He can have dinner with Wayne and his family."

"And with my family too. They'll all be there. There'll be an empty chair. Mine. And where will I be? Off with a soldier in London. Wayne will be delighted to say anything and everything he wants about it."

"He's not just a soldier. He's an officer in the elite SAS. You seem to really love the guy and he sounds great, from all you've said. How could you consider not going?"

"Easily. There's another thing. What if he doesn't show up, like in Edinburgh? That could darn well happen. I haven't told you, but he has a three-week patrol that will keep us out of touch until we meet in London. Think how dumb I'd feel if he doesn't make it again. I feel like a trapeze artist having a go at it for the first time without a net, and I'm not sure there'll be anyone on the other side to catch me."

"He'll be there. And if he isn't, you can just have a nice trip to England. Do more research. You'll find something to do. Then lie like hell. Tell everyone how wonderful it was. Look, I'm writing the date down on my calendar and I'm going to be sure to put you on that plane."

"Thanks, Margie. I really need all the pushing I can get right now. I'm very scared, but if Jim can jump out of planes, I guess I can get on one. It somehow seems similar in this situation."

Jim's phone calls were infrequent, and the letters had stopped. The British Army had tightened pressure on the gunmen. Unknowing, she sensed the tension in his voice when they talked. But they were both excited about the meeting. His slightly suggestive comments, founded in honest lust and desire, added fuel to the fire building in both of them. Their last phone call before they were to meet was as spicy as the military phone line could handle.

"Now be sure to bring some sexy lingerie. Bring a long black lace gown and plenty of perfume. I love perfume."

"What's your favorite? I sure wasn't wearing any when I was alone and we met."

"Your favorite, whatever that is. Bring several. But look, I'm afraid this is the last time we'll talk before then. I'm leaving in the morning on that patrol, and I've got to run now. So this is goodbye until London. See you at the Hyde Park Towers on the 27th. Okay? Be strong! Ciao!"

Ginny found herself wandering around the shopping mall searching for the perfect black nightgown. Or what about red, too? It had to be special, better than the one she hurriedly bought in Edinburgh. And she was sampling perfumes. This was a soldier's fantasy after a long period of celibacy. That should make it interesting.

But she had her fantasies too. She shut her eyes and began dreaming:
*What will our meeting be like? Nothing could be like the Highlands. They both knew it was a once in a lifetime encounter. But she had to believe this would be special, too. She would leave Miami on Wednesday the 25th and her flight would arrive in London on Thursday morning, the 26th. Jim couldn't get there until late Friday afternoon, and his court case was scheduled for Monday. She would rest on Thursday, then on Friday, she would amuse herself by going to the Tate Gallery for a look around, and lunch in the elegant dining room with a friend who was a Keeper of ethnic art there. She would return to the room and wait.*

She could close her eyes and let the fantasy tape roll. The hotel room was an average tourist-class room, although it looked nice in the brochure.

*Enter Ginny. What's she wearing? A black dinner dress, cut low with a single long strand of pearls. Seemed appropriate, but she changed her mind and outfit each time she ran through the fantasy. Yes, and lots of perfume! She would turn on the television and watch a comedy on BBCTV, to pass the hours. She would ice some champagne, to greet him. She loved champagne for special occasions even if the bubbly was not the most expensive. Time would drag by, and she would get more apprehensive. Would he make it? Could something possibly come up? Could she be stuck in London alone, holding the bag again?*

No. It just couldn't happen.

*There would be a knock at the door. She would ask cautiously, "Who is it?"*

*The voice she loved so much would simply answer, "Jim"*

*The long agonizing anticipation would be over. She would open the door and he would look wonderful, in spite all of all that he'd endured.*

*What would he be wearing? A uniform? That would be more Hollywood than the three-piece suit he said he wore in London. He would sweep her off her feet with the most glorious kiss ever shared. Then he'd shut the door, and fantasy thoughts always ended there.*

She would save the rest for the real thing. But she could close her eyes and play the scene any time she wanted to. It kept her going. She knew he had his fantasy of the meeting too, and she was sure that his was a lot more explicit. It just might be closer to the real event, recalling their first and only time together.

Again, she felt she was living in an old black and white World War II movie from late night television. What was she doing here anyway? Those movies often crossed her mind when she thought about their predicament. She could picture them dressed like other ill-fated lovers, Bogie and Bacall or Bergman, trench coats and foggy days in London town or Casablanca.

Ginny drifted through the days, spending more time in fantasy than reality. It was all she could do. If she dwelt too much on the disaster her life had become, she might simply lose it. Dr Johnson kept a close eye on her, looking for signs of her cracking, but she somehow held together.

Departure week was the roughest. Ginny felt like she must be verging on cardiac arrest. To ease her anxiety, she remembered a stress management class she took, and took deep abdominal breaths. Inhale. Exhale.

On Monday, she packed *Liberator* with cold weather clothes and stowed it back in the luggage closet.

Tuesday morning before departure was cursed with the weekly session, with Wayne and Rhoda.

"One more hurdle and I'm almost there," she said to herself, as she turned her car into Rhoda's driveway. She gritted her teeth through the entire session, while her mind was thousands of miles away.

When it was finally over Rhoda pulled out her calendar to schedule next week's meeting. "How about next Tuesday? Any objections?"

The atom bomb dropped.

"I won't be able to make it," she said.

Rhoda and Wayne stared at her in disbelief, saying in unison, "What?"

"I said I won't be here. I have other plans. Perhaps you two should meet without me anyway. I think it would be helpful to Wayne."

"Outrageous. How can you sit there and say you're really going?" he asked.

"It just didn't seem fair to go without letting you both know, and this seemed like the most controlled environment in which to discuss it. I'm sorry, but I've got to go. I've given this a try, but it's too late. Too much damage was done. I'll never be happy if I don't go."

"But this is Thanksgiving week. Eric will be home tonight. What are you going to tell him? What will he think?" Wayne asked.

"Eric knows about Jim. I told him this summer. I've written to him about this, told him that I'm flying to London. He knows where I'll be and with whom. I have to be up front about this. I'm not sneaking around here. I can only hope I've raised him right and he's mature enough to say, 'Whatever makes you happy, Mom.' He knows the problems here. He's lived with them too. I'll see him tonight, have a nice dinner waiting, then I leave tomorrow.

It was Ginny's coolest performance to date.

The session ended with Rhoda pleading with Ginny to change her mind.

"Don't you think about anyone else?" Wayne asked.

"I have too much for too many years. But now it's my turn, and this's something I must do. That's that."

She drove home, outwardly cool, but shaky inside.

Wayne was crushed, unprepared for the bomb to fall, especially on a holiday. Her heart bled for him. It tore at her to think about what she was doing to him. Cruelty to someone she had spent most of her life with was not her strong card. Thanksgiving had always meant so much to both of them. She usually fixed the big turkey dinner, the house filled with blending smells of varying foods prepared with love. The bands, floats, and balloons of the Macy's Thanksgiving Day Parade on television enlivening the kitchen as she cooked alone.

Preparing the table was an art. The silver was always shined, the linen perfectly pressed, china and crystal gleaming, and an appropriate centerpiece of fresh flowers in a basket cornucopia in the middle of the table. It took days of work to get ready, and to clean up afterwards, but she was always proud of her work when the whole family gathered. It made it all worth it.

This year, though, she had passed the reins back to her mother, and left the event in her hands with a brief explanation. There would be a lovely dinner; she just wouldn't be there to participate.

Eric arrived at the house with a carload of friends in the late afternoon. When the two of them were alone, Eric eyed his mother.

"What's up?" he asked. "When are you leaving?"

"I've got to be at the airport tomorrow at three o' clock. Margie is taking me. I know my timing's terrible. I wouldn't do anything to hurt any of you for the world, but this just can't be helped. This is the only time Jim could get away and I wouldn't miss seeing him for anything. The British don't celebrate Thanksgiving like we do, obviously. If you remember, the pilgrims were celebrating with the Native Americans because they had survived settling in America, *far* from the British. But that's beside the point. This was the only date we could plan this meeting. It's all killing me, but I would be worse if I didn't go."

"I understand, Mom. I really do. You and Dad have had it, and I don't see how you've lasted this long. But how's he doing?"

"Awful. Please be kind to him while you're here. He's still your father. I guess he could see that the marriage counselor wasn't getting through to me this time. It's too late, and Rhoda sure couldn't change my mind, hard as she tried. Yet, your father seems resigned to it. I don't know if he's been on the phone with his attorney to file for divorce yet or anything. I'm terrified and sick about all this, but there's no other way. I don't want to warp your little psyche with all this. Are you okay?"

"Too late for that. Yeah, I'm fine. But be careful."

It was all too civilized. There were no scenes and they got through dinner without incident. Wayne was obviously shaken but maintained his cool, which surprised Ginny. In some ways, she found it a bit unnerving. Was she making a bigger mistake than she realized?

She tossed and turned through the night in the guest room, alternating anxiety and apprehension with brief patches of restless sleep.

Wayne dressed for work. Hell could freeze over, but he wouldn't miss a day in the office.

"Have you changed your mind? I hope so, but it's too late to beg you. Have you no shame? What do you think your son really thinks of you?"

"I can only hope he understands. If not, I'm sorry. I really am. Look, why don't you come home for lunch?"

*Now why in the world did she say that?* She wondered. Whatever did she want to talk to him about at this point? They usually didn't talk anyway. After all, she was leaving him, wasn't she?

Then the old fear gripped her. How could she leave her rock, her supposed stability? Could she get through this?

"No way," snapped Wayne. "What's there left to talk about? You've said it all. Unless, of course, you want to change your mind."

"No. But think about coming home. I'll fix a nice lunch for the three of us."

She moved through the morning like a robot, tried to think ahead to London, and call up her fantasy. Instead all she could think about was what she would leave behind: Miami, her home. It would be easier if they had argued, if there had been a scene or fight. It would make her angry enough to remember why she was walking out the door in the first place.

Dr Johnson had asked her to call him at ten that morning to tell him how she was doing. She poured her apprehensions into the phone.

"You aren't backing out, are you?"

"I hope not. I can't, but I'm so unsure. My little drama's moving to its grand finale and I'm afraid I'll blow my part or just blow apart. I think I'm verging on both."

"Look, call me if you need me, or if you change your mind. If you change your mind, you'll really need me. You know where I am, and if I don't answer I'll get back to you as soon as I can."

She hung up and tried to remember what she had to do next. There was that suit she had decided to take at the last minute. She had to pick it up from the cleaners. She was organized, but glad to have an errand to pass a few minutes.

The morning seemed so long. Margie was to pick her up at three. Would she jump out of her skin before then?

She returned home and packed the suit into *Liberator*. She put the suitcase and London Fog in her study and shut the door. Her change of clothes was set out, and she waited, ready to go at three.

Margie called.

"Are you ready? You must be excited."

"I wish I could say I am. I'm too nervous to be excited. I guess I'll be fine after I settle on the plane and have a glass of wine or two. I just don't know if I can go through with this."

"You'd better! I don't want to hear another word from you if you don't. Frankly, I can't take any more of this stuff you put up with. Now I'll be there at three, so be ready. Think of the fun you'll have. Think of Jim. Go get ready. See you then."

Ginny's gut wrenched a notch tighter. She did what she always did when she was afraid. She called Wayne.

"I'm fixing nice sandwiches for lunch," she told him, as if it was any other day. "Won't you come home?"

"I don't want to get all upset again. I have an important client this afternoon. How do you expect me to take this?"

"Please. It won't be emotional. Maybe it'll ease the pain for both of us."

"What pain can you have? You're off to see your lover! Why do you want to see me? Is this a test of my pain threshold?"

"You can't imagine how bad I feel. Will you come?"

"Okay, but I'm probably making a big mistake."

Ginny fixed the lunch and mechanically set the table by the pool for the three of them.

*Why am I doing this? She wondered again. Am I deliberately sabotaging my trip? Do I want them to lock me up and throw away the key? I'm laying my own land mines. Am I begging, 'Stop me. Stop me before it's too late, before I self-destruct?*

Just another sun-filled day in paradise. She was never immune to the beauty of her world. The turquoise pool water sparkled and the vivid green of the palms and lush tropical foliage stood out against the brilliant blue sky. The friendly chirping of cardinals and the melodic cling-clang of the wind chimes were the only sounds. Though there wasn't a cloud in the sky, a dark cloud hovered over the table, the joyless cloud of a Last Supper.

Conversation was about college and Eric's upcoming exams. They might never sit down to a table again as a family, dysfunctional as it was, and they were all keenly aware of it. Everyone was present and accounted for and made an effort to get through this last time together, but it was bizarre. Eric thoughtfully ate and ran, leaving Ginny and Wayne alone.

She felt tears well up in her eyes. Why did it come to this? In theory, they had everything going for them. You couldn't ask for a more attractive and healthy family. In theory. Happy was the missing ingredient. Why was she throwing this all away? Was there still a chance things could work out?

*Can a leopard change its spots? No. And wouldn't.*

What about the big unknown she was running off to face? She had identified the problems here, knew the enemy, the pitfalls. Would she just be exchanging one set of problems for another? Was she jumping from the frying pan into the fire? She had no idea what the future could hold if she walked out to meet Jim. He had said so himself. No promises. Was love, worse yet, lust, enough?

Suddenly she paused. Was it love for Jim, or for the way he made her feel confident about herself. Which? Was she sure? Could she feel that way alone?

"I'm not going," she suddenly said.

"What did you say?"

"I said I'm not going. I just can't."

"I'm not begging anymore. That's a decision you have to make, and I can't stop you. You've said you're a big girl now and I have to believe that."

"I'm a woman now, Wayne, no longer a girl. Accept that. I really am heartsick. And I'm confused. I guess I can't throw all of this away, throw the baby away with the bath, no matter how bad things have become. We still are a family. Having Eric here made that all clear to me. If we can, I have to give this one more try. Here. In Miami. Not in London. Much as I want to get on that plane, I don't think I can. Rhoda's right. Marriage is glue, and we can't dislodge ourselves so easily."

"Are you sure this is what you want?"

"Yes. I don't feel comfortable with leaving like this. Maybe if it wasn't a holiday. I'm not trash, as you'd like to think. I do have a conscience. This isn't guilt, mind you. I just don't think it wouldn't be right for me to go, if there's a chance we could work things out. After all, Miami is my home. I have a lifetime invested here. Go back to work and I'll try to figure out how to cancel my plans."

What had she just done and said? Was she really crazy this time?

She thought first of Jim but knew she could not get in touch with him now. How would he feel? Would he be there, and she not? Heartbreaking as it was, she had made her decision, and was going to live with it. She would at least put her life in some kind of order and try to take control of her destiny. But her story was in Miami, not on a boat in Greece, as romantic as it sounded.

It was 2:00 PM.

She picked up the phone and called Margie.

"I'm sorry. You won't have to pick me up. I'm not going. I just can't do it."

"Goodbye, Ginny," said Margie, slamming down the phone.

Ginny knew she meant it and she might never hear from her again.

She had never felt so alone in her life. She had just turned her back on her lover and alienated her best friend, all in order to try and make the best of a bad situation. But now it was the only alternative she could live with.

She cancelled her reservation with the travel agent, knowing she would have to pay a stiff default penalty, but that couldn't be helped. Just a bit of salt in the wound.

She called Dr Johnson to tell him of her decision. She could sense the concern in his voice as he set up an appointment for the next week.

Ginny floated through day and night. Wayne adopted the kindest course and said little. If he felt victory, it was shallow and empty.

Ginny had to say something to Jim. She had to apologize, and explained that to Wayne, who agreed it was the decent thing to do.

She called the hotel and left a message. "I had a reservation for today, but had to cancel it. My name is Virginia Thomas, and a friend was to meet me."

"Yes, I see you as a cancellation."

"I need to leave a message for my friend, Lieutenant James Evans. Say, 'I'm sorry that I couldn't come but I want to explain. Please call me at the usual number, collect.' It's urgent that he gets this message."

"I'll see that he gets it, don't worry. Sorry you couldn't come."

Ginny and Wayne were the quietest members of the family at Thanksgiving dinner, through everyone pretended not to notice, and the festivities went on as if nothing happened.

Friday morning, they sat at the breakfast table, silently absorbing the morning paper. Ringing of the phone in her study broke the silence.

Ginny looked at Wayne and scrambled to her study, shut the door and answered the phone.

"Hello," Jim said, sadly.

Her heart sank.

"You just couldn't do it, could you? You just weren't ready."

She knew he was hurt, his ego crushed, rightly so. She had stood up her lover, who desperately needed their meeting and to be out of Northern Ireland.

"No. No, I couldn't. I couldn't get on that plane and cross the ocean again, no matter how bad I wanted to. There's just too much at stake. You don't know how much I wanted to, Jim, more than anything else in the world. But you gave me nothing to hold on to. You have no idea of the depth of my insecurity any more than I understand your obligation to the army. No matter what the problems are here, if I left, I would have thrown away everything I have, for an uncertainty. Even if you did get there, which I doubted from past experience, you would've had to go right back to Ireland. I knew that.

"So what was I supposed to do with the rest of my life? My history, my family, friends, and my future are in Miami. My son came home from college and it was just more than I could handle. But I see you did get there. You can't imagine how sorry I am. That was the most difficult decision of my entire life!"

"Yes, I'm here. Even got here yesterday, a day early to surprise you. They said you had cancelled and gave me your message. I wondered what in the devil happened. Then I decided that you couldn't make the break. The hotel's quite nice by the way. It would've been fine."

"What will you do now?"

"Stay for my court case. They gave me a couple of extra days leave, but I've scheduled a military flight back after court. I'll just go back to Northern Ireland."

Nausea swept over her. "I guess there's nothing else I can say that will make it any better. I'll write you and explain what happened as soon as I can make some sense of this myself."

"Right. Well, I'll wait for that letter. So long. Ciao."

Wayne pretended not to notice her tears. Somehow they had survived the battle, but both were numb, tiptoed around like on egg shells, avoiding glances, saying little, much as if a sound would bring the house tumbling down. It was a very long weekend. They existed in separate cocoons, surrounded by webs of despair. All of their energy was sapped. But by Sunday, they had both mended somewhat, and tried to find a positive common ground.

Wayne sat at the kitchen table, reading a law journal. "The New York Bar Association's meeting in New York week after next, " he looked up and said. "You love New York. You can go to the art museums. See plays. Dinner in the Village. Why don't we go?"

"Fine. Good idea." A compromise of sorts, but the thought of going to one of her favorite cities lightened the mood of the day. She went to the news-stand and bought a Sunday *New York Times*, to check the plays and museum listings.

On Monday, she found the proper words to write to Jim. It was the most difficult letter she had ever written, but no match for the letter he wrote to her:

> *I'm sorry that you couldn't make it to London. As I said, I even came a day early as a surprise. I suppose that in a way it might turn out to be the right decision. I don't think now that we'll ever meet again. Perhaps that is right, because what we had belonged to a special time and place, never to be repeated.*
>
> *I shall now go back to Ireland, get back to what I do best, and from there maybe to the Sinai with a U.N. peace-keeping force. After that, I may resign and buy my boat and drift away to my Greek Island. Who knows, perhaps not.*
>
> *Please don't think of me anymore. Lead your life in your world as you have chosen. Take care of your man and your son. Pursue your career. You're now confident and capable of doing what you please. During quiet moments, look back to Scotland and dream of what was and then come back to reality. It's a hard, cruel world sometimes. Take special care.*

In December, Ginny received a Christmas card from Jim in her box. "To a Special Friend Across the Miles" opened the greeting. Inside it said, "From someone who thinks the world of you." Then silence. The ocean had won.

# 10
# Miami

Slowly, Ginny began to pick up the pieces of her life and weave them back together. She regretted not going to London to meet Jim, but it was the only choice she could make if she wanted live with herself.

Ginny and Wayne settled into a truce, and she stayed in the guest room. They made the most of a family Christmas for Eric.

The sessions with Rhoda and Dr Johnson continued. Rhoda tried to make Ginny and Wayne understand why they were still together, and now that they were, what they had to do about it. Dr Johnson just tried to keep Ginny from bashing her brains out on rocks of despair.

She was recognizing how serious and real her hang-ups were. Why did she back out? She knew staying in Miami was the wisest decision. But then there was her insane bag lady fear of the future. The lack of money. Money was the key. Although Wayne was financially very secure, she was still dependent on his "generosity," and he used it as a bargaining tool.

She became determined to get a job that actually paid enough to support herself, so she could get control of her life. She passed the word among friends that she was on an open job hunt.

It didn't take long. She started work as the manager of a respected small art gallery in early January. She loved working with the artists, and the salary was decent enough. The gallery was pleasant and it was interesting to have a try at business. The experience suggested new possibilities.

Ginny tried to put Jim out of her mind, but that was impossible. She was making every effort to build up the gallery clientele and smooth out her mixed-up marriage.

Her answering machine continued to collect her messages at home and referred calls to her work number, not that there were many calls on it. Her friends knew where to find her. There were a few strange calls that she thought started with the familiar beep, and then the caller hung up. She could never be sure, and she chalked it up to wishful thinking.

Winter tourists jammed the city, and business bustled. There were periods when she and her part-time helper couldn't take care of all of the clients who walked in at once, as if a bus had just dumped a load of art lovers at her door.

Then there were other times when she was the only person minding the gallery, with long lulls, hours or days when no one came in and she busied herself rearranging the art or updating client names, and sending out invitations to openings, or setting up displays. She caught on to gallery management rather quickly.

The phone rang during one of these dull spells and she welcomed the ring. A *beep* greeted her as she answered.

"May I speak to Ginny Thomas, please?" the male voice asked.

She couldn't believe her ears.

"Speaking. Jim?"

"Hello. I just left a message on your machine, but I wanted to talk to you. How are you?"

Okay. Well, honestly, awful. And you?"

"Same. Listen, I'm sending you some things. Do you still have your post office box?"

"Yes. Same number."

"Well, a friend's on his way to Belize. He's coming over to the States and I'll have him mail the package to you from there, to make sure you get it."

"What are you sending?"

"You'll see. Do you still have your micro-cassette recorder? I'm sending a tape."

"Sure. Great! I can't wait. Where are you?"

"England, London in fact, at the moment. The house my father left to me is vacant now and I'm leaving it that way so I can use it. But I'm stationed in Bicester and I'll be there for a while. They have me taking some courses at the university, so it's rather nice. Better than Northern Ireland for sure, but then, anything's better than that. Seems pretty well resolved now, by the way, at least for the time being. What are you doing?"

"I'm managing an art gallery. It's different for me, but I like it. Good full-time jobs in my field are rare, and I'll stick with this until something better comes up. I think of you so often."

"Right. Got to run. I'll call you in a few days to see if you got my package. Ciao."

Ginny felt that her face was flushed as she put down the phone. She knew her heart was pounding. The gallery was quiet and she settled down to write her first letter to Jim in a long time.

The pink notice was in her box on January 24th, but it was after work and the end of the day. The windows were closed. The next morning she dropped by the post office on her way to work and the postman handed her a large padded manila envelope from Jim.

It was too early to open the gallery when she arrived, and so she sat alone and opened the package, examining the mysterious contents one by one.

There was a boat brochure, a glossy production advertising a "go fast" boat with luxury living accommodations. In fact, it was far more luxurious than anything she had imagined Jim aspiring to own. A luscious blonde was featured, sitting on a king size bed in the owner's stateroom, brushing her long hair, then lounging with a drink and entertaining friends in the main salon. The brochure noted that photographs may show certain items not included in the standard specifications, and Ginny assumed that meant the blonde as well.

She found the micro-cassette tape and put it in recorder.

"Hi. I've been promising myself I'd do this tape for a long time. In the end, decided to wait until I came back from my Christmas and New Year's leave. Well, it's now January 2nd and this tape will cover the events up until today's date. I'll just space it with some music, which will give me time to think out what I'm going to say next.

"The first bit of news is that my tour of duty in Northern Ireland is finished. The security forces seem to be winning the battle over there. December was the first month since back in 1971 that was free from deaths attributable to terrorists' activities. The force levels are being gradually reduced, and I'm now back in sunny England.

"I came back in mid-December and decided to go to Scotland for some skiing and hiking. I decided to go by car, but unfortunately, Britain had its worst winter in living memory and I actually managed to get as far as the Lake District before being snowbound. I had to stop for a few days at a small inn until the snow plows could get out and clear the roads.

"Time for a little bit of music. This is one of my favorite pieces. It's actually the theme from a film called *The Deer Hunter*, a film about American involvement in Vietnam. The music is quite haunting."

And it was. If there ever was music to orchestrate their story, it was the bittersweet song he played, *Cavatina*. She had avoided seeing *The Deer Hunter*. It was the saddest song she ever heard in her life, and perfectly suited the mood of the tape and all of their ill-fated romance.

"Right," he continued as the music ended. "Back to my leave, which was a total unmitigated disaster, thanks to the weather. I eventually got to Scotland, but the only way to get around was by foot. The car was buried under five feet of snow and for days I was completely isolated and cut off from the rest of the world. For three days, Christmas Eve, Christmas Day, and what we call Boxing Day, I had no water, so cooking was a washout, pardon the pun. The only way to get water for tea or to even have a wash, was to boil up snow. You'd be surprised how much snow you need to shovel just to make a pint of water. The nearest civilization was eleven miles away, so it was a fair hike or ski to go to get essentials or a newspaper to find out what was going on in the world.

On the way back from Scotland, I even hit worse weather. My car eventually skidded off of the road and it cost a few bob to get that repaired. So all in all, it was not a very good Christmas.

"The New Year was just as bad. I went to a party on New Year's Eve, but the people were very boring, so I left fairly early. On New Year's Day, I found a log fire and alternated reading and sleeping. I actually just got back yesterday and began unpacking.

"As for my immediate plans, it seems as though I'll be based here for at least a couple of months. I may have a Sinai job, but I'm not sure because of the attitude of the Israelis, but that is in the melting pot. If the British do eventually send a contingent, I will probably go. After that, I don't know. I suppose Belize is still in the cards. I would be happy having a six-month spell in Belize. The next guy to go out there is going at the end of January, so he'll be due to be replaced around the end of July. I've asked my boss, anyway, if possible, I'd like to go out there. I suppose it's in the hands of the fickle gods. I'll just have to wait and see. Right. Time for more music."

The next song was George Harrison singing *All Those Years Ago*. Was there a message in it? The tape was too unclear to make out the words but she felt he must have had a reason to select it. The clearest words George was singing were something like "I'm shouting about love, while they treated you like a dog." He knew.

Ginny would have to listen to the song later to catch the rest of the meaningful words. Jim loved contemporary music and especially the Beatles. So many good sounds and analytical poetry came out of that generation in England.

He continued.

"What about the future, after next year? I've decided I'm coming out of the army at the end of my current engagement. Eventually, after all of these years, I've had enough of them and they've had enough of me. The next question, I suppose, is what I am going to do. I've always thought I'd get a boat and go live on a Greek island. I like Naxos. But I don't know if a Greek island is practical, and eventually there will be another conflict in Europe, and perhaps Greece isn't going to be the best place to be. But then again, where in the world do you go to be sure you're safe?

"I suppose the middle of the Pacific. I don't know. It's something I've got a couple years to think about. I certainly feel that I don't want to have to work. The biggest decision I'll make is what time I'm going to get up. I can read, perhaps even write. I can swim, just relax, and do the things I've missed all these years. But on the other hand, I'm sickened by what I see in places like London. The violence, murders, robberies, and rapes. Sometimes I think I'm going to be a cross between the parts Charles Bronson played in both *Death Wish* and *The Executioner*, one man against crime, but I don't think that's really on. I suppose one day I'll drift off into the sun, and like old soldiers, just fade away."

The next music, as haunting as *Cavatina*, was *Dolannes Melodie*, beautiful, slow, unwinding sadness. Ginny listened and wondered why he put this powerful package together. It had taken a lot of effort and emotion. Had he realized over that depressing holiday that he had feelings for her after all? Maybe he could best express his feelings in music. The tape was mystifying, an enigma, and almost more than she could bear.

He continued. "At least our weather's improved. It's been a beautiful day. I guess not as beautiful as Miami, but then again, we can't have everything."

He quickly slipped in two appropriate songs, with no question of their message. Michael Jackson sang the love ballad, *One Day in Your Life*. It sweetly and vividly recalled that magical day and night they shared in the Highlands. Jackson crooned, "You'll remember the love you found there."

How could they ever forget?

Diana Ross next sang the sultry *Ain't No Mountain High Enough*, a reminder that if she ever needed him, he'd come running. More to the point, she sang words that hit his meaning right on target, singing, "I know you must follow the sun, but if you fall short of your desires, you'll always have me." Words he couldn't say, but Diana Ross said them for him.

The tape wasn't designed to self-destruct, but it should have been. Ginny was devastated, trying to imagine how much worse it had been for him to put it together. Such depth, raw passion, an open wound, a bleeding heart. Did his work, which was life and death, make him more sensitive to the value of life and love? There couldn't have been a more effective message, sung openly or between the lines.

Side one of the tape ended. Almost three weeks elapsed before he recorded side two.

His plans, always in constant change, were supposedly set for the year. "I'll be here, attending a few courses, which seem like a bit of a waste of time. Then in March, I'm going to Cyprus for a few months to bolster up the British contingent of the U.N. force there. I'll be back in England and perhaps have a couple of weeks leave. I'm thinking of going to Teneriffe, to see my father's grave there. But that's not definite. As I told you, I've decided to leave the army, and two weeks ago I went to the London Boat Show. I've enclosed a brochure of the type of boat I intend to get. The important thing is that I'm leaving the army in a couple of years. Another couple of years in the army will see me financially independent for the rest of my life.

"I've also started going out more and decided that life has more to offer. I've taken out a few young ladies, to restaurants and the theater and life is looking better. I think now that I'm out of Northern Ireland and I know I won't be going back there, and the fact that I've made the decision to leave the army, perhaps it's lifting a burden from my shoulders."

Elton John played the next hypnotic melody on the piano, *Song for Guy*, a sad, moody song without words he had written for a dead friend.

Jim continued:

"I've been kept busy these past few weeks, looking after my lads. A few of them have gotten into mischief with the police, which is reasonable, considering the circumstances of their work, although one or two of them have gone slightly overboard. I've been in court this week with one charged with robbery with violence. Perhaps I should be a Perry Mason. He was released back to the army in my care. I've attended court and stood up for them all, explaining they've served in Northern Ireland in South Armagh and elsewhere in the world. Perhaps they weren't really back in the swing of things. Thankfully, the judges have been reasonable.

"By the way, did you ever get the book I sent you? I recall you said you'd never received it. There's a picture of me in it. I'm carrying a rifle in my right hand, but it's not very flattering. There is a priest waving a white handkerchief. It happened on what is known as "Bloody Sunday," when five to six thousand civil rights association marchers went on the rampage in Londonderry.

"Regrettably, through no fault of the British Army, IRA gunmen opened fire on us and we returned fire. We were very selective, in only going for the gunmen. We killed thirteen. The Irish community claimed that the thirteen killed had nothing to do with the fighting and were innocent bystanders. Of course it caused a lot of trouble.

"I've also enclosed a small poem. I hope you can find it among the brochure and tape. I think the words in it are very appropriate in our case. What we had, we had, and it was beautiful. Through various circumstances that we both know about, it's in the past. It was a wonderful experience, something that we both wouldn't have missed. It's something we can always look back on and can remember with a certain amount of feeling that only we know about, of course.

"I don't know if we'll ever get together again. I've given it a lot thought over the past two months since our abortive meeting in London, and I understand the reasons. Perhaps it was selfish of me to insist on you coming over at that particular date. It really was the only date that I could have made. Perhaps I should have gone for a date earlier this year. However, I didn't, I went for then, and it didn't come off. It's history now, and you can't change history. People have been trying to do that for years without success.

"What we had existed in Scotland. You called it a magical place. Was it just a coincidence? Perhaps it couldn't be repeated anywhere else. It was a wonderful experience, I admit.

"But in reality, perhaps if we met under different circumstances in America, or London, would we have even given each other a second look? I don't know. It's really difficult to predict. You've lived your life and I've lived mine, and I really don't know if we would have been happy or not if we tried to blend those lives. Maybe. Maybe not. Who can tell? However, it's passed. So I'll close now, Ginny, and," a pause, "I don't know what to say, really."

The music playing in the background seemed to swell with his emotions.

"I would like to remain friends with you. As you know, I'm not the world's best writer or communicator, although in this day of magic like telephones and radios, it's much easier to just pick up a phone. If I don't communicate for a while, fine.

"I honestly believe that it would be a mistake for us to meet again. All I would say is what we had, we've got, and no one can take that away. And perhaps it's best if we leave it, and as we grow old, it's a fond memory, one we can both look back on in our own worlds and say, Well, I did know happiness for a brief moment in time."

More sadness was yet to come. Ginny unfolded a piece of green lined paper and found a carefully penned poem. It was haunting, touching, beautiful. Was he the poet or was someone else? It didn't matter. He felt enough to send it. Without realizing it, Ginny began to cry as she read.

### LOST LOVE

*Each weary night the phantom fades, at restless dawn to rise,*
*Haunting the shadows of my mind with gentle, laughing eyes.*
*Veiled in stars your image glides before me through the day,*
*A mirage from a vanished land - yet I cannot turn away.*
*Though sightless tears drift down the years, for fragile dreams that died,*
*I now must stand forever damned by wishes I must hide –*
*Forever in my memory those priceless hours will last,*
*But I have not the power to call forth, again, the past.*
*Had time but stopped I could have dwelt in frozen ecstasy.*
*But I am left alone to long for that which cannot be.*

*The lingering pain must long remain, but nothing of regret,*
*For the touch and kiss that I shall miss, but never now forget.*

Reading the well-chosen words was heartbreaking. Jim was not the cold bastard he pretended to be. Just the opposite. His sensitivity and depth amazed her, but he also was so courageous. How had she ever been able to turn her back on him? No wonder it was the most difficult decision of her life. She had no idea what he had been doing since their aborted meeting in London, assuming he was still mired down in the Troubles of Northern Ireland. Suddenly he reappeared, back in England, and had gone through the holidays. He was actually thinking of life after the army, something he only briefly discussed. It was all too shocking for her to absorb.

Tears rolled down her cheeks. She had never experienced anything so moving, passionate, and sad, all rolled up and mailed in one package.

That day the ocean seemed wider than ever.

# II
# Florida

The letters and phone calls began again though there were more phone calls than letters from Jim. Ginny wrote to him almost daily to break the tedium during lulls at the art gallery. It also bolstered her morale in dealing with Wayne. Though he felt victorious when Ginny cancelled her trip to London, now he saw the control eroding away again, as she gained self-confidence in her job. His verbal attacks were renewed. In spite of that, she was neither financially nor emotionally ready yet to sever the ties.

More than ever, she realized the role Jim had played in her life, in her quest for self-understanding. *James Byrd Evans*, his name written on his passport. How ironic that his middle name was "Byrd," reminding her that in Native American stories, a bird can be a spirit helper. Be it as lover or friend, he had inspired her to find the best in herself, to set personal goals, as she worked on establishing a solid financial base.

Engaged in a deep trip within, for the first time in her life, Ginny seriously searched and examined the miscellany that comprised Virginia Thomas.

In spite of what was said, Ginny knew they must meet again, if only to set each other free. There was something each saw in the other that offered the possibility of a more meaningful life. The question of *what could have been* would haunt them both to their graves if they didn't meet once more.

The plan evolved quickly in the middle of a phone call. Suddenly Jim said, "I want to come over and see you. I have a week off before I go on a mission to Cyprus, at Easter time. Can I come over then?"

"Really? You'll come here?"

"Yes, I'd like to, if that's all right."

"Yes, of course. I'll work it out and find a great place to stay."

"Some place with a beach, right on the ocean. Something nice."

Another fantasy began to take shape in Ginny's mind. She didn't just want a hotel. She would find an apartment, with a kitchen where they could have leisurely breakfasts and make simple lunches. They could eat in or out, as they pleased. She wanted an opportunity to spoil him. To have long sunny days to walk the beach, and romantic moonlit nights. She played the fantasy when she got discouraged, frightened, or simply felt alone. She would look at the moon and imagine Jim sharing it across the ocean. Soon they would share it together.

By the end of February, the date was set. Jim would arrive on April 6th, spend Easter with her, and fly back to London on the 12th. Not quite a week, but the best he could do. Even though it was Easter, Eric was not planning to come home.

This time Jim would cross the ocean. That eliminated a huge uncertainty. Either he was here or he wasn't, and she was not as far out on a limb.

On a day off, Ginny drove up I-95 and got off at a Palm Beach exit. She drove to the beach and turned south down highway A1A. The drive was beautiful, the sparkling turquoise ocean lapping the shore in foamy white waves. The busy tourist season crowded the beach resorts with sun worshippers and gaily colored umbrellas. She was in no hurry and took her time to find just the right spot.

The coastline was glutted with classy unsold condos that were available for weekly rentals. From Deerfield Beach south there were stretches of sandy beaches and parks, areas reserved for picnics and bike riding. She knew she was getting close to what she wanted when she got to Pompano Beach. Suddenly she saw an appealing resort, with brightly colored flags fluttering in the breeze and a sign advertising "Weekly Rentals! Stop for Information!" Her car seemed to swing into the parking lot by itself.

She knew she had found their hideaway.

The clerk behind the desk was friendly and helpful. The resort was a motel converted into condo apartments, and no expense had been spared.

A nice restaurant across the lobby would be handy, serving only dinner and offering steaks and seafood. Ginny asked to see a condo.

The clerk grabbed her keys. "They're all the same, pretty and furnished down to the last spoon. The developers had top decorators from Fort Lauderdale do the interiors. They were selling fairly well, but all of a sudden there are too many time-share condos on the market, so the developers decided to rent them weekly until they're all sold."

The condo was perfect. The first floor had an attractive living and dining room combination. The kitchen was as complete as promised, with tastefully selected dishes, glasses, and stainless flatware. The bath and bedroom were upstairs. The bedroom had sliding glass doors that opened to a balcony with a spectacular ocean view. The other tenants or owners appeared to be snowbirds, nice, quiet, adult Midwestern or Canadian types, likely to mind their own business and hopefully be pleasant enough to be around.

"Of course, this might not be the condo you get. It depends on what's available when you come. What are the dates?"

Ginny gave her the dates. The price was unbelievably reasonable. She knew this was the right place.

"There is something open on that date. We'll need a deposit of half to hold your reservation."

Ginny wrote a check, handed it to the clerk, and gathered several glossy brochures to send to Jim. The warm sunny beach would inspire him, sitting in England.

"See you April 6th," she said. "What time can I check in? "

"Any time will be fine. See you then."

Happy and confident as she drove back to Miami, Ginny ran the fantasy through her mind, this time filling in the perfect setting. There was no way this dream would not become a reality.

Still, there was a rocky road ahead. The home front had to be reckoned with. As unhappy as Ginny had been, she never before considered having a lover. Just not something she would do. Her life had always been an open book. This was a bolt out of the blue. She had no intention of being cruel to Wayne, but too much damage had been done. While once her rock, now he was her captor. She would be living a double life and was not at all comfortable with that. Jim couldn't do that either. Despite the circumstances, she just wasn't the type to manipulate an affair and chose to suffer in silence. As usual, her coping mechanisms were deafness and detachment.

Ginny had never known a man like Jim. It was so unexpected, such a bolt out of the blue. No wonder she was overwhelmed and had to see it through. She had seen a glimmer of happiness, and had to pursue it, despite the consequences.

It was time to do the right thing and see her attorney again.

"Are you up for this, Evelyn? Here we go again."

"The real question is, are you up for it? No more backing down. Is Wayne giving you trouble again?"

"Yes, that too. He's as bad or worse than ever. He's so possessive and domineering. He never learns. But the big thing is that Jim is coming over here at Easter time, and we're going to experience South Florida and Miami together. This time it's different though, because there is one less risk. Either he makes it or he doesn't. I won't be stuck sitting alone in England, should he have something come up and has to cancel. Eric's not coming home from college this time. So I guess this is it. What do I do?"

"Nothing. Absolutely nothing. Just wait and see what happens."

Not again. She couldn't go on being a shady lady. That wasn't her style or manner. And Wayne really hadn't gotten better, and worse yet, he had reverted to old bad habits.

"I should get on with this thing, right? "

"Why? You don't know what will happen. How long since you and Jim saw each other? Over a year? Don't burn bridges until you have to. You might be sorry."

"But what will people think? We know Wayne will tell everyone in Miami how awful I am."

"Do you care at this point?"

Ginny paused for a moment, thinking. "No, not really. I've stopped allowing my life to be motivated by what other people think a long time ago. That went out the window with guilt. I guess that isn't an issue. You're right."

"See Jim and have a wonderful time. I'm sure you both can use it. Come see me when you get back."

"There's more. I'm quitting my job. I took that job to learn some business management skills, but I'm not sure it's the place for me. I'm giving the owner a two-week notice. I've saved some money but now I won't have a job. Where will I go when I return from this great honeymoon, as Wayne will call it. I'm still living at home in the guest room. I can't afford my own place yet. Do I just walk in and say, Hi, I'm back?"

"Exactly."

"What if my clothes are thrown in the pool?"

"We'll sue for damages. He'll have to replace them. He can't do that."

"Are you sure? This all seems so sordid."

"The whole situation is sordid. Look at the rough times you've been through. The worst that could happen is that it would come to an end, and believe me, you wouldn't miss the pain for a minute. At least this way you have a chance for happiness. Go check it out. I'll protect you. Let me worry about the legal complications. Anything is worth a try at this point. Just be careful. Stay out of Miami."

"That's taken care of. I found this great timeshare condo on the ocean in Pompano Beach. It should be wonderful."

"Just keep that in mind and call me when you need me."

"Okay. Here's to nothing."

"No. Here's to everything. What have you got to lose?"

Ginny left the office relieved, but she wasn't sure why. It still sounded so risky. Even Dr Johnson was encouraging, urging Ginny to do as she pleased, and accept the consequences as they came. All agreed that she had tried.

She knew now that Wayne would always be the same. What was the bond that held her there, remembering the Wayne she fell in love with so long ago when they were young? Whatever happened to him? Where did he go? Or was it really the strong pull of Miami, her home?

The sessions with Rhoda droned on, and Ginny realized the situation was hopeless. There was something that stood in the way of making the great escape unannounced. Was she again shouting, *Save me from myself.*

"I'm sorry," she said. "We've all made an effort here, but it isn't enough. I'm planning a meeting with Jim. I have to. This can never work unless I'm sure that I want it to. Too much damage has already been done."

Wayne and Rhoda were astonished. *Deja vu!*

Rhoda said, "Outrageous. See? You have to stir things up again!"

Ginny found the courage to stand up to the attack.

"I said I'm sorry. I really am, Wayne. I wouldn't hurt you for the world, and I know I am. That kills me because I never want to hurt anyone. But you wouldn't want me this way, always wondering what could have been. Neither you nor I could live with that. I didn't go to England at Thanksgiving, and I gave therapy another chance. I'm not bad, as you'd like to say. I do have a conscience. But I'm not sure you have caught on yet to the problems we have. Also, Jim is something special, and I have to see what it's all about. Nothing either one of you can say will stop me this time."

The room was quiet for a moment. Then Rhoda broke the oppressive silence.

"When are you leaving?"

"An undisclosed time."

Rhoda tried to keep the dialogue open.

"Okay. Will you both agree to meet with me until that time comes? Maybe something will work out yet."

Wayne readily agreed, but Ginny was reluctant.

"Why?" I said, "I'm leaving."

Wayne said, "Just give this a try. Leave the door open. It's only fair."

She was no longer sure what fair meant. She recalled the saying all's fair in love and war. Which was this? Then she remembered Evelyn's advice about not burning any more bridges than she had to.

She agreed to continue the sessions, though she was often amazed at the depth of her own masochism. In her heart, she knew that the bonds of love and trust that had been broken by years of verbal abuse had left so many invisible scars and loose ends that they could never be spliced back together again.

Her last paycheck from the gallery was deposited in the bank with the other money she was able to put aside. She had Evelyn's retainer fee and some money to tide her over when things really started hitting the fan, but that was about it. Family money had always been *his*, not *theirs*.

For once, the plan was set and she was on target. Ginny and Jim excitedly discussed their meeting on the phone, but with Jim still continually reminding her that the army could always change those plans. At the moment, though, it was unthinkable.

He was scheduled to spend March in England with a week off in April. May and most of June would be in Cyprus, returning to England at the end of June and on to Belize. It all sounded too good to be true.

And it was.

Argentine generals boldly decided to take possession of the islands that were remote British colonial outposts. The British knew the islands as the Falklands, but to Argentina they were the Malvinas. Ginny had never before even heard of those bleak islands in the south Atlantic. At first, little blips appeared in the headlines, hints of rumblings over ownership of the islands, but on April 2nd, Argentina invaded the Falkland Islands.

Ginny read the newspapers and watched the television reports with growing alarm. She knew what this could mean.

Jim was anxious on the phone. "I'm not sure what may happen. So far, so good. I'll get to come over, but that could change any minute. We'll just have to play it by ear. Things are really building up here. Margaret Thatcher is adamant to protect our islands. I'll keep in touch. Don't worry. You'll know if my plans have to change. By the way, do you have a stereo tape deck and radio?"

"No, but I can get a cheap one. Why?"

I have some tapes, with *Cavatina* and other music I like. I'll bring them and we can listen to them together. Okay?"

"Sure. I'll find one. Bye." Ginny loved *Cavatina* but had not seen *Deer Hunter* yet.

On April 5th, a British carrier group set sail to the Falklands from Portsmouth, but Jim called to confirm his flight to Miami.

"Looks like I'll be there, but you never know. And by the way, when we meet, nothing emotional at the airport. I hate scenes at airports. Let's save it for later, okay?"

"That's a big order, after all of this, but I'll do my best. I've seen enough nauseating arrival scenes myself, so I share your sentiments. You have my word. Nothing for a *Life* magazine cover."

The morning of April 6th was another sunny day. Ginny had played her finest performance, and Wayne had no reason to suspect the day would be any different as he left for his office.

She wrote a note, kind as she could word it, saying, "I will be away for about a week. Please try not to think about me and have as nice an Easter as possible. We can talk when I return."

What else could she say? She left the note in the foyer, where it couldn't be missed, loaded *Liberator* in her car and went to the grocery store. There were a few things she wanted to pick up to make the condo more personal. She bought breakfast and lunch items, croissants from her favorite bakery, champagne, and flowers.

She drove to their hideaway, checked in, and put *Liberator* and the groceries away in the condo. There was a clear view of the ocean.

She'd bought an inexpensive stereo tape deck and plugged it in by the sofa in the living room. She played a favorite tape and the stereo sounded unexpectedly good, especially for the price. She iced the champagne and put the flowers in a vase on the coffee table. There was a little time before she had to drive back to meet Jim's four o'clock flight, so she did her best to relax by the pool. Finally, it came time to shower, dress, and leave for Miami International Airport.

*Is this really happening?*

More than a year, and Jim was coming to see her. That year had been filled with incredible sadness, despair, disappointment, and a lot of world history had been made. The tragedy of war-torn Northern Ireland had been a daily reality for Ginny. Even though she did not understand The Troubles they were always in her thoughts.

Unbelievable assassination attempts had been made on the Pope and President Reagan; Anwar Sadat's enemies had been more successful. Had Jim been called to Egypt? The world as she had known it had become a rapidly changing place, and for the first time she was keenly aware of it. She had a better understanding of the threat of international terrorism. Heck of a time to fall in love with a British SAS officer, especially a career anti-terrorist, she thought, even though she admired him for his courage, and the strength of his convictions.

Her heart raced as she drove through the heavy traffic on I-95, thinking how they were on the brink of bringing their two different worlds together again. But there were so many doubts. Was it wise to see each other again? Or was Jim right when he wondered if they should have just lived their lives in their own worlds, cherishing the fond memory of their romantic day and night in the Highlands? No, they decided. It was better for them to examine the reality of things rather than just live with a lifelong fantasy.

The airport was jammed with Easter holiday tourists and college kids on Spring Break. Ginny circled the parking garage several times before she found a parking space which was a healthy walk from the Customs exit.

*Will we even recognize each other after a year?*

The monitor flashed incoming international flights, and British Airways flight 824 was arriving late, at 5:05. That left a good hour to kill before it arrived, and then would be the wait while he was cleared at Customs. She headed to the bar for a glass of wine to calm her nerves.

The minutes seemed like hours. Would he even be on that plane? She never was sure. He hadn't been exaggerating when he said he was always on alert. With the deepening Falklands crisis, there was a chance his leave could have been cancelled at the last minute. This time she wasn't sure that she could face the bitterness of one more disappointment, but at least, this time, it was on home turf.

At five, she finished her wine, paid her bill, and walked to the international passenger exit. The television flashed that flight 824 had arrived at the gate. Judging from the many people waiting for the flight, it must have been a packed 747. The man next to her said that he was waiting for his wife and children.

"Waiting for your husband?" he asked.

"No," Ginny said. "Actually, I'm waiting for a British army officer, and I'm concerned he might not have made it because of the Falklands crisis." She realized she shouldn't have said that as soon as the words were out of her mouth.

"That is a mess. Good luck," he replied.

The doors slid open and Jim walked through first, his eyes anxiously searching the crowd. When he saw her, he nodded his head, indicating where to meet.

He was even better looking than she remembered. Why was that such a surprise?

She respected Jim's request and with typical British reserve, the greeting was only a quick hello.

Their eyes said it all.

"How was your flight?"

"Fine, but a little bumpy at the last. That's why we were late. Hit a bit of turbulence."

He handed her his carry-on bag, threw his topcoat over his arm, grabbed his suitcase, and they started the long walk to the car.

"I want you to know this right away. There was a message to call my boss when I checked in at British Airways. He said, I don't want to spoil your holiday, Evans, you're going to the Falklands on Wednesday after you return. Your men have been given leave too."

The news was not totally unanticipated, but still one more shattering blow.

"Does our getting together precipitate international crises, or do you think they would happen without us? We first met and you were called off to Northern Ireland, and now this, so unexpected. Do you realize that we're star-crossed lovers?"

She wondered how they would deal with this. Nothing would spoil their visit, no matter what, not even the Falklands or if it comes to it, World War III. This was their time to enjoy life, He put his luggage in the trunk and she drove through the congested maze that led to the airport exit.

They had agreed he would be in the driver's seat for the visit, but she decided to drive to their condo, giving him time to unwind and take in the Florida landscape. Both were happy just to be together again, at long last.

The sunset was spectacular, and she commented on it. "We rate our sunsets in Florida. That's a ten on a scale of one to ten. There also will be a full silver moon this evening."

"We sometimes have one of those in England, too," Jim said.

"I think about that often. It has been the only thing, besides the phone, that we could share over these long months. I would look at the moon and wonder if you were looking at it too, across the ocean. There's a little song we sang about that at summer camp when I was a girl:

*I see the moon,*
*The moon sees me,*
*The moon sees the one that I want to see.*

"I've thought about that too," he said.

Their chatter was light, as they gradually became more comfortable with each other again.

"The Customs agent asked, 'What is your business in America, Mr Evans? I answered, 'I'm visiting my American girlfriend. He said, 'Enjoy, and handed my passport back to me. Now wasn't that nice of him?"

That made Ginny tingle. Following their aborted meeting in London, Jim said they would only be friends.

That was seeming a joke now.

"Who's your boss?" She had so many questions to ask him.

"I answer to a General, who must remain nameless. I answer to him and whomever says, *Send Evans!*"

Ginny turned off of I-95 at the Atlantic Boulevard exit and concentrated on the small town traffic of Pompano.

"You're pretty pale. Let's stop and get some suntan lotion so you won't burn to a crisp."

She pulled into the parking lot drugstore. Jim slid his arm around her and held her close as they as they walked. The first time in all of those agonizing months. They selected a suntan lotion that smelled like Piña Colada, something that always made her think she was on vacation. Hurrying back to the car, Jim gave her a look and put out his hand for the car keys.

No question of who was in control here.

Ginny co-piloted, giving him directions to turn left on A1A as they crossed the bridge and reached the oceanfront highway. Soon they pulled into the parking lot and he unloaded his luggage. She led the way along the beachfront walk to the entrance. It was dark now and the path was lighted with twinkling garden lights. The full moon filled the sky, reflecting a shimmering silver ball on the black Atlantic. They stopped on the patio deck to share the view.

"You're right. This is beautiful."

She sighed with relief.

Inside the condo, Ginny, turned on a light.

"Very nice. In fact, this is great. Where do we put this stuff?"

"Upstairs." She led the way up the narrow stairway to the bedroom. The curtain was open and the panorama of the moon on the ocean was spectacular. After appreciating the view, she pulled the curtain closed for privacy.

"I have champagne in the fridge. Let me get it while you freshen up. You must want to use the loo."

"Right."

She went down and got the chilled champagne and two glasses, carried them back up and set them on the nightstand by the bed, just as Jim emerged from the bathroom. He took her hand and looking squarely into her eyes gently drew her close. Then he began to kiss her with the same intensity she had remembered for over a year. The frustration of that year seemed to melt away.

Once more, passion took over, the kisses multiplied as they sank onto the bed. Moments later, they were undressing. And then their naked bodies were one.

Somehow, they managed to talk as well as make love and then they sipped champagne, talked, and made love again.

Play. Repeat. Play some more.

Sip, talk, dip into each other some more.

Later on, dressed for dinner, Jim said that the aroma of steak was steal-ing into his subconscious mind.

"You're just hungry," Ginny said, chuckling. "Let's go downstairs and have some."

They had one more glass of champagne, and then, arm-in-arm, they went down to the lobby.

The restaurant was popular with locals, and very busy, even on a Tuesday night. Jim left his name with the hostess, and they went to the bar for gin and tonics.

They sipped their drinks in silence. Soon Jim's name was called and a cheerful waiter recited the day's specials.

"Just give me a steak, the biggest you've got," Jim said.

Ginny ordered broiled snapper. Their conversation was light, the food was slow in coming. Suddenly Jim snapped out of their revery. He said to their server in the purest Cockney accent imaginable, "Where's me steak? I want me steak!"

Ginny giggled like a school girl. "I can't take you anywhere, I can see that."

He grew serious. "Wait a minute, don't misunderstand. I love to kid like that, but you must know that just before we met I had to deal with royalty on the closest and yet most formal levels. I have a Christmas card personally signed by the Queen. I brought it to show you. I doubt if you know as much as I do about protocol and etiquette. I like to joke in Cockney."

"Who wouldn't?" she said. "I would if I could. But the way you say it, well, it has a certain edge."

"By right," he said.

After dinner, they strolled by the pool once more to listen to the sound of the ocean, and to appreciate the scintillating moonlight.

Back in their condo, they looked out the window at the sea. Jim slid his arms around her waist from behind and held her close. The sound of happy diners floated up from the restaurant below, and somewhere a camera flashed.

"Must be a birthday party," Ginny said, then closed the curtain.

Soon they were wrapped in each other's arms and again lost in lovemak-ing. That night, the hurt, disappointment, and anguish of a long, withering year dissolved. Then there was nothing but the soothing sound of the sea.

Morning. Filtered silver rays of the early morning sun peeked through the slit in the curtains and awakened them. Jim was jet-lagged just enough to not be in a hurry to get up. He gave her a wink and a smile, pulled her close, and they began the day in each other's arms.

*If only every day of our lives could begin this way.*

After a little while, Ginny opened the curtain so they could look out at the sea and sand. Seagulls cried and circled in the sky, and an occasional pair of pelicans skimmed the shallows.

"What would you like for breakfast? I'll have coffee, tea, orange juice, strawberries, croissants, and eggs." Ginny hated to cook breakfast but it seemed a small concession for such a special morning.

"Tea, not coffee. You Americans and your coffee. You shower first. Then while I shave, you can decide what to fix. I really don't eat that much for breakfast. Off with you, woman."

She was not under his command, but under his spell. With a laugh, she darted to the shower. That established their morning house rule: she would get the bathroom first. She showered, put on perfume and her favorite coral-colored bathing suit and cover. Bathing suits would definitely be their morning attire. Jim stirred and she went down to start breakfast. Just as she did every morning, she turned on the TV to watch the *Today Show*.

The news was dire. The crisis in the Falklands had escalated. Jim came down the stairs to listen, said nothing, and went back upstairs to finish dressing.

*Let me think. He wants tea. How in the devil does an Englishman like his tea?*

She wasn't really sure. It was just one of many cultural differences between the British and Americans. Although she had fought so hard for her liberation, here she was, dying to please his every whim. Worse yet, she loved it. She genuinely wanted to spoil him; but then, of course, that was her nature. It also had been her downfall.

He taught her how he liked his English Breakfast tea, and they ate marmalade on warm croissants.

Their condo faced a large pool deck shared by all of the other tenants. Several other couples were already seated at tables under umbrellas, or on lounges, reading their morning papers or just soaking up the sun. Several small children splashed in the pool with their parents. The families seemed nice, quiet, and occupied with their own concerns, flashing smiles but otherwise showing no interest in the new arrivals. Jim set up their lounges outside their glass door, then got the stereo and a few of his tapes. He turned it on softly and settled into the morning paper. After putting dishes in the dishwasher, Ginny made turkey sandwiches for lunch and joined him, content simply to watch him read or to stare out at the ocean.

She also wanted to plan their day. Seeing how pale he was, she gently slathered Piña Colada suntan lotion on his white skin. A sunburn was the last thing he needed. She noticed a nick in his shoulder, pink and still healing.

"What's this?"

"Nothing much, just a little souvenir from the IRA. Actually, I was lucky. It barely broke the skin."

There were so many unanswered questions. There had always been the possibility of someone monitoring their phone conversations, so there were many things he could not discuss.

"Where did you go for those three months? You vanished and I was so worried. I kept the faith and continued to write to you. But what were you doing?"

"I still can't say. There are so many things that are secret. I'm sorry. As you know, I really can vanish for long periods of time with no explanation."

"Where did you go after Sadat was assassinated? Can you tell me now? Your friend said he thought it was the Middle East, but he wasn't sure. I appreciated that you had him call me. I asked you when you got back and you were very evasive."

"I still can't tell you about that either. I can just say the weather was warm, very nice. Sometimes I'm loaned out to other governments for special assignments, to eliminate troublemakers. That's all I can say."

"I still have trouble imagining what your life must be like. I'm reading a lot, things you've suggested, like *The British Army in Ulster*. The copy you sent never came so I ordered it and got it recently. I read *Battle Cry*. There's so much I want to know. Like what does it take to become so darn dedicated?"

"With me, a sad beginning. How did it all start? I guess it was back in my first tour of Northern Ireland when a young lad named Mick Gardiner died in my arms. He was my partner in an undercover job. We were set up by an IRA gunman named Sean O'Hara, who killed him.

"O'Hara's as dangerous a terrorist as you can get. I've had multiple encounters with him, one quite recently, in fact. I had set up an ambush in Northern Ireland, not knowing he was involved. If I had, I would've been there myself. It was carried out by less experienced soldiers, and he slipped through the net. I'll get him someday, though."

"That's horrible. And frightening," Ginny said.

"I grew up after that first incident with O'Hara. I had a cause, something I've believed in for the rest of my life. There's no place in this world for terrorists. Kill them all. I turned out to be good at it. I'm a damn good soldier, Ginny. Call it whatever you like, defending my country, a guardian of freedom, or just a plain killer. Whatever. It sustains me."

"You're just doing your job. You can't take the blame for what they tell you to do. You often seem to see yourself as just a killer. You're too hard on yourself, unless you enjoy doing it, and I don't think you do. I see you more as the guardian of freedom. We sure need that now. I've never seen so many crazies out there."

"This is just the beginning. The world is full of O'Haras, and their day is coming. He's one rat I'd like to exterminate. Make the world safer."

Ginny had hoped to help Jim relax, get over jet lag, not stir him up. This was to be a restful day to become more familiar with each other, talking, not on a phone or just through letters and an ocean away.

"Why don't we take a towel and sit on the sand near the water?"

"I hate sand. If you'd spent as much time in the desert as I have, you'd understand. Instead, let's walk the beach to the lighthouse down the way."

It was a long walk in the warm sun. He entertained her with funny stories of things he had done with his army buddies over the years as the calm surf splashed silver bubbles around their feet. Ginny stopped from time to time to pick up seashells and a small piece of driftwood. She took them back to their condo, saving them in a paper cup. The air conditioning felt wonderful. They talked while looking out the window at the pool, ocean, and waving palms as they ate lunch, drinking chilled white wine.

House rule: No TV.

"Shower time," Jim said, heading up the stairs, taking her hand. She followed.

He turned on the tape deck to play the music he brought, pulling her close and giving her a longing kiss. The room was lit by sun through the curtains. Slowly, they undressed each other to the piano melody of *Cavatina*, then

*One Day in Your Life*, and his other favorite songs he taped and sent to her.

"I've wanted to be with you like this for so long. You can't imagine," he said, touching her face, locking their eyes.

Hugging, kissing, hands exploring, their nude bodies blended into one on the bed, making love, passion unleashed. Fantasy became reality and he led her into the shower, smoothly lathering each other, tingling, to the mood of the music. The ecstasy was all Jim promised it would be, and much more. The soldier was romantic beyond imagination, as they left the troubled world behind.

During the week, they lazed about in the mornings, walked or sunned by the pool listening to music, read or talked about favorite places, travel books and spy novels. Some mornings or afternoons they poked around in the touristy stores of Pompano Beach. They ate lunch out, with Piña Coladas, and returned to the condo mellow, ready for love and a nap. Evenings were in the convenient restaurant downstairs, drinks overlooking the ocean and dinner with a favorite server. Back in the condo, they watched TV until bed beckoned. Just what a man off to war needed.

The days flew by, and suddenly it was Saturday morning, sunny, but not for long. Before noon, dark clouds gathered in the sky, as a cold front rumbled in. The wind picked up and the palms began to furiously shake.

"The weather forecast is terrible. Looks like a good day for some indoor sightseeing," Ginny suggested.

"I didn't come to see the sights. I came to see you."

"That's nice, but you can't go back to England without seeing some of Florida. Let's drive up to Palm Beach, less than an hour away, and see how the other half lives. We'll look at the elegant shops along Worth Avenue. Just tourists -- lookers, not shoppers. Easter week the shops always have beautiful things on display. I know a nice restaurant, Taboo. Name seems right doesn't it?"

Jim nodded. He seemed less than enthused but gave in to her plan without complaint.

The sky opened wide as he drove the A1A highway. Gale force winds drove torrents of rain against the windshield, and at times visibility became so poor that Jim pulled the car off of the road for a while to let the worst parts pass. By the time they reached Worth Avenue, the rain had slowed to a drizzle.

The Avenue was jammed with tourists and shoppers, picking up last minute gifts or designer clothing for Easter Sunday. The haughty sales people at

Gucci were no friendlier in the Palm Beach store than at any other Gucci store she'd been to, but it was a good stop for a free shot of their wonderful perfume. Jim found a matching tie and scarf he fancied … until he saw the price.

The other stores were filled with the trappings of the good life, sequined gowns, diamond and ruby or emerald necklaces, earrings, tiaras, very expensive clothing, gift boutiques, and art galleries. Jim seemed particularly allergic to the art galleries, but they readily agreed on their love of bookstores.

Jim was intrigued with a glossy book on the royal wedding, and eagerly turned the pages, stopping at a photo of Charles and Diana kneeling at the altar.

"See this chap?" he said, pointing to one of three soldiers in full dress uniform guarding the royal couple. "He's the fellow who replaced me. Looks like he had his work cut out for him. I haven't told you this before, but when we met, I had just received my commission. My boss had talked me into becoming a commissioned officer because he felt I could deal with my responsibilities better than as a non-commissioned officer. At first, I was against it, but after the fact, I'm proud."

"I can see that. As you should be."

Taboo had a line of people waiting at the door, but there was a surprisingly short wait for a table. Ginny thought the food was incredible.

Jim's take was different. He made a face. "Too rich for my taste," he said, "makes me nervous."

Ginny smiled. "You'd rather have toast and tea?"

"To be honest, I'd rather be out in the open air after having eaten another steak."

"The rough life has roughed you up, I see."

"A little of this goes a long way."

"OK. I can see now that this was a very bad idea and the weather's made it worse. You really balked at the art gallery and I just wanted to get a little closer to that Picasso they had. You don't see many of those for sale in store windows, not even in Miami."

The return ride was better. The winds were worse, but there were open patches of sunshine as they streaked along admiring the oceanfront mansions that lined A1A. Jim relaxed a bit they approached familiar turf.

"I read about a bar with wonderful exotic drinks a little farther down the way. Let's go try out their Piña Coladas."

The cocktail lounge overlooked the stormy ocean waves that pounded the shore. The icy Piña Coladas came in large, stemmed glasses and were topped with a shot of Myers rum, flaked coconut, and a cherry.

"Perfect! Now this is a Piña Colada!" Ginny said.

"Did I tell you that I tended bar in a pub once?" Jim asked.

"When did you find time to do that?"

"Time off, on weekends. It helped, because they paid me nothing in the army then. I was also a London cabbie, in one of those big black cabs. You learn a lot about people from odd jobs like that."

There was still so much to learn about each other, and time was slipping away. How do you cover two lifetimes in six days?

"Let's see," Ginny said, "I was a model and sales girl in a department store for two summers when I was in college. I guess I never worked that much.

Starting a career changed my life but led to chaos. Now I have to decide what to do next, and fast! I can't imagine what you face when you leave. Likewise, you can't imagine what I face when I put you on the plane on Monday. No job, little money. I'm not even sure where I'll go. It should be interesting! But our time together has been worth it all, Jim. I had to make changes, and this is sure a catalyst."

"But where will you go?" asked Jim.

"I honestly don't know at the moment. I'll figure it out and just face the music when the time comes. Let's go back to the condo and decide what we want to do about dinner."

The drinks made them feel sleepy and romantic. After which they tumbled into bed. The room was dark and the howling wind rattled the windows. They fell asleep listening to it.

When they woke, the wind had lessened, the sun was out and Jim rolled up his sleeves and made a dinner of steaks, mushrooms, baked potatoes, peas, and salad. Jim was an experienced mushroom cleaner and he added sugar to the peas. Ginny was surprised that he was so adept at handling and cooking the food she'd brought for the trip. But then Jim was full of surprises.

*How wonderful life could be*, she told herself, though didn't dare say it out loud. After eating and sipping Beaujolais, they watched the news, which continued to worsen on the Falklands front. They turned in early, enjoying every moment of their time together.

It was an ugly Easter Sunday. The angry Atlantic pounded the shore and the palms bent in the wind. The seagulls and pelicans had taken refuge. Jim bought the thick *Miami Herald* and poured over the front section as Ginny fixed breakfast. The Falklands situation had intensified. The 3 Commando Brigade had sailed on April 9th.

"Things look bad," he said. "Thatcher's more determined than ever to keep the islands."

"Do you realize what an impact Thatcher's decisions have had on your life, and ultimately mine? You say you are a 'Soldier of the Queen,' but you're also are a pawn of Thatcher. She's unpopular here. Think about it. Why ever would you want the Falklands? It's desolate, bleak. There's no economic gain in keeping them. They're a drain, in fact, and there are more sheep than people there anyway. I just don't understand."

"No you don't. It's the principle of it. Thatcher's right. Argentina can't just come in and say 'I want your islands' and take them. Then what? Any country in the world might try the same thing. You have to defend what's yours."

"But is that unimportant hunk of land worth the lives that can be lost there? I shudder to say that even you could be killed. I don't think it's worth that. What a stupid reason to die!"

"People have died for less, Ginny. You have to understand the price of freedom. You're for peace and I'm a warrior and want action."

"Think how long the war could go on, and it's so far from the UK."

"It's amazing what it would take to stop something like that, or to overthrow a regime. Just five or six good, well-trained men and the right equipment could create havoc. We're trained to do that, you know. Blow a few things up, pick off the right people, and the victory's ours."

"But this couldn't be that simple. I'm counting on our Secretary of State, Alexander Haig's peace negotiation efforts. I just don't want to think of you going there. Northern Ireland was bad enough. This is different. It could be a full-scale land, sea, and air war. I don't know if I can handle this one, and America is not even involved."

"Don't worry. I'll be fine. We have the training and they don't. We can throw them out in a couple of months. You'll see."

"I'd rather not have to see. Please come to breakfast and bring the Sports section or something else."

The day was long and lazy. The grayness outside fueled their need to be close and cozy. They read the newspaper for a while and talked. Jim put his head in Ginny's lap as he stretched out on the sofa, watching sports on television. He was intrigued with American television, especially the commercials. It was a totally relaxing day. They never left the apartment. To top it off, they decided to have a last dinner celebration in the restaurant downstairs which had been a consistent winner.

Ironically, the Sunday night movie on television was *My Fair Lady*. As Professor Higgins gave Eliza Doolittle lessons in proper English, Jim gave Ginny lessons in the most outrageous Cockney. They laughed and loved away their last night together.

D-Day. Departure. The time had to come, and even though they both knew it, they had done a pretty good job of putting it out of their minds. They quietly packed their clothes and emptied out the refrigerator. Ginny saved the seashells she had collected along the shore.

Jim's flight was at 6:30, and they planned to spend most of the day in Miami.

After three months without contact. Margie and Ginny had realized how important their friendship was and had mended fences. Ginny had invited her to have lunch with them on that last day so that Margie could finally meet him.

"I'm going to the car to get my running shoes," Jim said. "They're in the trunk and I need to pack them. I'll take a load of things to the car when I go."

He soon returned with the luggage he had carried out.

"It's not there."

"What's not there?"

"Your car. It's gone."

"You must be kidding! We didn't use it yesterday. Maybe you forgot where we left it."

"No. It's not there. I looked all over the parking lot. You're welcome to look, if you want."

They checked the lot. Sure enough, the car was gone.

"Big problem. We'll have to call the police. Just what we don't need now." Ginny could only imagine the problems that would create. Then it quickly dawned on her that Wayne probably found out where they were and had the car stolen. She told this theory to Jim.

"How could he? Couldn't he leave me alone for once?"

"I have to be careful, Ginny. I haven't told you, but seeing a married woman is not allowed in the British army. I talked to my boss about this, and he knows how much you mean to me. His best advice was to just be careful."

"Now you tell me," she said.

They went to the lobby and Ginny talked quietly to the desk clerk, asking her to call the police. Jim thumbed through the Yellow Pages to find a rental car agency.

The policeman met them in the lobby. He was a pleasant man and agreed when they asked him to go with them to their condo so they could explain the circumstances in privacy.

Ginny began, "My husband and I are negotiating a divorce, and the car is in both of our names. I think he had it stolen."

"That complicates things. If it's in both names, you both have to report it stolen. Why would he do it?"

"Jealousy."

"Oh, I see. And who are you, Sir?" he asked Jim, pulling out a report form. "Where're you from? You sound British."

"Right. I'm Lieutenant James Evans, on leave from the British army. I have a flight back to London from Miami this afternoon, and then I'm scheduled to leave for the Falklands."

"This is sticky. Sounds like the old boy's as crazy as my ex-wife, to have the car stolen. I can sympathize. You have a lot ahead of you. I'll see what I can do. What're you going to do?"

"I guess we'll rent a car and I'll take him to Miami for his flight. I'll check back with you tomorrow. Any suggestions?"

"Well, we can call your husband and tell him the car's been reported stolen and see what he says. We'll try to smoke him out and tell him that you've reported it stolen and that anyone who has it is in danger if they're stopped driving a stolen car. Then if he backs down and admits that he knows where it is, it's problem to work out with your attorney."

"That's awfully nice of you and a great idea. Let's hold off on it for today and get Lieutenant Evans safely on his plane before you do that. I'll come up here tomorrow morning and we can figure it out then, if that's okay."

"Fine. Here's my card. When will you be up?"

"I'll see you around ten, depending on traffic."

"Don't worry. We'll take care of this. There aren't many car thefts here, and it sounds like you might have figured it out pretty well. See you then."

Jim was rightfully annoyed.

"I will get him one day. He's really in for it now. Those were my favorite running shoes in the boot. Now what?"

Ginny was amazed for being so clearheaded and in control of the situation. She was strong enough to not fall apart, and this was one day in her life she had to be strong.

"First I'll call Margie and cancel lunch. We have to be careful in Miami. We might have been tailed. I had no idea. I thought we'd pulled this off so well. I'll call my attorney and see what she suggests. Did you find a rental car?"

"There's a Hertz right down the street. They said call back and they'll pick us up when we're ready."

Margie was disappointed and shocked. Evelyn was aghast and urged Ginny to be very careful where they went. The Hertz driver took them to the rental office and Ginny signed for the car.

"Cheer up," she said, trying to make light of it. "I know a super spot for lunch on the other side of town. We can't let this get us down."

Jim had loaded the trunk of the rental car with their things but insisted on bringing his briefcase into the restaurant with him, in case that car should be stolen too.

"There's some heavy-duty stuff in here. I'd have real security problems if this is stolen. I'll tell you about it over lunch."

Food Among the Flowers was a picturesque restaurant. They were seated at an intimate corner table and ordered a bottle of Chardonnay.

"This briefcase has my Cyprus mission in it. I was going to study it, in case the Falklands thing cleared up, but I never got around to it. See, my cover will be as a colonel commanding a Greek outfit. I was to have an American major serving under me in this operation. We all speak Greek and had been assigned Greek names. One of my men is supposed to be my younger brother. We have several objectives that are targeted. Here's what I mean."

He handed her a list of names with information by each. She wondered if it was a hit list of some kind.

"What the heck is this?" she asked.

"This is the list of my men, and there are some serious problems we have to clear up, wipe out bad elements. It'll probably be more dangerous than the Falklands ever could be, so my alternatives are limited."

Food arrived and they turned their attention to their meal.

"What are you going to do now?" he asked. "Your situation sounds pretty dangerous, too."

"I guess I'm going to take charge!" Ginny laughed. "It's past time, isn't it? If you can face that, I can face this. At least I know the enemy and his capabilities and limitations. I've learned so much from you. How I'll miss you!"

"No. Don't start that. I hate 'hellos' and I hate 'goodbyes' worse. Please just drop me at the airport and don't even look back. It will make it easier for both of us. Promise?"

"I promise. Any way we say goodbye will hurt." She felt the sting of a tear and quickly wiped it away before Jim could notice. They ate in silence.

"There's plenty of time. What do you want to do before I take you to the airport?

"Could you take me to a department store? There are some American cosmetics that I said I would take back to our secretary. Maybe you can help me get what I need. She types all of my reports and I sure want to keep her happy. And I need a haircut."

Wine at lunch blotted out the unpleasantness of the morning, and they went to the Dadeland Mall to find the things he had promised to take back to England.

The haircut was next on the list. The only barbershop Ginny trusted was the old one her son Eric used to go to. She dropped Jim off there and when she picked him up an hour later he was well-shorn, as they used to say.

"Scalped me, he did," Jim quipped in Cockney.

They laughed about it as Ginny drove him to the airport.

"There's one last spot we have to go to," she said.

She turned the car into the parking lot of a restaurant named Aero Squadron. It was a popular place with a World War II French bunker theme that overlooked the runways at Miami International. They ordered gin and tonics and listened to the control tower on the earphones provided at each table. Ginny's sadness was growing, as hard as she tried to suppress it. She had been doing pretty well until now.

*Don't blow it. Be cool. But she knew she couldn't do it.*

"Please be careful," she said as she always did out of anxiety, even though it sounded trite. Of course, he would be careful, but the danger was very real and ever present. It was all around him, wherever he went. Danger was his way of life, he wouldn't have it any other way, she couldn't change him if she wanted to. He was what he was.

*But how can I accept the fact I might lose him … forever?*

In the midst of these dark and frightening thoughts, Jim offered his own advice to Ginny. "You be careful. It sounds like you have some big problems ahead. Is your lawyer tough enough? I think you need a killer attorney."

"I think she is. Time will tell. When will I hear from you again?

"Call me when I get back to London, tomorrow. We'll keep in touch until I leave for Ascension. Then you may not hear from me for a long time, months even, you know."

"Unfortunately, I'm getting used to that by now. I guess it will give me time to straighten things out. I'm sorry this turned out to be the way it is, but I've had to live one day at a time for so long it has become normal. On the other hand, our time together has been so wonderful, hasn't it? For me it has anyway."

"Yes, it's been great for me as well, but there's so much ahead. I have no idea what the future holds. But I can't imagine us completely apart after this time together."

He shook his head. "I don't imagine any more. I just try to live full in each day that comes. Please try to understand my uncertainties."

They stared at their empty glasses and then their eyes met. They knew the time had come, and there was little left to say. She excused herself, went to the women's room, while he paid the check. Ginny closed the door and took a long, deep breath. When she exhaled she remembered the word of a song by Bob Dylan. Of course she had the words wrong, but the ones that came mattered just as much.

*Hang on, kid. You feel like you're dying and you're busy being born.*

They were at the airport in no time and she pulled up in front of the British Airways departure sign at the terminal. They got out of the car to collect his luggage from the trunk. As if rehearsed, they looked into each other's eyes one last time, understanding that the moment had come. He gave her a swift kiss.

"It's been wonderful, Ginny. Thanks for everything, honestly. I'll be at Bicester, so call me tomorrow night. Ciao."

That was it. He was gone.

She turned to the car, the tears starting to flow. But she kept her vow. She didn't look back.

୬୨୦

She drove through the airport traffic in blinding tears, then steered the car toward home. Where else could she go? Pulling into the driveway, she was relieved to see a darkened house, giving her time to consider all of the unthinkable thoughts she'd tried to put out of her mind.

The locks had not been changed, a good sign. Quickly she unloaded the car and put her things in the guest room. The house was hers too, legally, and she had every right to stay here. Changing into jeans, a white shirt, and sandals, she knew it was going to be rough. But then her soldier had it way rougher. Rough to death. Rougher than death. Tougher than life had ever been before, and maybe would ever be again.

The seashells and driftwood clinked together as she put them in a pear-shaped glass container on her desk. She flipped on the pool lights and sat in a chair on the patio in the darkness, sipping a glass of white wine and staring at the starry sky.

Her fantasy was fulfilled. Soon Jim would be on his way across the ocean, then far down under. She considered the harsh reality of her future and wondered what she should do.

The rattle and opening of the front door startled her.

It was Wayne.

*Now what?*

*Calm yourself, hold your ground.*

She felt his fury as he tore out onto the patio.

Wayne erupted

"What're you doing here? You have your nerve. Whose car is that out front? Where is our car?"

"What am I doing here? Well, let's just say I live here. This is my house too, remember? And you know very well where my car is. You had it stolen."

"What do you mean, stolen?"

"Cut the act. I want my car back right now!" Ginny felt herself in that quixotic danger zone between livid rage and trembling panic. Her world was spinning out from under her.

"You can't stay here," Wayne said in his coldest cutthroat voice.

"Oh, yes I can. I'm staying in the guest room. Legally, this place is mine too until we sell it."

"You're a tramp," Wayne shouted. "You're a whore."

Then he closed the gap between them and slapped her face.

This was the first time he'd ever hit her.

Then he suddenly turned away with a sob. "I hope it was worth it."

She held a hand to her stinging face, her eyes full of tears.

Realizing what he'd just done, Wayne stifled a sob, shook his head.

Ginny said softly, "I never meant for our lives to come to this. But you never listened to me. Not ever. I'm no tramp and you know it and I want my car." Wayne looked blankly at her. He shrugged, as if none of this meant anything to him. The sudden emotion that had made him cry out in pain was gone. He looked at her with hard, unforgiving eyes.

Ginny said, "Everything's yours, is that it? You have the new Mercedes. I want my car back tomorrow."

"Go find it then." He grabbed his coat and slammed the door on his way out.

Round one. Ginny was shaking. But she'd held her ground.

She asked herself, *Why can't I just move out and be done with it?*

But she knew the answer.

She was neither financially nor emotionally prepared to move yet. Her sheltered life had left her totally unprepared to survive in the real world, her next leap of faith. Even though life with Wayne was difficult, she also loved this home.

Finally, Ginny went to the guest room, dressed for bed, and turned out the light. There was comfort in darkness. But she tossed and turned, unable to sleep. Once she heard Wayne open and close the refrigerator. She was relieved when he went into the bedroom across the hall. The door finally clicked shut. The stillness was like a nocturnal tide.

In the morning the beeping of Wayne's alarm clock reminded Ginny of where she was. She lay in bed, motionless, wondering what would happen next. She heard Wayne rummaging around in his closet. She knew the drill. He then went out the front door for the morning paper. Soon she smelled coffee brewing in the kitchen.

At last she put on her robe and headed to the kitchen, as if nothing had happened.

"Good morning," she said.

She poured a cup of coffee and glanced at the paper. The headlines were focused on the Falklands, British ships steaming to the south Atlantic.

Wayne was reading the business section. Without looking up he asked, "How can you just sit there?"

"Easily. I live here." Hopefully, her fears were well masked. She buried her head deeper in the front section of the paper and silence reigned until Wayne finished his cereal, paper, and went to the bedroom to get ready for work. Ginny's heart began beating out of sync again.

As he was leaving, she asked him, "When will I get my car? I want it today."

"Who do you think you are? You go off on a despicable honeymoon with your lover, get your car stolen, come back here as if nothing's happened, and now say I've got your car. Find our car, because I don't have it. And it's our car, remember that. It's ours."

He slammed the door as he left.

She dressed and drove through the I-95 morning traffic to the police station. The officer at the front desk was expecting her.

"Well, how did it go? Is your friend off to war?"

"Yes, and I have my own war here. And my husband won't admit to knowing where the car is."

"Didn't think he would, did you? Okay. What's his number? I'll get on the phone."

He dialed the number and asked for Mr Thomas.

"I'm calling from Broward County police. Your wife has filed a report that her car's been stolen. Since you both own it, I have to check with you to see if you know anything about it. Is it stolen?"

Wayne answered that he knew nothing about it.

"Well, since it's been reported stolen, I'm going to put an alert on it. Anyone driving it could be stopped and arrested; there could be real trouble. Someone could get shot, you know. She says you're an attorney and know the laws, but I just want to make sure that you understand the situation. If you have any second thoughts, I'm Officer Bryan, and I'll give you my number here in Broward. That alert will go out immediately, so I'd appreciate your co-operation." He gave the phone number and hung up, then looking at Ginny, he shrugged.

"Now we wait," he said. "Fill out the forms and let's see if he has a change of heart."

She hadn't completed the forms when the phone rang.

"Yes, sir. You say the car's not stolen? How do you know? Do you know where it is? You do?" He nodded to Ginny. "Will it be at the house today? Not possible? Oh, I see. Well, this becomes a matter between you and your wife now. Thanks for calling back. I'd hate to see anyone hurt or killed over this. I'll cancel the alert."

He hung up the phone and turned to Ginny. "Well, you heard it. Now I suggest you either get him to produce the car or have your attorney handle it. We've done all we can do. Good luck."

She thanked him. He'd been very considerate and saved her a world of headaches. She drove home and called Evelyn from her studio to fill her in.

"That bastard!" Evelyn said. "Demand that he return your car to you or we'll go to court and get it. Are you ready to file for divorce?"

Ginny considered it. "Yes. But Jim's off to the Falklands and God only knows what might happen there. I have to get my life in order. I'll work on getting my car back now and you can work on the legal action. Might as well go ahead."

She could only cope with one or two crises at a time.

# 12

# Jim / England
# Ginny / Miami

*Dear Ginny,*

*Thank you for a wonderful time. You can't imagine how much I enjoyed being with you. I've never known such peace and contentment. But now my thoughts must turn to other things. I'm really not that special, Ginny. I'm just a soldier, a cog in a big wheel, one man among many, and I only have a job to do...*

The flight to London was as expected, long and boring. Jim had already seen the movie. Sleep, which usually came easily, was impossible. Two children in front of him squabbled, cried, and ran up and down the aisle for much of the flight, the exasperated mother having long ago given up on controlling her brood.

His thoughts turned to Ginny.

He realized after their time together, that he really was in love with her. There were not only the moments of pure passion, but he considered the possibility of a future with a beautiful and interesting woman, enjoying the peace and contentment he secretly longed for after army life. If, of course he lived to see it. Would he be off to a dangerous job in Cyprus, or suddenly on his way to an unknown assignment in the Falklands? Either was possible and either could be a suicide mission.

Ginny would never understand the gravity of his work, even though he tried to make it very clear to her. These were not war games; it was real, tough, deadly, dirty business. As much as he loved her, he had to protect her by setting her free. It was not fair to leave her suffering over wars that weren't her problem. He also had to put her totally out of his mind if he was to survive. He knew what he had to do, but how to write that letter?

The big surprise came at Heathrow. Not expecting to be met, the sight of Barry Wells waiting at the Customs gate was a shock. It could only mean that the Falklands job was on.

"What's up, Barry? Need I ask?"

"You can probably guess, James. I was asked to meet you and take you directly to Duke of York's. The Old Man's waiting for you. Seems we've been selected for quite a job. You're to attend a special briefing on the operation right away."

They drove straight to Duke of York's Headquarters in Chelsea, home of the Director of the SAS regiments. Without delay, James was ushered into his presence. A big man, a good six feet tall and broad shouldered. His list of military awards was impressive, and he was a true warrior, a serious student of military history who thoroughly understood his profession.

On this day he had reason for concern and was totally keyed into the job at hand.

"Welcome back, Evans. How was America?"

"Not bad, sir."

"Seems we have a big job for you. Let me introduce you to everyone."

Aside from the three members of his team, the group included the key people who were vital to the operation: the Quartermaster, the Communications Officer, and the Operations Officer. James was familiar with the reputations of all the men. They were well prepared for the meeting. The Director brought James up to date, and explained the situation.

"Evans, for the task force to be successful, the carrier based Harriers must be supreme in the air. The Argentines have some pretty useful planes. They're flying Super Entendards, Mirages, and they also have Pucaras to launch a very effective ground attack. The Pucaras are actually based on the

Falklands and could be used to strafe troops. The Mirages and Entendards are based on mainland Argentina. Although they are based in Argentina, they are in fact controlled from a site on the Falklands. The eyes and control of all Argentine aircraft are from one point on the Falklands. That crucial site is a radar installation on the top of Mount Kent, which has been identified by satellite. Evans, that radar site is your first mission."

James could tell that he had his work cut out for him.

The Director continued.

"Unfortunately, the defenses of the radar site are not known, but from what was picked up on satellite, it's estimated there could be up to a full company dug in around the radar site. We have no ideas of their defenses, though we're hoping that the next set of photos will give us a better idea."

"How do I get in? I suppose a HALO drop would be best."

"No. That's been considered but ruled out. Dropping from twenty thousand feet and opening at one thousand is just too risky with winds sometimes in excess of a hundred miles an hour. To gauge a drop zone would be very difficult. So that idea has been discarded. Oh, another little surprise for you.

"You also have to be there in advance of the task force. You and your team will fly from Brize Norton to Ascension by Hercules. From there you're to be connected with the nuclear submarine Conqueror, and will be let out some five miles offshore. You'll go ashore by Gemini, bury your boat, and hike to your target. You're not to come in contact with the Argies until the execution of your task, so you can only move at night.

"Now Evans, how you accomplish the operation will be left entirely to your discretion. It could actually be a standoff attack, using the missiles you'll carry. But this is the way I want it done. You'll want to get right in, use plastics, PE, for total destruction and cause as much havoc as possible. That should have the added effect of spreading panic among the Argentine garrison in the Falklands, when they realize that British troops are somewhere in their midst. Any questions?"

"No Sir. That sounds like the most effective way to handle it."

"Now, if that isn't enough work for you, you're to rejoin the *Conqueror* after you've destroyed your target, and sail down to South Georgia, which by then will have been taken by regular SAS troops and commandos. They should have a package for you to pick up and deliver back to England. You're to take into custody a navy captain, Captain Alberto Gomez, who is in command down there, and bring him back to Ascension by way of submarine. Gomez is a nasty character, wanted for atrocities on mainland Argentina. There are also a couple of other allies that have some questions to ask him, including information on the murder of two French nuns. So it's absolutely urgent that he's brought back alive, with the possibility of standing trial."

The briefing was quite complete and detailed as they got into the nitty-gritty of planning the operation. The Quartermaster ran through a list of state of the art equipment that would be supplied. Using a "spurt" radio, they would transmit a twenty-minute message in four seconds. The message would be transmitted to any designated spot in the world and played back on another machine. The Communications Officer provided communications instructions, including the frequencies that would be used, issued the code name that was needed, and the fixed schedule for transmissions. The Operations Officer went through a map briefing to familiarize James with the planned submarine drop and route to his objective. He had already figured out the compass bearings, which would save James from the time-consuming chore of worrying about that.

The briefing lasted three hours. It was long and tiring, and after a trans-Atlantic flight, Jim was exhausted when it was over.

His four man Sabre Squadron would be made up of Barry, Corporal Geordie MacDonald, and Corporal Neil Lee. Each man was a specialist; Barry, a radioman, Geordie an expert in demolitions, and Neil a marksman, as well as first aid man. A Spanish language speaker was unnecessary on the mission because they were not to come into contact with the Argie forces until the actual execution of their task, and if successful, that would be a brief encounter.

The four men knew each other well, having worked together in Northern Ireland. It was a well-matched patrol and they had high regard for each other's capabilities. That went a long way in inspiring confidence when your life depended on it.

Jim had one week to get his team organized, get the equipment needed, and learn the operation. Later in the week, they would rehearse in the ideal spot, the Welsh Brecon Beacons, near the SAS headquarters at Hereford. Brecon Beacons was a hilly site, inhabited only by sheep, with terrain identical to the Falklands. It was where all SAS selection training takes place, and over the past few years, several potential SAS recruits and a SAS major had died from exposure there. The harsh climate and wildness of the area made it perfect for training for the Falklands. Within twenty-four hours, a mock-up of the Mount Kent radar site had been constructed by Royal Engineers, enabling the team to rehearse at their leisure.

The operation was crucial, risky, and top secret. The soldier in James took over, and Ginny could not be a distraction. She became the least important thing in the world to him. Success and survival were of the utmost importance.

∾ఌఌ

On Wednesday, Ginny picked up the phone and called him. He must have been sitting by the phone, because he answered on the first ring.

"Are you okay? What's going on over there?" she asked.

"War talk. Everyone over here is taking up arms. It isn't just headlines, like in the States. Here it's very real. Argentina can't just walk away with our islands.

"Since my outfit sailed on the *Canberra*, they're trying to figure out how to get me to Ascension. I'm not even sure I'm still going. They may still want to send me to Cyprus. That job was pretty important too. Just depends on where I'm needed most. How are you? What about your car?"

"I was right. He has it. The officer smoked him out and he admitted to knowing where it is. Getting it back is another story. Needless to say, things are pretty rough. I'm back at home. I love this house. It's the only home I've known for so long. I have nowhere else to go. For a while, I set up camp in the guest room. I'm standing my ground until I sort things out and figure out what to do."

"What about your attorney? What does she say?"

"I'm working on it with her. When do you leave?"

"My kit's packed. I could only have a few hours warning. Same old story."

"I miss you. Thoughts of you and our wonderful time together are all that's getting me through the day, you know."

"I've thought of you too, on the way over. But understand this. All I can think about now is what's ahead. That's the only way I can survive. If I don't concentrate on everything my men and I need to stay alive, if we forget one thing, it could cost us our lives. I'm responsible not only for myself, but for each of my men, and that's where my thoughts have to be. Understand that."

"I do. Believe me, I'm trying." She could tell that the training and military mentality had taken over, and knew it had to be that way. Nothing was more important to her than he survive his mission.

"Call me tomorrow, same time. I should be here at least for a day or two."

She put down the phone. That tenuous line and a satellite were once more all that joined them across the sea. Soon even that link would be lost and the ocean would become vaster.

The frustration had begun to grow anew.

Jim sat down and composed a goodbye letter to Ginny. He had no idea what the outcome of his operation would be. The only fair thing he could do was to set her free, encourage her to plan her life without him. The last thing on earth he needed now was to think she was caught up in this. He couldn't think about her. She couldn't be expected to understand that mentality.

Again, he reasoned that as an American, the war in the Falklands was simply not Ginny's problem.

The letter was short and to the point.

*Dear Ginny,*

*I don't know if you'll ever see me or hear from me again. I can't say how this will end. But put me out of your mind, forget about me, and go on with your life. I know that might not be easy, but you must do it. I'm not trying to hurt you. It is for your own good.*

*Again, thanks for a wonderful time. It has been special knowing you. You are someone I'll never forget. Take care.*

*Ciau,*
*Jim*

Ginny moved most of her clothes into the guest room's dresser and closet. She was entrenched for the duration of both wars, on the home front and abroad. She brought in two framed prints from her studio and hung them on a wall. They helped brighten up the room.

If you've lived with someone most of your life, how do you suddenly stop living with them, no matter what the circumstances? Ginny thought about that and thought of Rhoda. She was right; their marriage was like glue. But Ginny had made a small break, just in moving across the hall. If you have shared so much with one person for that many years, the gap can seem impossible to fill. Ginny and Wayne had a choice. They could make a wrenching decision to divorce, or sidestep each other, overlooking the circumstances as best as possible, and see what time would tell.

When Wayne came home, Ginny did not mention the car. Like nothing happened, they went out for dinner, and said little as they ate.

On the way home, she said, "I know you know where my car is. I called the police and they said you have it somewhere. I want it tomorrow. I can't afford this rental car and would hate to have to take you to court. It would be a foolish waste of money and I have a feeling you've spent a fortune already if you had a detective following me. It really wasn't necessary, you know. I told you that I was going away in front of Rhoda and couldn't deny it at this stage of the game. What did you want?"

"I've got more stuff on you than you can imagine. Even photographs. You shall soon see."

Ginny remembered the camera flash that first evening in the condo with Jim.

"Why? Are you taking some sort of sick delight in this? 'See, Judge, see how bad she is?' Well, this game doesn't work for me anymore, and I doubt if it will work for the courts. You should know that. No fault, right? When will you learn?

"Yes, I made the mistake of falling in love with someone else and finally went off with him. I'm truly sorry that hurts you, but I have no regrets. You had treated me badly for so long. Now he's off for the Falklands. What if he gets killed? I would spend the rest of my life living with a fantasy, a phantom, a ghost. Now at least I can accept reality, no matter how good or bad that might be."

"You aren't supposed to fall in love with anyone else. You're mine."

"Yours? A possession? That's the fatal flaw. Just because your Southern ancestors had a slave or two, you think you can own me. Well, that's become pretty damn unrewarding. You've become too self-important, and you're never home, always off to meetings or out of town. And when I made the effort to stand on my own two feet, you fell apart. All I wanted was the same chance you had, to have a career and some control my own future, be able to support myself because everything is yours."

"I gave you everything!"

"You gave me nothing. I worked hard raising Eric, managing our home, making it as nice as it is. At least I would get paid for my effort if I had a job. And I want my car! Keep your expensive Mercedes. But no court in America would let you have both cars, even if I walked down Biscayne Boulevard naked."

"You'll get your car when I'm good and ready. Sweat it out some more."

"Creep!" she said, slammed the car door and went into the house.

At least she had finally vented her anger.

Jim sounded more somber than ever when Ginny called him the next day. He was worn out from the day and night briefings and skull sessions, with intensive physical training thrown in to keep the team in peak condition.

"I'm leaving tomorrow. They're flying me to Ascension and I'll catch up with my group there. Looks like Cyprus is on hold for a while."

"Please be careful. What can I say?" Her throat tightened. No matter what she thought, she couldn't let him know how scared she was but sensed the fear showed in her voice.

"Try not to worry. You can't spend your life worrying about me. This could be long and bloody. I just don't know. And you won't hear from me for a long time. All of my concentration is on this, and has to be on this. I've told you that."

"I know. I'll just get real busy. There's a lot I've got to figure out anyway, to get my life straightened out. Maybe I'll be squared away at least to some degree, by the time you get back."

"I hope so. I leave tomorrow night. Call me at 11:00 PM, your time, and say goodbye, okay?"

"Okay. Bye."

Ginny had a sinking feeling like the world was caving in under her, inch by inch. Yet if she had learned to cope with her concerns over Northern Ireland, she could learn to cope with this. At least in the Falklands they could identify the enemy.

It was shaping up as a proper war, men in uniforms, speaking different languages. The British troops had the upper hand, all of the training for this, and would probably relish the opportunity to give it a try in a real combat. It was very different mindset to deal with, but she'd have to live with it.

The farewell conversation was brief.

"I'm packed and ready to go. We're leaving a little earlier than planned, so I'm glad you called on time."

"How will you get to Ascension?"

"By *Hercules*, a big military transport. It takes off from a Royal Air Force base near here, Brize Norton. They're running a lot of full flights down there. I guess it beats a long ship ride. I could've used a bit more sun though. I still have my suntan lotion. Piña Colada, was it?"

"Right. This is so final." What could she say? How do you send a man off to war? It was something she never expected, and had never aspired to do. But here she was, trying to think of the appropriate way to say goodbye to someone she loved, whose face she might never see, and whose voice she may never hear again. Words just wouldn't come.

The photos and television clips of British girlfriends, wives, and children waving their men off flashed through her mind. She couldn't picture herself in that scene at all, and understood why Jim had never married. He couldn't handle it either. You lose your concentration if you're thinking of the little lady back home wringing her hands over you. Soldiers end up dead that way.

*Stiff upper lip*, she thought, realizing she was thinking with a bit of British. "Well, I know that you won't end up a dead hero. You promised me that long ago, on the day we met. I guess all I can say is, 'Take care. ' Will I hear from you at all? Or when? Any idea? In the awful event that anything happened to you, would I even know?"

"Yes, I've asked a friend to let you know, but don't think about it, and don't look for letters. That would be the last thing on my mind. I've written to you, by the way. You probably won't like what I've said but read it carefully and know that I meant it. Please try to understand how I feel. I've got to go now. My transport to the air force base is leaving in half an hour. So you take care too, Ginny."

"Until then. Whenever. I love you, Jim. 'Bye!"

"Don't. It's too dangerous. Forget me. Ciao."

Ginny hung up the phone and all of the held-back tears engulfed her. The day was gray. The only thing that brought her in touch with reality was the reminder she still had to battle to get her car.

If Jim could be strong, she could be, too.

By Sunday, even Wayne could see that she was tortured enough on all fronts. After breakfast and the morning paper, he announced they would pick up her car. They drove to the Fort Lauderdale airport. He searched the expansive parking lot to locate the pre-arranged marker, and her car was waiting in the expected spot. Ginny was smart enough to not even question the circumstances. She was just glad to have her wheels returned.

Jim's letter arrived in the middle of the next week. He was right; confused and hurt, she neither liked nor understood it. She only wondered if she had failed or bored him. As usual, her insecurity reigned supreme. She had no idea that he had been assigned the most dangerous mission imaginable, and there was no way she could comprehend the risks involved.

Ginny looked at the seashells and driftwood in the glass jar on her desk, and realized that the ocean was not only wide, but long, and becoming very stormy.

# 13
# Jim / Falkland Islands

April 19th was the day of their departure for Ascension and by then they were all well prepared. The four men were in good spirits and quite confident.

They were taken with their equipment for their flight to Brize Norton in an unmarked van. Each man would be carrying almost one hundred and fifty pounds of gear, including four missiles. Their packs contained all special equipment they would need: radio, explosives, silenced Uzi machine guns, loaded pistols, black uniforms, food, and water.

It was a thirteen-hour flight to Ascension Island, with a stopover in Dakar for refueling, where no one was allowed off the plane and no one was allowed on.

Although the flight was uneventful, the time was well spent. The team went over what was going to happen, carrying on with the planning so that everything would go just as rehearsed. They continually checked their weapons. Jim always told his men that a soldier treats his weapon like a woman: he strips it down, oils it, and puts it back together again.

He was getting keyed up with anticipation. It was an assignment that a true soldier relished and at the same time feared. Their flight arrived at Ascension on the 20th. After a quick breakfast, the team was transported by a Wessex helicopter to the submarine which was lying up on the surface some twenty miles south of Ascension. Being put to sea by submarine added a nice twist.

A new captain on his first command of the nuclear-powered *HMS Conqueror* was at the helm, a reserved man to his crew, but with wisdom hiding underneath his reticence. The submarine had a crew of one hundred and three. When they left their home base at Faslane in Scotland, a surgeon also joined them, an unlikely member of a sub crew.

Jim and his team were taken aboard. Once everything was set and ready, the *Conqueror* steamed along at about thirty-five knots. It took nearly five days to make it to their destination, some five miles off of the southern coast of East Falkland.

A confirmation message of the retaking of South Georgia was transmitted to the sub. Just after 2000 hours on the 25th of April, the submarine surfaced in the inky blackness of the sea and the men unloaded their gear through the forward hatch, arriving well before the British task force.

"This is as far as we go, Evans. Good luck. See you in a few days," the skipper said.

"Thank you, Sir," He had every intention of making the rendezvous. If not, he would have to wait for the task force invasion, an unhappy prospect. They loaded their gear into the inflated Gemini boat and started the 40 horsepower engine.

The engine struggled on through the rough waters, waves pouring over the sides and into the small inflatable boat. Limited visibility did not help the problems of their wild ride, and with adrenaline flowing, the men hung on for dear life. When they finally touched the mainland, they were slightly relieved. They deflated their boat, dug a hole and camouflaged it under kelp, and carefully noted the site. Hopefully they would be back on time.

The move from the beach to Mount Kent was worse than expected. Their plan allowed two days to complete their fifteen-mile hike to a point about a half-mile from it, but it was pitch black and impossible to wear their night vision goggles all the time.

The terrain was peaty and with many rock outcrops, more so than on the rugged hills of the Brecon Beacons. They trudged on with their heavy kit, getting a feel of the land and gauging their time, their combat boots sinking in the mud. With a thud and a muffled grunt, Neil hit the ground, grabbing his shoulder.

Jim was the first to reach him. The heavy weight of his kit made it difficult to upright him.

"Good God, Neil! Are you okay?"

He eased the pack off of his back.

"It's my shoulder," he winced in pain. "I landed on my pistol and it hurts like hell!" He tried to move his shoulder but couldn't. "I think it's dislocated."

Jim carefully removed the shoulder holster and pistol. Obviously the impact of the pistol compounded by the heavy weight of the kit had caused an injury that would make it very painful for the first aid man.

"You're the medic and your diagnosis seems damn right. We've got to move along though. Think you're ready?"

"Sorry, Sir. I'm okay. Let's go."

The weather was far worse than expected. Their biggest fear was the possibility there might be snow on the ground, leaving tracks of their movement. They were in luck; although there was snow, it was very light and not sticking. Still, the weather conditions were miserable, with temperatures somewhere around 12-15 degrees below zero. The wind, sleet, and wet snow pounded against the men, making travel slow and difficult. Their heavy loads sunk them deep into the sloppy peat as they struggled up and down the hills, some as high as 800 meters.

Using a compass, they covered about six miles the first night, living with constant fear of running into a minefield. The men prodded several suspicious spots with knives, but fortunately the Argies weren't really capable of sowing a consistently effective minefield.

As daylight approached, the men found a suitable hide location. During the day, they spent their time lying motionless in their carefully concealed positions in the tussock grass and peat. There were no conversations between the men; once they hid, they were silent. They took turns sleeping, though sleep did not come easily. Freezing and wet, they ate cold food and drank the water they had with them. The only fortunate fact was that daylight hours were short.

They traveled only at night, pushing against the wind and sleet up and down slopes. They needed the full two nights they had estimated to cover the fifteen miles. Neil held up well, but the heavy load, was almost more than he could take.

By dawn, they arrived at a point a half-mile southwest of Mount Kent.

From that point, they could get a good look at Argie activities. Radio confirmation of their location was made and they dug in, ready to wait, watch, and plan how to take out the radar site.

The lax Argentine defense of such an important site was the first surprise. Although well dug in with their position on top of a hill they should have been impregnable. But they were poorly organized and their gun positions were not interlocking and one pit couldn't see the next one. Judging that the men casually moved around the installation, it seemed that there were no minefields out to protect them. They could have used claymores or projectile area defense.

Trip flares were out, but not well and the British patrol could breach the perimeter unseen by the Argentine force.

The troops guarding the site were also inexperienced conscripts. Their officers were safely in Port Stanley some eight miles away.

The Argentines had little training. Morale seemed bad. Frequently the Brits heard emotional flare-ups. Some of the enemy looked like young draftees, yanked into service and given a rifle. They were obviously poorly led by their NCOs, and had formed very low caliber troops.

It was decided that surprise would be the biggest determining factor. The Argies had no idea that the British had been able to put men ashore. It could well become quite a shock to inexperienced soldiers who felt set and safe on a mountaintop they thought they controlled.

The Sabre Squadron led by Jim thus had the advantage. Their enemy did not know where they came from or how they had gotten there.

On top of this, the Brits had vision goggles that gave them an extra advantage, since the Argies had no night aids at all.

The plan was thus to actually get in, plant explosives, use short fuse detonators, and in the ensuing chaos that followed, get out quickly.

"Here's how we'll take out the radar site," Jim explained. "We'll go in from the southwest, and establish a rendezvous about one kilometer from the site, where all unnecessary gear, bergans, and radios, will be left. Everything we've got will be stripped to a minimum. We'll carry our personal weapons, double magazines taped together for the 9 mm Uzis, grenades, and the plastic explosives.

"The plan's academic," he said. He then made a sketch dividing the site into a circle on a principle of a clock, from 1200 to 0400, 0400 to 0800, and from 0800 to 1200 again. Each man was assigned an area equating to a third of the clock face. "It should be just a matter of going around from the inside and spraying them with bullets. The thing we have to be careful of is to not shoot where our own men are, and we've identified those locations."

Luck was again on their side. It was a moonless, pitch-black night. When Jim finalized the plan and they readied their equipment. Each man knew where the others were and what their jobs were. Now their adrenaline started pumping like crazy. *Adrenaline's brown*! Jim thought.

Each in position, they formed a well-oiled machine, doing something they had trained to do a hundred times. Wearing their black suits and blending into the darkness, they were able to slip into Argie territory with no difficulty. Geordie got right up to the radar installation before any form of alarm was raised. From then on, it was left to Jim and the other two to keep the Argentines occupied while he placed his short fuse charges.

When the shooting started, the Argies went into panic mode. The Brits opened with each man throwing five grenades. There was no euphoria as the bullets thudded in the darkness. Moving on and firing at the next target as quickly as possible, each man fired ten pairs of magazines of ammunition, random shooting their un-aimed shots, and firing in short bursts. The noise and chaos grew boggling, as they continued moving, firing, and causing as much mayhem as they could.

The fact that Jim and his men were inside the perimeter caused added confusion for the Argies. They quickly found their arcs of fire were directed at their own men, firing inward. Since Jim's patrol knew where each of his men were stationed, they did not face that danger.

Once the short fuses started detonating, the heart immediately went out of the Argentine opposition, who all began to flee Mount Kent. As planned, the Brits finished their job and got out of there. Argentina had started this war and their soldiers paid the price.

Unopposed, the patrol's escape from Mount Kent back to the rendezvous was easy. They caught their breath, sat tight and slept through the day while Evans tried to figure out their next move. As expected, the alarm had been raised in Port Stanley and the hunt began. Some Argentine Special Forces were known to be on the island, and it wouldn't be long before they were on to them. Then there was also the fear of helicopter sightings or strafing by Pucaras, ground attack aircraft.

However, the Brits stuck to their plan of moving only at night. To be safe, Jim determined it would be better to cover as much ground as they could, as fast as possible, and make it back to their Gemini in the next night.

When darkness fell, they ditched most of their equipment, keeping only the necessities, and went hell bent for leather. Covering twelve to fifteen miles in one night might not sound like a difficult task, but it was complicated by having to make their way up and down hills, at times sinking up to their armpits in the soft peat. The weather remained abominable, maintaining a minus fifteen-degree temperature, with sleet and gusting winds. The only bright note was that the snow would not leave tracks.

The conditions made life unbearable, and the four men had to call upon reserves of stamina to meet their deadline. Taking another route, they made it in record time, arriving at 0500. Exhausted, they got into a hide near the beach to wait out the thirty-six hours before re-inflating the *Gemini* and moving out to rendezvous with the submarine.

The shore was a logical source of escape, and it was well covered. Argie helicopters, as well as Pucaras flew overhead. Ground troops came within twenty yards of them, but they were masters of concealment, and well- established underground. One of the arts they learned very quickly was to burrow like rabbits, which was exactly what they did, getting themselves underground and covering themselves with kelp. Kelp stinks, but it's very useful for concealment. The hide was not the ideal for comfort, but perfect for this situation.

Barry established radio confirmation that they were on the beach. Unable to light fires, they continued on with cold food.

At the end of the thirty-six hours, they were very tired, very cold, very hungry, and very cramped, but they were all still alive, and the success of the mission was worth the agony.

In the darkness of the morning on the 2nd of May, they dug up the *Gemini* and re-inflated it, glad to be pushing off for their rendezvous with *Conqueror*.

Rough south Atlantic seas and torrential rain again awaited them. At first the engine was reluctant to start, but after several tries, they were on the water, bucking waves and on their way.

The journey to the sub was a nightmare. Foul weather. Visibility poor at best. Angry waves lapped over the sides, sweeping away most of their kit, including the radio. It was 0700 and fortunately they had been in the water for only about an hour, bobbing frantically like a cork, when the submarine finally emerged.

It was a welcomed sight, like a great whale, coming out of the water. On deck, Jim punctured the *Gemini* and let it vanish into the ocean.

Inside the submarine, the men were greeted with welcome cups of tea laced with rum and a traditional English breakfast with bacon and sausage. The Captain did not waste any time ordering an immediate dive, and *Conqueror* slipped quickly and silently back beneath the churning sea.

The submarine had been underway for about an hour and a half when klaxons and calls to the action stations sounded. Jim as well as his platoon were startled, not knowing what to expect or how to respond.

The Skipper didn't keep them in suspense for long. He sent an aide down to inform them that a large Argentine warship was in close proximity, and they feared they would be picked up by sonar. He prepared battle stations, with the aim of torpedoing the warship.

The Petty Officer whose duties included ship identification, used copies from *Janes' Fighting Ships*. He'd had the base photographer enlarge them before *Conqueror* left Scotland, and identified the warship and her escorts.

It was the 10,650-ton cruiser *General Belgrano*, accompanied by two destroyers, *Piedra Buena* and *Hipolito Bouchard*. The ships were not only barring the exit of *Conqueror* from the Falklands, but also posed a potential threat to the remainder of the task force.

The directive to sink the *Belgrano* needed approval from London. Permission granted, Jim and his men sat back and watched another well-oiled, well-drilled team perform their duties, carrying out the order to torpedo the ship.

*Conqueror* attacked at 1500, firing six conventional MK 8 torpedoes at the ship from two thousand yards. She then plunged deep to make her escape. The crew heard two heavy explosions as the torpedoes struck the Belgrano, wiping out the ship's power and communication system.

The rest is history, and 368 men, mostly young sailors, perished. Argentina started the war and their sailors paid with their lives for it.

For two terrifying hours, *Conqueror* was pursued by the destroyers that had been accompanying the *Belgrano*. They deserted the sinking ship and drowning men to hunt the sub with sonar and Hedghog depth chargers.

*Conqueror* escaped, however, preventing a great loss to the task force. If the *General Belgrano* had let go of its depth chargers, it could have resulted in the loss of *Conqueror*, its complete crew, and sixteen Polaris missiles.

Jim and his team were given more than they ever bargained for. He assured his men that it was the worst experience he'd ever had in a sub. The crew of the submarine was welcome to their polar lives, ranging from total boredom to sheer terror.

*Conqueror* steamed on to South Georgia for its rendezvous with the *HMS Antrim*, and to pick up *The Man*, Captain Alberto Gomez. The journey took less than twenty hours, and Evans had time to read up on Gomez, the prisoner who was being handled with such care.

In reviewing his dossier, Jim wondered why they didn't just put the man through the torpedo tubes and make the world a better place, but not even the SAS operated like that.

Jim had studied the dossier before he'd departed from England. The notorious Gomez had earned his reputation as "Captain Death" for the role he played in the 1976-1977 Dirty War, the Argentine Junta waged against internal opponents. These were supposed terrorists who reacted against the decadent Peron government. After the military coup, the new government they established set about to eradicate that element. More than 18,000 Argentines and other suspected dissidents vanished into the night, never to be heard from again. The disappearances were denied or dismissed by the government as political necessities.

The atrocities personally charged to Gomez that were brought before Amnesty International and the Argentine commission on human rights, based in Madrid, included kidnapping, torture, and murder. Not only was he responsible for the disappearance of untold numbers of Argentines, but governments of other allies of Britain were seeking information from Gomez about the disappearance of their citizens in Argentina. The French and the Swedish government believed that he had shot a fifteen-year old girl from Sweden in the back as she tried to escape.

More recently, Gomez had arrived at Grytviken, South Georgia, on March 26th, commanding marines, faces blackened, in camouflage uniforms, and armed with rifles and grenades. They immediately set about to capture the island. The Junta had assigned Gomez that job with the idea of upgrading his reputation on the mainland to that of a hero, after Argentina emerged victorious.

Instead, he formally surrendered control of Grytviken on April 25th, and was held in custody until the arrival of *Conqueror*. Gomez was turned over to Jim, who found him incredibly arrogant, and proud of his achievements. He became increasingly reticent on the return journey, though, when it was made very clear to he would be standing trial for multiple murders.

*Conqueror* steamed directly back to Ascension with its prisoner of war, arriving on the 8th of May. The sub was being replaced on station by another nuclear sub. On the 9th, Jim's patrol and their prisoner boarded a *Hercules* for the return flight to England. The Director was in the welcoming party, and he greeted Jim as Gomez was taken away.

"Congratulations and a job well done, Evans. Pleased to see you made it back in one piece."

"Thank you, Sir. Bloody well knackered though. It was quite a job."

"You'll get to tell me all about it in the debriefing. I'm afraid you won't get much of a rest. We're sending you right out on the Cyprus job on the 16th. In fact, we were training another team, just in case anything happened to you. Not very comforting, I suppose. But you're the best for the job, and I expect you to be up for it."

"No problem, Sir. I just need some sleep and decent food. I'll organize my kit and be ready. I'd hate to miss out on this assignment!"

"Splendid. Now tell me about Mount Kent."

On the drive back to Duke of York's, Jim gave the Director detailed information about the Argentine forces he had encountered in the Falklands. In the back of his mind he was thinking about the assignment ahead, which was beginning to make the Falklands look like a picnic.

# 14
# Miami / England / Miami

Time heals.

Ginny's life was in order and she was determined to put thoughts of Jim out of her mind forever. The house she loved so much was sold, the assets split. She now owned a nice condo with a pool view. For the first time in her life, Ginny felt secure and enjoyed being on her own.

It had taken months for the museum to be ready for an opening. As the big day approached, though, the excitement grew and she was engrossed in her work more than ever. The complexities of planning a new institution were absorbing, and her mind had to deal a lot with decision-making. Her job was taking so much effort that she had little time to think of anything else. An occasional movie, or drinks and dinner out with her friends offered all the diversions she needed.

One weary night, she carried a dinner plate to her sofa, set it on the coffee table, and flipped on the television evening news. The phone rang.

"Ginny? Can you stand the surprise?" asked the familiar voice.

She had been able to keep her same phone number, but never expected this call. She looked at the phone in wonder, unsure how to respond. Could she take any more heartache?

"Jim. Not sure. Where are you this time, and whatever could you want?"

"I'm in England. It's quite late here, but I wanted to talk to you. I told them today that I've decided to resign my commission from the army at the end of this tour. That means I'll be out of the army by April 1st, 1985."

"April Fool! What perfect timing. Can I believe that?"

"Yes, you can. I've had enough of the army and they've had about enough of me. I mean it. I'm Captain Evans now, by the way."

"Well, congratulations, Captain Evans. Glad you're finally ready to join the real world though. Any idea of what you want to do?"

"Not a clue. That won't be easy. I'm going to be in England for several months training before my next assignment. Unfortunately, I have a job back in the Falklands for six months. I'll be directing an engineer regiment that is rebuilding the island. Can you call me tomorrow? They're going to hot box me, to get me to change my mind. I'd like to talk to you after that meeting."

"I'm not sure why I should go along with this, but okay. I'll give you a call. Give me your number."

As she hung up, she wondered why, after so long, had he called, and particularly with an announcement that was so important to him? The truly strange thing was that he wanted her to know if he stuck with his decision.

Here we go. Another roller coaster ride.

She ate her dinner in silence, studying her mixed emotions and the seashell reminders in the glass container.

What did he want from her? Why did he think he could just walk back into her life without an explanation or an apology? And why would she ever let him?

Curious as always, unable to resist, she called him the next day.

Jim was excited. "I told them no! They made some attractive offers, but I still said no."

"Good for you," Ginny said, but was not sure what the decision should mean to her.

"I'm going to write tonight. There's a lot to tell. I have a house now in the Lake District, a very old cottage. I'm starting to fix it up. The house in London that my father left to me isn't rented now, and I'm using it some on weekends. I've been seeing some theater. Have you seen the play, *Cats*? It's great."

"Yes. I get to New York some with my job, consulting with museum display designers. I saw it on my last trip and loved it."

Her favorite song now was *Memory* from *Cats*. The haunting words lingered in her mind, reminding her of Jim, their time together in the Highlands, and their aborted meeting in London. She sometimes feared herself becoming a tattered Grizabella, singing, "I remember the time I knew what happiness was."

Was she detecting a nesting syndrome in Jim? He was even enjoying London. It sounded like he might really be through with army life.

"When I write, I'll send a picture of my cottage and of me. Will you send a picture?"

"Yes. I'll have to get one taken." She glanced in the mirror and saw how tired she looked. Despite the fact she found her job fascinating, the strain of final planning and construction were draining.

There were more phone calls than letters. Jim called from London or his cottage. Some of his time was spent in Brecon Beacons, training his men in an environment similar to the Falklands.

Ginny put all of the hurt out of her mind and simply went along with the flow. She was not sure why, but she was happy to hear from him again. She savored memories of the good times, and forgot the bad. She would always love him, she knew that, but had to keep it in perspective.

England and Jim had a good summer, and his calls were upbeat for a change.

"I've had two weeks off, one in London, one in the Lake District, working on my cottage. I've sent a picture of the cottage, not as grand as some of the homes in Florida, but it's quiet, comfortable, easy to maintain, and I like it."

"I hear that the Lake District is beautiful."

"Did I mention that the weather here is superb? I can't understand what's gone wrong. We haven't had any rain for nearly a month, and I've got my tan back, though I haven't got any of my favorite suntan lotion left. Remember that? Piña Colada, is it? At any rate, it's perfect weather for my favorite sports every day, a few games of tennis, squash, cricket.

"I might as well enjoy myself. I'm scheduled to leave for the Falklands in mid-October. Imagine, last Christmas in the steamy jungle of Belize, this one in the isolation of the Falklands."

That was a line of conversation Ginny had no desire to pursue.

He could sense her feelings, and wisely changed the subject.

"My discharge file is getting thicker, as I weigh up all of the options of what to do when I retire. I've even been approached to go into politics. They must be mad.

"I'm having a resume done for me by a specialist company in London, although it's not proving easy for them. How do you put in a CV that you're nothing more than a trained killer? I suppose I could get a job as a hit man for the Mafia."

"Perhaps you're due a career change," Ginny suggested.

"Seriously, Ginny, you've got to understand I joke about my job. Helps to keep my sanity. When I'm ordered by the army on an assignment, it's to keep someone from doing something worse, something with graver and much more serious consequences. The world is a very dangerous place."

"You've shown me that. I understand and respect what you do. Also, I see how difficult it is for you, doing some things you're assigned to do. I know how brave you are. I'm really very perceptive. But it's good that you want out. You deserve a life."

The photographs arrived the next day. There was one of his new car, a sporty silver Toyota Celica, in front of the nondescript and cheerless brick Officers Mess that served as his home base. In the second photo, he was looking up from the morning paper, surprised. Ginny wondered who caught him so off guard.

She looked at the picture of the cottage, which qualified as quaint. It was two-storied, white, with a thatched roof, and two chimneys. There were rose bushes blooming in front and a neat pile of wood stacked alongside.

Who got to chop the wood? she wondered.

He was right; it was not as grand as a Florida home but had a charm all its own.

She had heard that the Lake District was not only beautiful but also tranquil. She couldn't help wondering if she could be happy living in a place like that, but realized she would probably never get a chance to know. Even though she had noticed a distinct change in Jim, she knew better than to ever think of it impacting her life.

Her office was the final target of the construction crew by the end of September. She decided to avoid the dirt and noise and work at home for a while. Jim had been in the Brecon Beacons for two weeks of intensive training with his men, and was due back in the Officers Mess. It was only two weeks before his six-month tour in the Falklands began.

The more she thought about the Falklands and Jim, the more depressed she got. The very name Falklands saddened her.

She sat at her desk and tried to concentrate on her work. The glass jar filled with seashells glistened with returning thoughts of Jim.

She put aside her work and called Air Florida, to check the cost of a round trip ticket to London. When the ticket agent asked if she wanted to make a reservation, something in her snapped.

"Yes," she said. "I'll depart on Thursday, October 6th, return on the 13th."

Ginny was shaking when she hung up the phone, her reservation confirmed. All she had to do was pick up her ticket.

But what would Jim say? What if he didn't want to see her?

*So what? I'll just enjoy London.*

This time, no one else would be affected by her decision.

There was no problem with missing work. It would take at least that week or more to finish her office, and much longer than that before the display areas were ready for artifacts and labels.

It was a perfect time to be away before she got swamped by preparation for the grand opening. She went to the travel agent and charged her ticket before she could change her mind.

❦

In late September, Sean O'Hara was sighted again. The word had been passed along by a most reliable source and was checked out.

O'Hara seemed to be living in Worthing, a coastal town just west of seaside Brighton. That curious fact seemed confusing at first. Why there? A valuable talented terrorist like O'Hara would not be sitting idle in Worthing on holiday. He was too dedicated to his cause to take holidays.

O'Hara had been put under discreet surveillance throughout the month of September. He was holed up with a girl in council estate housing, number 9 Willow Gardens. A check on the girl proved nothing. She didn't have a family. She was an orphan and drifter, only guilty of a poor choice for a partner, a bad decision that could cost her life, being part of a cover for O'Hara.

The couple seldom went out together. O'Hara seemed to be biding his time or waiting for some undetermined event. The girl handled their errands and marketing. O'Hara rarely left the flat but made several trips to Brighton. Most often he headed immediately to the Convention Center, where he mingled among the members of the various groups holding meetings in the facility.

With increased alarm, authorities came up with the answer. The Labour Party was scheduled to hold its annual meeting at the Brighton Convention Center from October 7th to the 9th.

Was O'Hara actually going for the leadership of the Labour Party? A successful assassination attempt would throw the British government in a crisis of unbelievable proportions. This time he had to be stopped at all costs.

Surveillance was intensified with the addition of listening devices. Number 10 Willow Gardens was fortunately unoccupied at the moment and an SAS team was able to slip in unnoticed during the night of Sunday, October 2nd. They set up their electronic bugs on the wall that separated the two flats and round the clock teams listened and waited.

Suspicions were quickly confirmed. The team got all of the necessary information from phone calls O'Hara made when the girl was out. He talked frequently to his contacts and carefully went over his detailed scheme, with no idea that his conversations were bugged.

It would be no problem for O'Hara to join the conventioneers at the Saturday night event. Meticulously disguised with his hair neatly trimmed and streaked gray, O'Hara was scheduled to open fire on the head table as the leader of the Labour Party stepped to the rostrum to welcome honored guests. In the chaos that followed, he would make his well-planned escape. He knew the Convention Center thoroughly, had mapped every escape route. He had even walked through it numerous times, all of it almost too easy.

The threat was so serious that it was immediately taken to Prime Minister Margaret Thatcher. An emergency meeting was hastily called at 10 Downing Street to deal with the problem.

On that dreary October morning, the somber participants were admitted quickly one by one. All had been briefed on the urgency of the situation and quick action was necessary. The convention was just days away. The heads of government, Police, and Special Branch were quick to make their position quite clear. They were not ready to deal with O'Hara. Their general consensus was fear of reprisals if he were lifted and then put on trial. The gunman had to be disposed of as quickly and unobtrusively as possible.

It was a well-known fact that O'Hara had long been a special project of the SAS. The eyes of the Prime Minister and all present turned to the Director of the SAS. It was the kind of job made for his well-trained specialists. Without hesitation, the Director spoke up. "Yes, Prime Minister, leave it to us."

The threat of O'Hara succeeding in his goal was such that there was no question the man had to be swiftly terminated.

The Director determined that the only man for the job was James Evans. No one was better qualified or more eager to blow O'Hara off of the face of the earth.

❧❧

He was elated about the exercise his boys had just completed in the Brecon Beacons. They had all worked hard and were ready for their Falklands tour.

He got the weekend to himself.

Ginny's call was a surprise.

"Jim, you're back! I was hoping I would catch you. Have you any plans for this weekend?"

"Not really. I was considering treating myself to a trip to Paris for a last fling before the isolation of the Falklands, but hadn't really made a decision yet."

"Would you like some company?"

"Company? What do you mean?"

"Well, I'm sitting here looking at an Air Florida ticket from Miami to Gatwick, departing Miami on Thursday night, October 6, arriving at 9:30 on Friday morning, the 7th."

"You're kidding. That would be fine. When did you decide to do that?"

"Today. It's one of the most impulsive things I've ever done. The dirt and noise from the construction where I work is really getting to me. My office is being completed and I'm working at home anyway, so I won't be missed. And honestly, I couldn't bear the thought of not seeing you again before you dropped off the end the ocean for another six months."

"That's a great idea. But we can just have the weekend. I absolutely have to be back here on Sunday to get my men ready for the Falklands."

"Fine. You know I can amuse myself in London. I'm looking forward to it. I have a few friends there that I can look up, and some things I need to see in the British Museum of Mankind. Since you called me again, I just know I'll be miserable for six months if I don't see you."

"Glad to hear that. I'll pick you up at Gatwick on Friday morning."

It had been almost ten months since they had been together, and her sudden announcement that she was flying to England the next evening perfectly fit into his mood at the moment.

He had just put down the phone when someone called his name.

"Captain Evans? Are you Captain James Evans?"

"Yes. Why?"

"I'm Corporal Moore. I've been sent to take you to London, Sir. The Director has some urgent business he needs to discuss with you."

It was 20:00. The situation had to be crucial to be called in by the Director himself at this hour. The drive to London would take another hour or more. James gathered his briefcase and said, "Let's go, Corporal."

He tried to rest on the ride to London. Whatever the situation was, the meeting wouldn't be brief, and James was too keyed up to sleep in the car. Arriving at the Duke of York's Barracks, he was ushered into the Director's study immediately.

"A dire situation has arisen that's right up your alley, Evans. Sit down. Let's talk about a friend of yours, Sean O'Hara."

"O'Hara? That rotten bugger."

"Fine. That's just the response I wanted. You're about to get your chance to take him. Got to keep him from making big trouble. But there's more. He has a girl with him. I'm afraid you'll have to take them both out. We checked her out. Not much turned up. She's a bit of a drifter, no family, no job. Seems to be someone he picked up, probably for a cover. We can't have anyone left around to tell what happened. Too bad, but necessary. Of course, you understand."

He was briefed on the gravity of the situation as a national security threat, and what they knew about O'Hara and the girl's activities.

"You have to get O'Hara before he gets to the Labour Party leaders. All facilities will be available to you. The date, time, and method will be left to your discretion. The bodies must be disposed of so there is no chance they could ever be recovered. O'Hara and the girl are to simply disappear. Make your arrangements. You're going to Brighton immediately."

Then Evans dropped the bombshell. "I've got my friend coming over from America on Friday morning. I'll try to cancel, but if I can't, I know I can handle that as well. I'd like to take care of it Saturday morning. Among other things, we'll need a boat, body bags, and concrete. We'll send both Sean O'Hara and friend to an appropriate watery grave."

"Well said. Anything you need is yours. The full authority of this office is behind you. Good luck."

Ginny could prove a big problem, but he didn't want to alarm the Director. He made several phone calls to tell her something had come up and he had to cancel their meeting.

Her phone rang endlessly. He would have settled to leave a message on her machine, but she hadn't turned it on. Not knowing her work number, there was no way to contact her. With the gravity of the situation, he would just have to figure out a way to leave her alone and get the job done.

There would be no tail at Gatwick, like they must have had from Miami International Airport. A tail could blow the whole operation. Jim arranged for a full surveillance team to cover Ginny's arrival. Even though she was divorced, he didn't dare take a chance. Anyone showing even the slightest interest would be swiftly and discreetly led away to the Special Branch office.

Likewise, the route down to Brighton was well covered. An army Lynx helicopter flew top cover and six high-speed cars sat at strategic points along the route. The message was quite clear. He was to meet Ginny unhampered, and get to Brighton without an incident.

Arrangements set, James briefed the participants. Chances of all chances, it turned out, a couple with family in London occupied Number 8 Willow Gardens, right next to Number 9. They frequently went to London to visit family for the weekend. Someone from Special Branch would drop by and explain there was an urgent matter of police business.

The cover was a plan to take the spies living next door into custody. The police needed their full cooperation, including access to their flat. In the interest of National Security, the couple was never to mention this to anyone. Well reimbursed for their trouble, they would leave for London after work on Friday.

By Friday evening, SAS units were ready in both 8 and 10 Willow

Gardens. All arrangements completed, Jim spent Thursday night in London, ready to meet Ginny 's flight.

He knew he had to tell her there was a problem as soon as they could talk. O'Hara was top priority, and without a question the most important thing on his mind.

❧❧

Ginny's eyes opened to the mauve orange of sunrise as the Air Florida flight from Miami began its descent into London. She liked the idea of landing at Gatwick. Less of a crowd and less hassle than at Heathrow.

But would Jim be there? The anticipation and uncertainty were building. She could never be sure. He could be sent to the far reaches of the world at the drop of a hat.

Baggage claim on a CD10 flight always took forever and this time was no exception. Hers seemed to be the last to arrive, but at least clearing Customs was no problem.

"What is the nature of your visit to England? Business or pleasure?"

"Definitely pleasure." Ginny said.

"And where will you be staying?"

"Good question," she answered. "I'm really not sure. I'm the guest of a British friend."

The agent stamped her passport and waved her through.

Clearing the door, she readily picked Jim out of the crowd. She was never sure how he would look. It was always so long between their visits, and he participated in so much. What toll had it taken this time?

Tall and fit, he sported more of a tan than she expected. He had said England had an unusually warm and sunny summer. She had never seen him so well dressed, in such a typical British manner: a beige wool topcoat, dark navy pin-stripe suit, crisp Oxford cloth shirt with his Brigade of Guards tie

As she pushed the luggage cart past the door, Jim moved through the crowd to reach her, guiding the cart out of the terminal. He glanced around to see if anyone appeared interested in her arrival.

"Ginny, something's come up. I have job to do. I tried to call you to tell not to come. Your blasted machine wasn't on and I don't have your work number."

Ginny was crestfallen. "That's a heck of a greeting!"

Had he changed his mind? Did he not want to see her after all? Surprised and hurt, she hid her emotions and shrugged. Things would work out; they had to. What was she supposed to do, re-board the plane and fly back to Miami? No way.

"But then I decided it would be okay if you were along. We can make a special trip of it."

"Where are we going?"

"Brighton. It's sort of Britain's answer to Miami Beach, but older, more sedate. You'll like it. Besides, I have some unfinished business to attend to there."

Ginny took his news as well as expected. He had trained her well. She knew not to ask many questions.

"No problem. I can always entertain myself. Brighton sounds fascinating. The Pavilion is there. I'd love to see it. Besides, that sounds like the kind of sightseeing you'd hate, so it will work out fine."

They chatted on the long walk to the garage, filling in the spaces of the many months since they had last been together. It had been a long time. They approached his shiny silver Toyota Celica that she remembered from a photograph. He tossed her luggage in the boot, and they sped off to Brighton.

With all of the chatting, the drive went by fairly quick. The countryside was beautiful, even if the weather was nasty.

Jim relaxed as he drove, and conversation helped make the trip seem quicker

"When I was a teenager, my friends and I used ride to ride motorcycles down here. In fact, a friend was killed on his motorcycle at this intersection, just ahead. I wasn't there but heard about it. We would all go down to the beach in the summer, just to hang out."

"You never struck me as a Hell's Angel."

"Not exactly that, but I liked to party and dance."

Brighton was a charming city. A park with a well-trimmed traditional English rock garden greeted visitors right inside the city limits. Before long they were by the sea, as well as a strip of hotels that lined the promenade and pier.

"Getting a place to stay should be interesting. The Labour Party's having their annual conference here and the city's probably pretty full. Let's start at the top."

Jim turned the car into a parking space at the entrance to the Grand Hotel, and left Ginny to wait in the car while he went inside to see if a room had become available. He had made a standby reservation at another hotel if the Grand did not have a cancellation.

Ginny looked at the old hotel and studied its curious ornate façade while she waited.

Soon Jim was back. "No luck. Let's keep trying."

They passed the sleek Convention Center next door to the hotel. Ginny read the marquee aloud.

"Labour Party Conference October 7-9. That sounds pretty impressive. Are you meeting someone at the conference?"

He laughed. "No. Nothing like that."

They stopped in front of the Old Ship Hotel, where he had been able to reserve a room. He went inside to register, and came out smiling.

"We're set," he said. "They even have a weekend package that includes breakfasts and dinners. This will be fine." He pulled his car into the parking garage, took out their luggage, handed it to the bellman, and locked the car.

The room was adequate but far from spacious. The yellow patterned drapes hid a view of the alley and brick wall outside the window. Ginny thought how lucky they were to get a room at all without a reservation. An ocean view was impossible at this time.

Inspecting their new surroundings, she sensed an unfamiliar tenseness, as if she'd crashed his party, like he didn't really want her to come. There was no longing kiss when the door shut. They simply sat on the bed, talking, waiting for their luggage to be brought up.

"If you don't mind, I'm dying for a shower. I must have two inches of construction dust on me. Can you imagine what it's like to dress up and go to work on a construction site? I had to leave for the airport from my office, and had no chance to change. I'm really gritty."

"Sure," Jim said. "You go in and shower I'll wait for the luggage."

The tub was large, with a hand-held showerhead that she was unfamiliar with. She had to figure out how to use it.

It felt wonderful, but then she remembered that her hair dryer needed an electrical adapter. She called out to Jim, asking if he could have one sent up from the front desk.

When the young porter delivered the adapter, he loudly announced, "Here's the adapter for the American with all of the fancy appliances." Ginny laughed as water cascaded over her but felt more like an alien.

After her hair was dry and she had dressed in wool slacks and a sweater, Jim suggested a walk. The weather was blustery and the angry ocean pounded against the shore and pier. They were the only people braving a walk on the promenade. The temperature had dropped, and her coat, with the warm gloves and wool scarf, were barely enough protection.

They hadn't gone too far when Jim excused himself to go to the public men's toilet, leaving Ginny to study the bronze plaque on a cannon monument. She waited, teeth chattering.

Odd, she thought, shivering. She was cold and alone.

The international signage on the facility indicated men's and women's toilets had telephones. Jim had taken the opportunity to call his team, report his guest had arrived, where they were staying, and make sure there were no problems. He learned all was okay on their end as well. Still, he knew the task ahead was formidable.

Jim rejoined Ginny at the cannon and they walked along the promenade, not touching. He was distant and distracted, his mind elsewhere, in a military mode, on the horrific task ahead. There was no friendly arm around her shoulder to warm her; no arm offered at all, and they didn't hold gloved hands.

They crossed the road from the promenade to an inviting narrow winding street full of stores and pubs.

"Let's turn up this little street to look for a pub and lunch," he suggested.

The dark pints with foamy tops were comforting. The pub was packed and they sat in the bar area at a small table. An odd twosome sat next to them; a son charming his antiquated blue-haired mother out of the last of her modest fortune so he could buy a car. It was a sad, semi-comical, conversation to eavesdrop on, and helped ease the tension between Ginny and Jim. They both enjoyed people-watching, and found the way the son presented his case somewhat amusing. After sandwiches and another pint, a few stories and laughs, they were again in sync.

Arm in arm, they walked through the light rain to the Old Ship. The narrow streets of the Lanes were lined with fascinating antique shops that Ginny wanted to explore later, but suddenly they were ready to begin anew, to pick up where they had left off so many months before.

Once in their room, Jim locked the door behind them and pulled her close. All of the feelings returned, pushing every obstacle out of the way as they melted together. Eagerly, suppressed longing found a path to expression, and the magic worked once more. It was as if they had never been apart.

Ginny awakened in a darkened room to the sound of Jim in the shower. A few minutes later he emerged in a towel, and drying his wet hair.

"Up! Time for cocktails and dinner. A lot of prominent people will be there."

He dressed in a dark three-piece suit, striped shirt, with matching tie and pocket square. His father's gold watch and fob and were the finishing touches. An accomplished raconteur, he once more enchanted her with tall tales as she finished putting on makeup and brushed her hair.

At one point, she grabbed her camera and caught him mid-story. Ginny wore a black cocktail dress with an expensive gold necklace and earrings she had splurged on to celebrate her independence. A bit of Chloe perfume and she was ready.

The lounge, oak paneled and dark, was very crowded. Jim surveyed the crowd and recognized some well-known Labour Party members in hot debate. He pointed them out to Ginny as they sat at a table for two near the pianist. Jim headed to the bar to get their drinks.

Ginny looked around her. The conventioneers were having a good time, but in a subdued way. They acted more like conservative Republicans than liberal Democrats, but she knew that opinion probably didn't really correlate. More simply a difference in British and American behavior.

She looked at Jim at the bar and couldn't take her eyes off him. She loved to study him from across a room -always standing above the crowd. There was something about the way he moved with the simplest of confident gestures that aroused her, always a surprising response.

Jim returned with two gin and tonics.

"Tell me more about Belize and the jungle. How does a boy from London know so much about jungles?"

"From Borneo, actually. I learned all you need to know about jungles there. That experience qualified me as a jungle warfare advisor to the Americans in Nam. Once I led a patrol deep into the jungle in Borneo. When you lead a patrol, you aren't in front. Young soldiers break ground.

This particular patrol was in a region inhabited by a tribe that not only killed but mutilated their enemy first in the most horrible ways. So, yeah, hostile territory.

"The jungle was so thick that you couldn't even see the man in front of you. The tribesmen started picking us off, one by one, until it finally got down to two men, a corporal and me. Then they killed him, right in front of me, but I managed to escape. I climbed a tree and at one point had ten of them around the base of it. Imagine, being the only one out of seven to survive."

"Gee, Jim. Surely someday your luck will run out."

"Skill, madam. It's not luck. It's skill. I've told you I'm a damn good soldier."

The pianist began playing "Cavatina," the melancholy song that Jim recorded on the tape he sent so long ago. It seemed ironic that the pianist selected this particular old melody.

"Did you request that?" Jim asked, surprised.

"No. Did you?"

No. But how perfect. Remember the tape I sent to you?"

"How could I forget it? It broke my heart. Both beautiful and sad. I guess if we have a song, it must be this one. Very haunting, like 'As Time Goes 'Bye,' from Casablanca. Bogie and Bergman, and an incredible love story.

"The biggest regret I'll ever have in my life is that I didn't make it to London, but I just couldn't."

"I know. It was wrong of me to expect you to go. The timing was bad, but it couldn't be helped. That's history now."

They finished their drinks, recalling memories of the past two and a half years.

Dinner included five courses, with all the silver set. Looking at the many forks, knives, and spoons, Ginny felt totally and completely socially inadequate, realizing how casual life was in America. As child, she had been raised dining in the finest restaurants and nightclubs that her grandfather owned in chic Miami Beach; but the sudden array of silver confused her.

"Who can't take whom anywhere?" Jim teased her, and proceeded to give her a lesson in using the fork and knife continental style.

Both were full and finished off the bottle of German wine Jim ordered. Jet lag returned, and Ginny was relieved when they went back to their room, made gentle, tender love, and finally crashed for the night.

Ginny's eyes popped open. In the dim light, her eyes and mind adjusted both to Brighton and to having Jim beside her. She reached and stroked his thick dark hair.

He stirred, opened one eye and said, "It can't be morning, can it?"

"Afraid so. Eight o'clock, in fact. What time is your appointment?"

Jim groaned and jarred himself into wakefulness.

"Around eleven," he said. "Off to the shower with you. We need a good breakfast, too. Up!"

Ginny laughed when he jokingly ordered her around. He delighted in being a tough taskmaster, a true drill sergeant, an act just for her. She showered, brushed her teeth, put on her makeup, and returned to find Jim had fallen asleep again.

She gave him a kiss on the cheek and gently shook him. He woke up with a start and said, "Through so soon? Go put on some nail polish or something." He was not eager to face the day.

At breakfast, they read the morning *Times* and said little. Ginny looked outside at the gale lashing the large picture window. Across the road, violent waves crashed against the promenade.

"Definitely not Miami Beach," she said. Of course, it seemed the oceans were always stormy when they were together. Some kind of warning?

By 9:30, they were back in their room, and Ginny could hear Jim talking softly on the phone while she was in the bathroom.

The message was brief. The SAS unit confirmed that all was going on schedule. O'Hara was in the house and the girl had left for her usual round of errands. It was a busy day for the twosome, and this was his big night. They had heard the girl say she would return around 11:00, and Jim was going in with her.

"What are your plans, Ginny? Hate to leave you, but this won't take long."

"Don't worry about me. I thought I might go to the Pavilion, but now I'm not sure. The weather's just awful, and that's pretty far away. I could take a taxi, but it looks like there are interesting things to see in the antique shops on the little streets and alleys around the hotel. When will you get back?"

"Sometime after noon. If you don't mind, here's a list of things I need for the Falklands. Would you pick them up for me? That should keep you busy." He handed her two twenty-pound notes and a long list he'd prepared.

"Okay. What are you doing, might I ask? Of course I'm curious, but you don't have to tell me."

I'm just having a chat with a fellow. I have to convince him not to make trouble. No problem. You wait here for me around noon, and if I'm not back, I'll be back soon. Okay, I've got to run. Good luck with the shopping."

Jim shut the door behind him and Ginny looked at the list. Toothpaste, shampoo, deodorant, and the likes, for roughly six months in the Falklands.

She shuddered. That was a long time to be there. But it gave her a rare opportunity to do something for him, so she bundled up in her coat and scarf and faced the blustery weather outside. The narrow winding streets intrigued her.

❧❧❧

Jim opened the boot of his car and unpacked his *Walther PPK*, concealed among his cricket equipment, now putting it inside the car with him. He had been briefed on the exact location in Worthing and had rehearsed the operation in his mind numerous times. He had no trouble finding the address and parked his car at the end of the quiet empty street.

Casually, he strolled toward Number 9, quickly blending himself in a row of bushes near the front door. He waited in place and ready, with his SAS team in numbers 8 and 10.

The girl arrived right on time. She carried a shopping bag and the suit from the laundry. At the door she rummaged through her purse and came up with the key. As she pushed the key into the lock and opened the door, two silenced explosions from Jim's gun hit her in the back, propelling her face down in the flat.

Jim leaped up the stairs into action. O'Hara came out of the kitchen just in time to see the girl explode in front of him.

Then he died as violently as he lived. The first bullet hit him just above the heart, followed by one through the throat and another through the mouth.

Jim stood over the terrorist's dead body, sprawled in a pool of blood, eyes rolled back. He didn't feel a twinge of remorse.

Mick Gardiner's murder was finally avenged, but the bigger issue was that he had saved his country from a national disaster of grand proportions.

The girl was another matter. He was only doing his duty.

The job had taken a matter of minutes. A furniture removal van arrived, two minutes later, and Jim watched as they efficiently emptied the contents of the house.

The bodies were loaded into body bags and hauled out with the sofa, in-route to the waiting boat. That evening the weighted bodies would be dumped into the English Channel.

Except for the carpet now cut in an odd shape no one would ever have a clue to the grisly event that took place at Number 9 Willow Gardens.

Killing women, even in the line of duty, was especially depressing for Jim. Even women involved with terrorists. Women involved in terrorist activities usually were every bit as dangerous as men, sometimes more so. Killing them was sometimes an awful necessity that made the world a safer place, but it was a part of the job that often sickened him.

He thought about the dead girl as he drove back to Brighton. She had been rather plain, and must have been lonely, simply making the wrong choice in a companion.

Had he joined the army to kill women and children? He remembered the teenage boy he had unwittingly killed in a night ambush during a drug bust on the border of Belize and Mexico.

No question, he had made the right decision in resigning at the end of this tour. His mood was more than grim as he headed back to the hotel.

Ginny had bought all the items on the list. Between the squalls, she enjoyed the luxury of exploring the Lanes, poking in and out of the little shops that lined the streets. The buildings once were fishermen's cottages. Now the narrow byways were lined with antique shops, pubs, and cafes.

Keeping an eye on her watch, she had to tear herself away from a collection of small silver lidded crystal boxes to return to the room by noon.

She hadn't been there too long when she heard the sound of Jim's key in the door.

He immediately headed for the bathroom, without so much as a hello or removing his topcoat. He filled the sink with hot and cold water, then very carefully soaped and repeatedly washed his hands.

Ginny observed the action with fascination, and somehow found it disturbing, but didn't say anything.

Why is this so familiar?

Her mind suddenly raced through college knowledge. Shakespeare.

Of course! Lady Macbeth! "Out, damned spot! Out I say! ... What, will these hands ne'er be clean?"

God, what had he done? She tried to push the thought aside, as Jim emerged from the bathroom.

"Well, I got everything on your list. I hope you like the shampoo I selected. You sure will smell good in the Falklands." She tried to sound cheerful, not to think the unthinkable. Something very bad happened, and she really didn't want to know, but still asked, "How did it go?"

"Oh, fine. No problem. Now the rest of our time is free." He turned on the television to a Saturday golf match, changed to casual a red sweatshirt and gray pants with white paint splattered on the gray pants.

"Sorry about the paint. I was rather sloppy when I painted my cottage. I did a better job on the walls than on these pants. Those walls are two feet thick."

"Tell me about your cottage. How is it decorated? I have the picture of it, and the one of you at the dining table, but couldn't tell what kind of furniture and accessories you have."

"Period furniture. I guess you'd call it Queen Anne. I like brass ornaments. I've just done over the kitchen and put in a microwave. It's really coming along. If this trip had been planned, and if we had warning, or this job hadn't come up, I would have taken you there."

"Have you taken many women there?" Ginny wondered who took the picture.

"No. No one really."

She wondered if she could believe that either, but she let it ride.

Jim stretched out on the bed and changed the TV channel to watch a very formal snooker match. The participants wore tuxedos. He lit a cigarette and became engrossed in the slow, deliberate action of the sport which emphasized the importance of precision and aim, skills he shared.

She could tell it would be a while before they left. Cigarette smoke bothered her and made her cough. More than that, a heavy atmosphere hung over the room, more powerful than gloomy weather and tobacco smoke.

Loud shouting outside in the alley drowned out the voice of the snooker match announcer. Ginny opened the drapes and looked out. A large, outrageous crowd of punk kids marched along, many dressed in black leather, with chains or fake animal skins. Some of the guys had weird Mohawk haircuts, or gaudily colored orange, hot pink, or lime green hair. The procession moved down the alley. Ginny knew the police could not be far behind for crowd control.

She was right. They herded the gangs to the stadium for a soccer match. The shock of it all reminded her of how confused and crazy the world had become. She couldn't help snapping a few pictures.

Ginny looked at the sullen man on the bed, his eyes narrowed, unfathomably sad, staring blankly at the TV. He was almost a stranger. Perhaps he always had been a stranger, a tangible figment of her imagination. The Jim she knew and loved was intelligent and deep, warm, caring, affectionate, and passionate with her. He said she really didn't know him, and now, finally, she could see he was right. The reality was that he had a violent and deadly side she could not imagine and never wanted to know. He had just done something, carried out an order of some kind, that was revolting to him. What he had to do was not who he was. She had seen his pain.

She was really seeing the two sides to both Jim and Ginny.

*Can I live with this?*

She opened a dresser drawer and pulled out some hotel stationery.

"Let's see. Why don't we just do the goodbye letter together this time?" she asked, sarcastically.

Had she finally passed her limit? Had she come this far to be hurt so badly? "I'm sure you have a form letter you use for situations like this. Dear Ginny, I have given a lot of thought about our time together."

"Are you really this masochistic?"

"I guess so, or I wouldn't be here. I thrive on hurt. I don't know how to act if it stops. You know me, 'Come on, hurt me again! Harder!'"

"Stop it."

"Sorry. You just seem different."

"Let's get out of here."

He dressed in jeans and a jacket and they walked down the main street of Brighton. The rain had stopped and they wandered in and out of the department stores, bookstores, music, and electronics shops. Instead of a lunch of fish, chips, and dark beer in a pub, they had hamburgers and French fries at the gleaming new McDonald's.

Ginny stopped in front of Woolworth's.

"Let's go in. I'd love for you to buy something for me, just any cheap little thing from you that I can touch while you're in the Falklands. You've still never given me one thing. Please? Just a reminder of the day."

"I don't want to remember this day. You have no idea. You wouldn't understand. Come on." He took her hand, ducked down an alley, and lead the way back to the hotel.

Confused, Ginny followed.

They dressed for dinner. Jim brightened. He started another round of storytelling. The tension began to melt and eventually they were both laughing, all the way to the lounge for cocktails.

There were too many drinks before dinner and two bottles of wine, white and red, with dinner.

Back in the room, desperation and urgency pervaded in their lovemaking. They fell asleep entwined, clinging to each other as if for the last time.

The next morning, they packed before going to the dining room for breakfast. An air of finality hung over the table as Jim searched the Sunday Times, looking at the news about the Labour Party conference, or maybe for a story he hoped he wouldn't find.

While Jim paid the bill, Ginny reflected on their time in Brighton. There would be no seashells to save as reminders of the sweet memories of this time together.

She shrugged it off.

The bellman carried their bags to his car.

In the car, on the way to London, she said, "I'll think of you often, Jim. You'll be so far away, an ocean away. There's something about the Falklands that freaks me out. It seems beyond the end of the earth. What will you actually be doing there?"

"I'll be an operations officer for an engineer regiment. We'll be rebuilding the island, finding and destroying undetected land mines, and re-establishing a radar site on Mount Kent."

"It seems I've followed your trail to so many places, one way or another."

"If you really love someone, Ginny, you'll go anywhere to be with him."

Was that true? Sometimes circumstances are too overwhelming.

Reaching the outskirts of London, Jim's attitude changed. He began to get enthused about showing her where he grew up.

"These are the woods where I played Robin Hood or soldiers as a boy. Sometimes we played cowboys and Indians."

"Did the Indians ever win? Or become your friends?" Ginny had to ask.

They crossed a small stone bridge.

"And this is where I fished."

"What did you catch?" It was a brown, murky stream.

"Disease!" Jim said, and laughed. "This is the hospital where I was born. Around the corner and down a way is the slum where I grew up. Mostly foreign families now."

They passed a large cemetery.

"Most of my family's there, except my father, of course. He's buried in Teneriffe. This was my school. They were as glad when I left as I was. And see that laundry over there? It was a disco, a real hangout. Sure doesn't look like one now."

Ginny studied the shabby neighborhood. The runaway boy from the slum had come a long way. They truly were from two different worlds. She could better understand that now. Once and for all, she knew it was impossible for the star-crossed lovers to merge lives from two such different worlds. Her world was sunny, while the whole entire world was his milieu, from rainy, gloomy England, to the hedgerows of Northern Ireland, the jungles of Belize, and the barren hills of the Falklands.

Ginny had lived her life and Jim had lived his. When they came together, they created a new reality, a storybook tale that was probably rooted somewhere in nineteenth century mentality He was her fantasy and she was his. She was the romantic princess, entranced by the British adventurer, the knight in shining armor on a white horse, the role he personified. He enchanted her with his stories and inspired her with his courage.

Yet that reality could only exist for short periods of time. Duty and the demands of the twentieth century always brought it to a wrenching halt. Then they had to escape back to familiar territory.

Their encounters opened patches of heaven, but this time they both quietly knew it had to end. The agony and despair were never ending. It was unwise and unhealthy to linger in this fantasy.

Jim was right. The dream had to be cut out forever.

He broke her train of thought. "We'll find a hotel for you in this section near Victoria Station. It's in central London, near many sights, and it will be easy for you to catch the train to Gatwick when you leave."

He stopped in front of the Lime Tree Hotel, in a Georgian townhouse, a modest bed and breakfast on Ebury Street. He went inside, then came back out a minute later with a key for her room.

As he opened the boot and carried *Liberator* into the lobby, Ginny looked at the pleasant street, noting the wine bar next door. She drew a deep breath, then went inside the hotel while Jim took her luggage to her room.

Inside, he pulled her close and gave her a long kiss.

"Wonderful to see you again, Ginny. Sorry this is so short, but I've got to get my men ready to leave. They really need me. I have to make sure their bank accounts and love lives are straightened out before we depart. I'll call you tonight and every night before you leave England. Who knows, maybe my last tour will be Belize and I'll see you in Miami again."

"I won't hold my breath, but that would be nice. Thanks for everything. I've enjoyed seeing you."

Did she? There were such mixed emotions about their time together.

"For God's sake, be careful in the Falklands. I'm sure you're tired of hearing me say that. Please call around six."

They kissed again. Then he left her staring at an open door.

Jim called her at the hotel each evening as he promised. Although still in England, for all practical purposes he might as well have already been in the Falklands. The distance was only relative. The thought crossed Ginny's mind to catch a train to Oxford, rent a car, and find out where he might be, but knew it was unwise to intrude. Plus, she had never driven in England.

The rest of the week in London passed fast and pleasantly. Museums, sightseeing, shopping, pubs. It was over before she knew it. Once more she was ready for her flight to Miami, ready to get on with her work and her life.

I'm not sure what really went on there, she thought as she waited to board her plane.

I know I've finally had enough pain.

What happened between them? What was the pull, the catch, the turnoff?

Finally, Ginny understood. Aside from just the passion and interesting conversations, they were two very different and needy people who, in spite of their differences, had strong feelings for each other and fell deeply in love.

They were like a puzzle, both recognizing the missing pieces in the other, and trying to fit them together.

Both were loners, in their own way; he as a soldier and she as an artist. They could read each other silently, without a word but just a look, a nod of the head where to meet in an airport. Telepathic. Both were storytellers, with great stories to tell.

When Jim was with Ginny, she offered the peace and contentment he had never known. He helped her find in herself the courage and strength that had always been there, untouched.

It was a story as old as time, just new characters. He was the Tin Man who needed a heart; she the Lion who needed courage.

Ever since he was a young soldier, Jim was never the master of his own fate. His life had been dictated by others, and by duty. He was a passionate defender of freedom, dedicated to ridding the world of evil, loyal to his country and Queen.

Though she so loved and respected Jim, his guiding force, his noble sense of duty, was not her destiny. He was a hero, but a shadow. He once described his role so well:

After living rough in the field for days, the soldier is unwashed and unshaven, unrecognized, and unrewarded, just performing his duty. No one would ever know all he did.

Jim's service wasn't quite over yet.

She remembered that in *A Farewell to Arms*, Ernest Hemingway wrote of the American character, actually himself, who was finally fed up with the heartbreak of foreign wars that weren't his. Hemingway so poignantly said with finality, "It's not my show anymore."

God knows we tried.

Once more faced with reality, things would never really change, but the love and good memories would always live forever.

Ginny quickly settled back into her routine at work, glad to be back in Miami. Her office was finished, clean, and ready when she returned. The big opening was soon and the excitement growing all around. Ginny knew she too would never be given acclaim. A cog in a wheel. She was just proud to be playing a role in developing a major cultural center in the city in which she was born and loved so much.

She didn't expect a letter from the Falklands for a while. It was a long month before it finally arrived. The beautiful stamp on the envelope gave no hint of the barrenness, or of the message the letter carried. The news was not unexpected, and in a strange way, she was relieved.

He began:

> *I know you didn't want any more goodbye letters, which is the main reason it has taken so long to write this. Our relationship will end; that's not being cruel. It's letting you off of the hook. There are other fish in the sea all right, but you latched on to the wrong one in in me.*
>
> *Friends, yes. I'll always remain a friend. But you don't want me for just a friend. So, the best way is for you to cut me right out of your life. I know. I've tried it and it works. This is how it must be.*
>
> *I won't be staying in Fort Stanley for much longer but going to the hills. I wish you success in your job and in your life. I'm sure you'll be very happy, as I will with my life. Whatever I do and wherever I go. I will always remember you, and the special times we've shared together.*
>
> *Goodbye, Ginny, this time forever.*

She had resolved her feelings but was totally unprepared for the letter that arrived from the Falklands in early January. Puzzled, Ginny looked at the date and unfamiliar handwriting. She went to her desk, hurriedly tore the envelope open, and looked at the signature. Barry Wells had signed the letter. Her stomach knotted in a wave of fear as she read it:

> *"Captain James Evans asked me to write to you in the event anything ever happened to him. Unfortunately, I regret to inform you that he was killed on December 22nd. I waited until after the holidays to send this bad news to you. He was killed instantly in an ironic and tragic accident. He was leading an operation near Mount Kent and stepped on an undetected land mine. James was very respected by his men and we are greatly saddened by his sudden death. I know he would have wanted you to be informed. We share your loss."*
>
> *Sincerely,*
> *Barry Wells*

A sudden chill crept into her entire body and she shivered, as when told that her father died.

Jim's unrewarded life of service and dedication ended in an instant, by a meaningless blast of explosives.

This was the goodbye letter to end all goodbye letters.

Ginny put it back in the envelope, tears streaming down her face. She touched the jar of seashells and driftwood, the only tangible reminders of the man she deeply loved, even if always so distant, an ocean away. Such a short and tragic life, but she realized the world has always needed loners and heroes, good and dedicated men like Jim. He was in a league of some of the bravest men in the most dangerous jobs in the world.

Having known him gave me the courage that made me strong. Now I fill my own needs with choices that make my life better and living the life I was meant to live. He was right all along.

I was blind. Isn't love blind? It never would have worked in the real world. Never. The magic would have ended. Still, I'll always wonder, why did he keep coming back?

Jim set me free to follow my own path, wherever it takes me. He'll always live on in my heart, and I'll forever be grateful. I can live with that. Maybe someday I'll write our story.

A storybook romance, from the stories Jim told me and wanted written.

Her thoughts turned back to the Scottish Highlands, and the magic of how their souls first danced as one. As Jim had so eloquently expressed.

What we had, we've got, and no one can take that away. And perhaps it's best if we leave it, and as we grow old, it's a fond memory, one we can both look back on in our own worlds and say, "Well, I did know happiness for a brief moment in time."

# Dorothy Downs

Dorothy Downs is an art historian, author, artist, who has worked in a number Miami museums and art galleries. She has published three nonfiction books and numerous articles on Native American art. She has also written and illustrated an historical children's book, *Canoe Back in Time*, about the Everglades in the early 1920s. Dorothy Downs' newest work is *Her Soldier of the Queen*, a romantic novel of empowerment, love, loss and adventure in Scotland, Northern Ireland, England, the Falkland Islands, and Miami.

# Other Books
# by Dorothy Downs

*Miccosukee Arts and Crafts*
Miami, Florida: Miccosukee Tribe of Indians of Florida, 1982.

*Art of the Florida Seminole and Miccosukee Indians.*
Gainesville, Florida: University Press of Florida, 1995.

*Patchwork: Seminole and Miccosukee Art and Activities*
Sarasota, Florida: Pineapple Press, 2005.

*Canoe Back in Time*
Santa Fe, New Mexico: Irie Books, 2017.

Made in the USA
Columbia, SC
27 December 2020